LEST NOBODY LIVES

GRIPPING POLICE COLD CASE MYSTERY

DS LIZ MOORLAND.
BOOK 4

PHILLIPA NEFRI CLARK

LEST NOBODY LIVES

AN IMPORTANT NOTE...

This series is set in Australia and written in Aussie/British English for an authentic experience.

Like to discover more about Liz, other titles, and Phillipa's world? Visit Phillipa's website where you can subscribe to her email newsletter. www.phillipaclark.com.

PROLOGUE

The night air reeked of death. Three bodies lay somewhere behind Liz Moorland, their lives snuffed out before they had a chance to offer up a prayer – should they have a higher power – or even see their assassin. Wasted lives.

She stood motionless beneath a tree. Her senses reached into the dark, desperately seeking a sign, any sign, of where he was, the man she hunted. Sight gave her nothing, not even with infrared binoculars. Smell was too focused on what was in her wake to be helpful. And sound? Not even the branches above were moving nor night birds calling. But her intuition was on fire. Her spine tingled and the hairs on her arms were upright.

Where are you, Dad?

There was a choice of direction. Continue along the trees lining the long, brick driveway, or cross in the open to the building. Neither were safe. Nothing was safe.

Her phone vibrated in a pocket, and Liz ignored it other than to cover it with a hand in the hope of muffling its soft buzz. She had to move before anyone else was harmed… or worse. For a second she glanced back, her heart heavy with loss but needing to compartmentalise the hurt for now. If she was to survive this night, she had to push everything aside.

In the distance, a drone flew low and slow. It was seeking her father, and probably looking for Liz as well. She wished they'd move a bit away, having no doubt there were snipers on the sprawling property who'd not think twice about taking down the only eyes helping her.

She needed to get inside the mansion. Somehow.

What was hidden within it was key to everything. The answers to a million questions raised over the years about the man behind a secretive and deadly organization.

Overhead, the clouds abruptly parted, and moonlight spilled across the open ground. There was still no sign of life and Liz made her choice. Watching the sky, she waited until the night was again cast into darkness and then flew across the twenty or so metres to the side of the abandoned mansion, throwing herself against the wall.

She was alive. Not shot. Not pursued.

What is he waiting for?

Her phone vibrated again. She couldn't turn it off as it was showing her location to the only people who might save her, if her father or his hoons got what they wanted. Liz in their clutches. Quickly, she lifted it from her pocket and read the last of many messages.

> Stand down! Wait for back-up. This is Ben's
> order. Confirm, Liz.

> Soon. I'm safe for now.

Knowing that response wouldn't go down well, Liz turned off the sound and buried the phone in a deeper pocket. Unless she completed her mission, the past months would be for nothing. Kyle would not only escape – again, but so would the best chance they'd ever had of quality intelligence about the Australian chapter of a terrible organisation.

People had died tonight because of him. People had been dying for a long time.

Liz edged along the wall. Built decades ago, this mansion once echoed with music and laughter. Now, it was a ghostly mockery of a happier past.

At the door she hesitated. This wasn't supposed to happen… she'd come here with a plan and fellow members of Operation Nobody. Yet she was alone and it fell onto her to finish the job. Liz couldn't permit the last half hour of shock and betrayal and deaths to be the final roadblock.

I will avenge you.

Heart pounding, she slowly turned the handle and let herself inside.

ONE

Two weeks earlier

Doctor Candace Carroll's apartment was a surprise. It was a penthouse, taking the full top floor of a gorgeous old building near the Yarra River. In the months she'd known the psychiatrist, this was the first time Liz had been invited to visit, and to say she was impressed was an understatement. For some reason she'd imagined Candace living in a townhouse in Port Melbourne or a house along the bay in Black Rock or Chelsea.

'Feel free to explore,' Candace handed Liz a glass of white wine. 'Only my office is locked because of client files. Security and all of that. Or I can show you around later.'

'Dinner smells wonderful. Anything I can help with?'

'Not a thing. The others are on the balcony if you wish to take in the view. Go on. I'm in my element cooking.'

Somehow that didn't seem at all like the woman Liz knew… yet didn't really know.

Tonight was important. This was the first opportunity the core senior group of Operation Nobody had to discuss recent events and the fallout – specifically, whether a member of the covert team was connected to Liz's father, criminal Kyle Moorland. Liz sipped her wine. The conversation was going to be difficult because no one wanted a mole in their midst.

Candace hummed as she returned to the kitchen, which was huge and surrounded by the most beautiful marble bench.

Taking her advice, Liz stepped through open French doors to a wide balcony which appeared to wrap around the penthouse. The table and seating was empty. The other guests leaned against the ornate railing.

'Hi there.'

'Oh, Liz! Hello!' Forensic analyst Meg Mackie came in for a hug. She had her hair loose, which was unheard of, and she'd changed its colour to dark brown with rainbow ends. 'Can you believe this view?'

'Get over here and join us.' This was Pete McNamara, beer in hand, back against the rail as he grinned. He'd been her partner on and off for years when she was a Homicide detective.

Making up the last of the small group was Ben Rossi, head of *Operation Nobody* and a man Liz had enormous respect for. It was Ben who'd asked her to be part of the covert team and she'd known him from his days running Missing Persons.

Meg was right about the view.

The Yarra River was a darkening ribbon, lit from either side by streetlights and buildings. With night closing in, it reflected the last of the sunset.

'It is an ever-changing painting.' Candace stepped out onto the balcony. 'I bought the apartment because of this and spend as much time as possible out here… particularly during difficult times. There's a certain peacefulness being high enough to miss the worst of the traffic sounds, yet almost able to reach out and touch the water.'

For a moment they all gazed at the river. Candace had a way with words which touched Liz's imagination. She didn't have a permanent home but lived in an Airbnb apartment on a month-by-month basis. A penthouse was unnecessary but perhaps a normal apartment on a lower floor which faced this way?

'I have an entrée to serve if you'd all care to come inside?'

She led everyone to a dining room with a table large enough to seat a dozen guests but tonight was set all around one end.

'Please sit anywhere. If someone would open the wines and pour?' Candace returned to the kitchen. There was a servery between kitchen and dining room, its doors open.

'Anyone driving?' Meg did the honours. 'I'm afraid to let Pete do this because he'll fill each glass to the top.'

'And what's wrong with that? Beer glasses are filled to the top.'

'And water. Shall I get you one instead?' Meg held the wine she'd just poured out of Pete's reach.

'I'm not driving. Just back from time at home so will go to my hotel, which is just over there.' Ben pointed.

These windows also overlooked the river.

'Uber for me,' Pete said. 'I won't leave you a tip nor a review if I don't get the wine.'

Meg passed the glass to Ben. 'Better be five star, dude.'

Liz laughed. This was the best of being part of the team. The group knew each other and didn't mind teasing and having fun, and Pete was both the one who gave the most and received it.

'Do you need a hand, Candace?' Ben asked.

Candace's face appeared for a moment through the servery. 'Actually, yes. I'll put some plates here if you don't mind finding space for them in the middle of the table.'

Once everyone had a goat cheese and tomato tart, the banter dropped away. The food was delicious and Liz was impressed. She could cook but couldn't remember the last time she'd had anyone over for a meal. It had to be when her twenty-something niece was a child and she'd have her sister and brother-in-law visit.

It couldn't be all that time ago.

Too long. Far too long.

. . .

With the last dinner plate cleared, the small group settled in the lounge room but not until Meg had wandered around the space with a hand-held detector.

'They'd have had to break in to plant any,' Candace said. 'You've seen how good my security is. And none of the rest of the team have ever been here.'

'I know, but we managed to miss cameras in Lyndall's house after her abduction. Thanks to Reuben's connections I have an even fancier device which is telling me this room is indeed free of nasty bugs.'

Only very recently Operation Nobody had its first case, the disappearance of the neighbour and friend of Vince Carter, Liz's first partner in the police force. Lyndall was a remarkable woman with a dark history and during the search for her, suspicions rose about a possible breach of security from within the team. There wasn't a person here who wanted those suspicions to lead to one of their own.

'Before we start, I want to thank you, Candace, for a wonderful dinner.'

Ben raised his glass to her and everyone copied. She waved it away as if it was no big deal but was smiling.

'On to the more serious reason for our meeting. I value the opinion of each of you and know you have your own thoughts about how we proceed.' Ben placed his glass on a coffee table and settled in his chair. 'If you could each talk through what, if any, concerns you have about our first case pertaining to other members of the team. Anything you observed. Even just hunches.'

'I have to say that overall every person did a remarkable job and any distrust I had for Hamish is gone.' Meg had finished putting her bug-checker away. 'He's a pain at times and has a terrible sense of what is appropriate but I can't find any evidence of him breaking protocol. I've found no digital footprint connected to the operation which doesn't belong.'

'What about his mystery phone call at the pier?' Pete asked. 'He was on a call which he claimed was to Reuben but wasn't.'

'Are you certain?'

'Hamish told me that Reuben was bringing in Tony Shaw for questioning,' Liz said. 'There was a definite implication he'd heard it direct. But then a minute later Reuben phoned me and was surprised Hamish knew.' Liz had conflicting feelings about Hamish and was unsettled about this process but the team integrity was more important than her misgivings.

'Do we have an explanation for that?' Ben looked around and everyone shook their heads. 'What else.'

'I told Liz ages ago he plays down his intelligence. Puts up this obnoxious front as a Bond-like ladies' man which effectively keeps people at a distance. And he mentioned Lyndall's real name when it had never been said in front of him.' Pete crossed his arms.

Liz knew he'd never liked Hamish.

'There are explanations though,' Candace said. 'I agree he understates his intelligence. My original evaluation of him revealed this along with several other traits which combined, make for an interesting human.'

Pete made a scoffing sound which he quickly covered when Candace gazed his way.

'Hey, Pete,' Liz said. 'Everyone has something to hide.'

'Not me.'

'You sure? Anyone can make themselves look suspicious. At the start of the last case you told me you'd been to Lyndall's house multiple times but not why.'

There was a sudden interest from the other people in the room. Pete groaned.

'You said you'd been there for dinners. Plural. But not with Vince and Melanie.'

Meg's mouth had dropped open. Candace smiled slightly. Ben leaned forward.

'Do you really want to know?' Pete rolled his eyes when everyone nodded. 'Fine. But if you laugh, then I'll quit the team. Serious.'

'We won't laugh.' Liz hoped they wouldn't.

'She was giving me art lessons. I always wanted to paint and she was teaching me. Still is, if you must know. Happy?'

You absolute dill for keeping it secret. That is wonderful.

'Oh… I would love to do that! Good on you for following a dream, mate.' Meg was beaming. Supportively. Not laughing at him. 'The extent of my creativity is all software based.'

'Which you do better than anyone.' Pete relaxed. 'Should have said, earlier.'

'Back to Hamish's early intel on Lyndall and different aspects of the operation. Is there a logical answer?' Ben asked.

This was where it got a bit messy for Liz. 'He told me Annette gave him Lyndall's real name, as well as linking the different relationships such as the husband and child. It was just before he and Reuben went to find Marcus Bonner, and Hamish was deadly serious. I'd never seen that side of him as we talked strategy and he dropped the façade.'

Candace picked her up wine glass, eyes on Liz. 'Did you ask Annette if she told him?'

'No. Too much happened too quickly, but…'

All of the others were watching her. However she said this, it would sound odd.

'I did ask Hamish if Annette told him about having been to Bonner Gallery in her school days, because she made a throw-away comment that she had let him know. But he said no and was clearly puzzled.'

'She disappeared a few times when I needed her that last day of the investigation,' Meg said. 'Left Phoebe to manage both their jobs while she went to the roof to smoke. But then she worked her heart out until we secured Lyndall and was brilliant when we captured Tony Shaw at the pier.'

'Thing is,' Pete said. 'Everybody has off-days. People say or do something which comes over as sus yet there's a perfectly sound reason. Like me. And Lyndall.'

Ben chuckled but Candace raised an eyebrow and he tilted his head at her in question.

'I agree with Pete—'

'Knew it!'

Pete shut up under the stern look she sent his way.

'We don't have a whole picture. There are multiple people involved and conversations may be lost among other memories. Annette *may* have told Hamish she had been through the gallery as a teenager and he might have forgotten or not been listening. Or lied about it. Alternately, she may *not* have told him but intended to, forgot she hadn't and her memory, under pressure, was faulty.'

'Or she lied.' Meg was grim. 'This is hard.'

'Yes, however there are ways to gather better information. I recommend we write a debrief questionnaire for each member of the team. If we are sensible about our wording and approach we won't upset anybody, nor alert a person with dubious motives.'

Liz and Ben leaned forward as one. This was good. Plans were always good.

'If you will all give me leave to do so, I'll create a document, which on the surface is simply a way to gather information about each person's experience during the case. In addition, I'd like to offer the opportunity for responders to add anonymous content about their observations.'

'Which won't be anonymous because I will be able to identify the person,' Meg said. 'As I said, this is hard. How can we create a cohesive team without being transparent?'

. . .

The small group agreed on a course of action and with that out of the way, began to disperse. Meg left first, hugging everyone. Then Pete and Ben together.

'Do you have to go just yet?' Candace asked Liz. 'It is pleasant to sit outside with a glass of something decent, if you'd care to join me.'

'I would, thank you. But are you implying that the drinks you've supplied up until now were less than decent?' Liz couldn't help gently teasing. 'I rather loved the white wine.'

'You did? My auntie owns a vineyard which supplies grapes to that winery, so I shall tell her you enjoyed it. So many people love the Barossa or Hunter wines but I do enjoy those from the Macedon Ranges, where she is.'

Liz joined Candace at a well-appointed bar. She'd known the psychiatrist for a few months but tonight was telling her more about the woman than the times they'd worked a case together. People showed more of themselves when they were under extreme pressure or relaxed.

'What is that look for?' Candace asked. 'Are you analysing me?'

'Ha. No. Yes. Maybe. I was thinking how nice it is to see you relaxing a bit.'

'And you. Now, I have almost every type of liquor under the sun, so do you have a preference?'

'Quite honestly, I don't have a large repertoire of drinks.'

'How about a brandy?'

'Actually, yes please.'

Sitting outside in the early autumn air, her hand slightly warming her brandy balloon, Liz was overcome by a sense of peace, something she rarely felt. Traffic sounds were less here than her rooms, and the lights of Melbourne twinkled as if encouraging her to stay a while.

'Tell me something about yourself, Liz. Something I don't know.'

Liz smiled at Candace. 'Is there anything?'

'Goodness yes.'

'I like eating chili for breakfast.'

Candace laughed. 'Oh that is good! At university I would heat up leftover pizza for breakfast, but chili sounds delicious.'

'Your turn.'

For a moment Candace swirled the brandy. 'I once saw a black panther while visiting my aunt. I was ten.'

'Not the aunt who grows grapes?'

'The very one.'

'In the Macedon Ranges in Australia… a black panther?'

Did you become a psychologist to work out why you were hallucinating back then?

'Bit of a legend up around the Mount. I'd never heard such a thing but the story goes that some escaped from a private zoo many years ago. You should ask Vince Carter because they've been seen up his way as well.'

Candace was serious.

'So where was it? The one you saw?'

'Strolling between two rows of grapevines at dusk. I was picking roses from the plant at one end and we suddenly noticed each other and it gazed at me as if sizing me up, then about faced and fluidly trotted away. Turning point in my life because it was the first secret I ever kept.'

'You didn't tell your aunt?'

'She had a shotgun. That moment the panther shared with me was magical and somehow I knew it wasn't there to cause harm.' Candace finally sipped her brandy.

'And you chose a life where you not only help… but you do no harm.'

A comfortable silence settled between them. The brandy was enjoyed. The breeze picked up, cooler than before.

'I should head home,' Liz said. She could just as easily have spent another hour here but Candace would want some sleep.

'When are you going to find a real home?' Candace stood, taking their glasses. 'You look quite comfortable.'

'Oh, I am.' Liz got to her feet and followed Candace inside. 'This is the most beautiful building and has me contemplating finding something similar. Not as large, but I love the peacefulness.'

'Pretty sure one of the apartments is for sale. Shall I find out?'

'In this building? Yes. As long as you don't mind me living here.'

Putting the glasses to one side of the sink, Candace made a snorting sound. 'I'd love to have you here, Liz. I'm pretty solitary and so are you, but I miss having people I care about close by.'

So what is your story? There's pain behind your words.

At the front door, Candace suddenly hugged Liz. 'I've enjoyed this evening. Should I give you some leftovers for breakfast?'

'Not unless there's chili.'

They laughed, and for the first time in a long time, there was a smile in Liz's heart.

TWO

At just before six the next morning, Liz was still not first to arrive at the series of offices and rooms hidden deep inside a nondescript old brick building in a rarely-visited part of a Melbourne inner suburb.

The rich aroma of freshly ground coffee beans was a pleasant welcome. Most of the team had taken a short break after their difficult first mission. As a brand new unit, they'd been thrown into it, under-prepared.

The main room was in darkness but the kitchen light was on, and Reuben whistled as he made himself breakfast.

For a moment Liz watched him move between fridge and bench and cupboard. She liked Reuben. He had a confidence which wasn't overbearing, a sharp mind, and a kind heart which made for an interesting person, particularly as he had worked in intelligence for years. There was so much to learn about each member of the team… although the three days searching for an abducted friend had gone a long way to feeling out their strengths and weaknesses. He had the former in abundance and none of the latter. Not that Liz had noticed.

'Coffee?' He didn't look up as he turned on the stove. 'Pancakes?'

'Really, you're making pancakes?'

'Come and see.' Reuben swirled a pan, grinning at Liz as she stepped into the kitchen. 'I've already made a dozen which are keeping warm in the oven and figured another dozen will keep everyone happy.'

'Are you related to Candace?'

'Er… no. Why?'

'She loves cooking.'

'Best therapy, plus sometimes you get to make another person feel special. Ticks some decent boxes. Coffee machine is pretty much set to go if you don't mind making your own.'

'One for you as well?'

'Thank you.'

By the time Liz made the coffees, Reuben had more pancakes cooking and was cutting up fruit on a board. He'd added maple syrup in a glass bottle. 'Do you think I should add some butter and ricotta to the board?'

'Aren't you vegan?'

'I am. Unless I missed something, the rest of the team are not. And cooking is about sharing bounty and enjoying food together.'

Where have you been all of my life?

'In that case, butter and ricotta sounds great. I might get the lights all on and then I'll come back and set the table up.'

By seven the whole team was gathered around the large table in the second room. This room was part conference room, and part relaxation, with a pool table, a couple of pinballs machines, and a bar. Until now, the only part which had any use was the table, as Candace had commandeered it during the last case.

'Already had brekkie,' Pete said. It didn't stop him snaffling a pancake and piling it with a bit of everything on the board. 'Dessert. Love the idea. Dessert after a real Aussie breakfast of toast and vegemite.'

'These are *vegan*?' Hamish poked at his with a fork as though expecting an answer from the large fluffy pancake.

'They are. So is the fruit. And the maple syrup is pure, so also vegan.' Reuben wasn't perturbed. 'Feel free to toss it my way if it doesn't meet your needs, mate. Always room on my plate for one more.'

Phoebe Renshaw, the youngest member of the team, and usually the quietest, stared at Hamish. 'Or me. I can't remember ever tasting a pancake so delicious.'

'Thanks, Pheebs,' Reuben said quietly.

'Is this a new tradition? Breakfast conferences at the start of each new case?' Annette Benski picked up a cup. 'Pretty decent idea, I reckon. Do we take turns? Make a roster? I cook a mean French toast.'

Ben's eyes met Liz's across the table. He was amused, but she knew him well enough to see a shadow of concern. The group at dinner last night would be taking special note of interactions, no matter how simple or innocent. If there was someone here who worked for the wrong side, then finding them was critical. He slightly nodded as though reading her thoughts, then pushed his now-empty plate back a little.

'Keep eating. I want to run through a few things if you don't mind.'

'Boss, you're interfering with my enjoyment,' Pete said. He was eyeing off a second pancake and Hamish pushed the board closer to him.

'Sorry, Pete. Not sorry. Once we've all eaten, we'll reconvene in the hub and have a strategy meeting about our next case.'

'Going on a bad guy hunt.' Reuben seemed pleased at the prospect.

'Later today each of us will receive a debriefing questionnaire from Candace. This needs to be completed within the next three days, please. Going forward, we'll refine it to use immediately after each case but with this being our first, please bear with us as we sort out what questions are relevant or less important.

Some may seem unrelated to our rescue of Lyndall Smith, but will help Candace build a better system.'

'Is it online?' Annette asked.

'It is.' Candace smiled at her. 'And completely anonymous, unless you wish to be known. There is a second link you'll receive to send me any thoughts, views, feedback of any kind from your experiences so far as a team member, and that will need your name but will only be seen by me and Ben.'

'Cool. I can complain about the lack of pancakes.' Pete was still eating and winked at Reuben.

Ben continued. 'Each of you did an amazing job with what was a difficult case, both mentally and physically. The result is a safe return home for Lyndall, likely long prison sentences for several people who were involved in her abduction, and the removal of one very violent and evil criminal thanks to the sharp shooting skills of Hamish.'

'From a moving helicopter, no less.' Liz knew she was being too quiet and she genuinely was impressed by how Hamish handled himself that night.

Unless it was done to silence Marcus on my father's orders.

'Thanks, Lizzie-beth.'

'Liz. It's still Liz, Hamish.'

There was a ripple of laughter among the team.

'Okay, finish up and we'll meet in the hub in fifteen.'

Liz was still in awe of this central part of the building they called the hub. Long workstations with multiple computers and other devices were in a rough semi-circle. Toward the middle of the room was a table about the size of one used for billiards, but this was far from something to play a game on. Topped by a thick panel of glass, at the touch of panels on either end a screen would appear – two actually. The first was vertical and perfect to display maps and navigation with outstanding clarity. The second was horizontal and quite science-fiction in style to Liz.

Meg had explained that it worked thanks to minute cameras creating a visible barrier. This could be opaque or transparent and images, text, and diagrams and the like set in place or moved by touching and holding… a bit like a phone screen.

Her very first day as a member of Operation Nobody had turned into a frantic race against time to locate Lyndall, leaving little chance of settling in and getting to know her new team mates under normal circumstances. But today they were starting fresh with a case waiting and the intention to also track down her father.

As the team gathered around the table, Liz collected a notepad and pen. She still preferred to hand write notes. Several years as a street cop and working with Vince – who was as traditional as they came – had formed habits she still followed.

Everyone stared at the horizontal screen.

Upon it was the image of a property, a series of photographs, and a couple of newspaper reports.

'Welcome to our new case,' Ben said. 'It was supposed to be our first case but as you all know, Lyndall's life was the priority and this is most definitely a cold case.' He pointed to the photographs, which were individual headshots of three people. 'Meet Ilona and Joseph Baxter. German immigrants arriving in the early 1950s with the original surname of Berger, changed presumably to please his employers who were merchant bankers in Sydney.'

'And protect them from the fear-based prejudice against all things German at that time,' Candace added.

The photo of Joseph was of a man in his forties with a rather stern expression.

'Joseph was an exceedingly clever man when it came to money and was well liked by his clients, quickly rose to senior manager and eventually came to Melbourne to open a new branch, before starting his own investment company. Ilona wasn't one to sit around, and created a line of women's shoes and handbags which were popular among the mega-rich. By the time they retired, their wealth portfolio included properties, stocks, and cash, making them extremely well off.'

Ilona was almost as stern as her husband.

Annette gestured toward the third image. 'And that is our past Chief Inspector Ronald Baxter.'

'He would have been before your time, Annette.' Liz asked. 'I think Vince Carter knew him in passing, not that any of the street cops tended to mingle with the higher-ups, but the inspector retired when I was a teenager.'

'So this really is a cold case.' Her own notebook in hand, Phoebe gazed at the images. 'I've read the brief but I'm unsure why we are investigating what happened.'

Ben nodded. 'Fair question. As a quick background… the inspector was the only child of the Baxters and they were a close family. The murder of his parents one night not only devastated him, but sent him on a path he never deviated from. He was a special kind of cop, one who was expected to go on to even greater things, possibly even politics of the highest level, but he lost everything with his laser focus on solving the crime.'

And he needs us to finish what he couldn't.

'How awful to have an entire police force at your command yet not find the killers of your own parents. Where do we start?' Hamish gazed at Ben. 'And how do we bring justice to this poor man and his family?'

Pete was staring at Hamish, his eyes half-closed. He did that when he wasn't sure. When he was shutting everything out other than whatever had his attention. Liz got the feeling he was every bit as conflicted about Hamish as she was.

'Justice may not happen and I want each of you to understand this case may have no resolution… certainly not in the respect of arrests. The murders happened more than thirty years ago, so even finding the killers might not be enough to lead to prosecution.'

'It's about ending a terrible chapter. Proving that the inspector should have been supported and believed rather than pushed into early retirement.' Reuben shook his head in frustration. 'He needed help, not disdain for not bouncing back and getting over the deaths. Had a killer been found, I am certain he would have lived a much different life.'

There was a murmur of agreement around the table.

Ben increased the size of the property image on the screen. It was overhead image of a house and outbuildings on a parcel of land. 'This is Heberden House. Fancy name for a fancy property. The house… mansion if you like… was already old when the Baxters purchased it, and they completely renovated it. The gardens are as ancient as the house and until Ronald Baxter died, they were maintained. In the past the gardens were open twice a year for visitors to enjoy.'

He glanced at Meg.

'There's not many images from back then,' she said. Using her tablet, she cast a photograph onto the screen of a stately home at night, lights all on. 'That was taken a week before the murders by the local press as the Baxters were hosting some dignitaries. And this was taken a couple of weeks ago. Unloved and not lived in for decades.'

The deterioration was sad. Neglected, the house was showing signs of disrepair and the gardens were overgrown in some parts and barren in others.

'Why is it empty?' Phoebe looked ready to cry. 'Surely it should be sold or rented and returned to its past beauty?'

Candace watched the younger woman with a slight tilt of her head but said nothing.

'There is a trust in place set up by Ronald Baxter,' Ben said. 'The rates and insurance are paid up and apparently people go through four times a year to check the place is secure and the grounds meet local council regulations. But the trust has instructions not to sell until the truth of his parents' deaths are revealed.'

'Then we'd better find them. What do you need from me?' Phoebe lifted her chin, eyes shining. 'How can my team help?'

THREE

'The photos looked better.' Pete hadn't even climbed out of the car and had made up his mind. 'Bulldozer is needed, not solving a murder. If it was murder.'

Meg and Reuben were already standing on the cobbled driveway and Liz wasted no time joining them. Pete had hypothesised the whole trip here and she needed a break, however short.

Despite a forecast for a warm day, the air was crisp in the higher altitude of the Dandenong Ranges. There was a sense of quiet all around… until Pete got out of the car.

'Where do we start?'

By being less annoying?

Liz loved Pete in her own way. They'd worked together on and off for years and there was a mutual respect and understanding which she hadn't shared with anyone other than Vince Carter. A lot of people misjudged Pete, and he only had himself to blame. But she knew his years undercover had shaped him and one had to dig a long way beneath the crusty exterior to find his good heart.

'I mean, we don't even know this was murder.'

On the other hand…

Reuben was behind Pete and grinned at Liz. 'Mate, how about we do a walk around the grounds?'

'Walking is overrated but if you need me to hold your hand, then sure.' Pete loved nothing more than stirring the pot. Another reason he'd not been popular in major crimes. 'What are we looking for?'

'Dunno. Guess we'll find out when we see it.'

With just their tablets, the men chose a direction along one fence line.

The car was parked inside wrought iron gates. They'd been locked with a heavy chain and padlock but Ben knew about it and provided a key, along with several others to gain internal access.

Meg was lifting bags from the back of the car and slinging them over her shoulders.

'Do we need all of this?'

'Unsure, but unless we're going to drive to the house then I'd rather carry them up once rather than come back and forth. We'll need that case there.'

Liz dutifully picked up the case. 'It isn't a drone?'

'Nah. Clever new portable workstation.'

'It weighs a ton.'

'It weighs six kilograms. Do you want me to take it?' Meg had a smirk on her face as she pushed black sunglasses onto her nose.

Sliding her hand through the handle, Liz made a show of struggling. 'Getting old you know.'

'Poor love.'

'So much sympathy.'

'I know, right?' Meg chuckled and began walking toward the home.

Liz caught up after collecting her tablet from the car. It was her decision to walk the hundred or so metres to get their first observations on foot. The driveway was wide and made of cobbled bricks, some in poor repair. On either side were expanses of grass, punctuated by derelict flower beds and rows of trees.

'Are those all oaks?'

Meg glanced over. 'Think so. There's gums along one fence line and I think pines behind the house. Shame the gardens haven't been maintained because the photographs from when the Baxters were alive were stunning.'

It seemed both ridiculous and sad that an estate such as this was pretty much left to fall apart, yet Liz also understood the determination of Ronald Baxter to keep people engaged in the life – and death – of his beloved parents. What a pity he'd succumbed to cancer before seeing justice. Well, she was going to bring it to him, one way or another.

'I really like Pete but geez he can be insensitive,' Meg said. 'Everything points to murder.'

'Yes... but no. He sees things on the surface first. And the lack of interest and support by the police was continually backed up by a belief that this was a bungled robbery. Murder generally has a solid motive and that just doesn't add up. The couple were well-liked and had no history of dealings which might attract the wrong people.'

The closer they got to the house, the more uneasy Liz felt. She shook the feeling off. This was just an old building. There were no people hiding in the shadows. No bodies buried in the base-ment... at least the original investigation had discounted such things.

'I'd live here,' Meg said. 'At least I would if it was closer to the sea.'

'Where *do* you live?'

Meg gave her a disbelieving glance. 'I think I need to host the next dinner party. I'm in St Kilda, across the road from the beach and in sight of the pier. You thought Candace had views to die for.'

'I'm easily impressed because just about anything is better than the old apartment I had, but now I want to know where everyone else lives. Apart from Pete because I already know.'

'He doesn't have a view other than of the shops around his place yet he's happy there.'

Liz phone buzzed. 'Did he hear us talking about him?' She answered on speaker. 'Did you get lost?'

'I wish. We found a well.'

'Does that make it a *wishing* well?' Meg asked.

'Hysterical. Once we've finished the parameter check we're getting some gear from the car and taking a look. Unless you need us at the house, that is.'

'Finish your garden stroll, then come and find us and we can work out the next steps.'

Before Pete could argue, Liz ended the call. Unofficially she was second in command to Ben and didn't mind taking on the role. Candace was outside the usual chain of command as a consultant, but Liz would defer to her in anything other than operational decisions. And Pete was used to being told what to do… more or less.

The women stopped at the bottom of a dozen steps leading to the entry of the house. It was an eclectic design featuring curved walls and porthole windows as well as a lot of straight lines. The steps were to one side, curving up to a tiled open area about ten metres square. The rails were white stone, matching the majority of the outside of the house, other than dark grey trimmings and roof.

'Can you imagine this place all lit up for a gala dinner?' Meg gazed around. 'This tiled area would be perfect for servers to hand out welcome drinks and guests to mingle before going inside.'

The tiled area reached around a protruding, glassed room and to one side, double doors led inside.

Liz went through the keys to find the one with a tag saying 'front'. She unlocked the glass doors, pushed them open and went in. Meg was right behind and they stopped in awe after a few more steps.

The glassed, semi-circle room was a grand foyer and open to a mezzanine level. A wide, sweeping staircase led up with marble steps and polished timber railings. The largest chandelier Liz had ever laid eyes on hung from a long chain, and wall lamps sat over half a dozen small tables, which were the only furniture in the vast space.

'Why did I think it would be left intact?' Liz gazed around. 'No furniture as such or personal touches.'

'Because it is decades. Inspector Baxter probably couldn't see the point in keeping it all. He wouldn't know forensic technology would advance so much, but guess what? It has.' Meg held out a hand. 'May I have the case? I don't want to set down my equipment until I've checked the floor.'

They did a swap as Meg piled her bags onto Liz and took the case. She had no choice but to place it on the ground to open and chose a spot along a wall. In a few minutes she'd constructed a narrow table, a bit like a card table but on thin, adjustable legs and a top which slid apart like an extendable dining table. Ending up about a metre long, it made it easy for Meg to unpack her bags onto it.

'That is clever.'

'Figured it would have many a use and is better than contaminating a table or bench. I want to do a quick sweep of the floor and walls in here first but as long as you don't touch anything, go right ahead and look around.'

Liz left Meg to set up the hand-held device she used to look for blood and other substances, which was a bit like a metal detector but with a built-in analyser and camera. She might be a forensic analysist by description but Meg had several degrees and was continually adding to her tools of trade. The team was incredibly fortunate to have her.

She was drawn by the staircase and followed it to the mezzanine. It was easy to watch Meg work from here and for a minute she had the oddest urge to sit on the floor and peer through the balustrade… as a child might when there's an adult party below. There'd be a string quartet playing and people talking in small groups, white-shirted waiters offering drinks and trays with tiny, delicious bites of grown-up food.

And I'd be so quiet nobody would notice me.

With a jolt, Liz stepped back. Her heart thudded and she drew in a long breath.

There was only Meg down there. No music or waiters. What on earth had gotten into her?

'Slacking off already?' Meg grinned from below.

'Um… admiring your work.'

The second Meg returned to her task, Liz spun away, almost running to the nearest room.

'I don't think you should have to manage getting my weight up and down the well shaft,' Pete said. 'Best if you go in and I'll shoulder the efforts up here.'

Reuben snorted but didn't bother replying. Pete didn't blame him. He'd complained a lot this morning and was beginning to annoy himself. Something wasn't sitting well and he couldn't decide it if was the cold case, the waste land they were walking around, or the potential issues with the team itself. He wasn't one to need security or safety but he valued loyalty. Heck, even some of the underworld bosses he'd associated with as an undercover cop had loyalty. They might kill you, but they'd have a good reason, and if they didn't they'd defend you to the death.

They'd followed the boundary of the property along the front, one side, and the back and were heading in the direction of the car again. Other than the well there was little of interest. A handful of locked outbuildings. Neglected garden beds. A glasshouse so overgrown it was impossible to open the doors.

'Just needs some love,' Reuben said.

'Who?'

'Not who. This property. It would make a wonderful place for a private school. Arts, culinary, that kind of thing. Young adults maybe, who need a hand getting started.'

'So they'd learn to grow their produce and cook it? Become chefs?'

'Yeah. Or draw or act or make films.'

'You're an idealist. Liz would like that. Me? I'm a realist.'

'Bulldoze it and build a supermarket?'

'With a giant apartment building above it.'

Pete actually agreed with Reuben's ideas but liked keeping his more humanitarian side private. His more *human* side. Better than letting people get too close.

They reached the front gate and at the car opened a chiller box and opened bottles of water. The day was unseasonally hot and humid and heavy clouds were gathering in the distance. Both checked their phones and as Reuben tapped away for a minute or two, Pete's eyes wandered over the closed gate behind them. It was wrought iron and tall, with pointed bits sticking up. He had no idea of the real name of the pieces and on closer inspection noticed they were shaped like arrows. A danger for anyone attempting to climb over.

The entire property was surrounded by ten foot high stone walls with smooth sides. The only regular way in and out was through this gate and the average robber would be intimidated by the obstacles. All reports were of the gate being locked that night.

This wasn't a theft gone wrong.

'Meg just said she's found something and to bring her camera bag.'

As they walked up to the house it was easy to see Liz at a window on the top floor. She wasn't looking their way but out over the grounds to her right. Pete followed her line of sight but there were shrubs in the way.

'Look at these mosaics. Absolutely stunning.'

Reuben was fixated on old tiles in a large area at the top of the stairs. He wandered to the far corner, eyes on the pattern.

'Yeah. Groovy.'

Pete joined him, glancing up to look for Liz. She was still in the window, her position unchanged. From this vantage he could see over the shrubs.

Liz was staring in the direction of the well.

FOUR

Hearing Pete and Reuben talking with Meg, Liz ran down the stairs. The other three were in one of the rooms which went off the foyer and they looked around when she entered.

'Oh good. Meg, once we're done here would you take your tool to the last bedroom upstairs?'

'You calling me a tool?' Pete asked.

It wasn't worth a response even if it was a half-hearted attempt at humour. He was in a mood and best left to sort himself out.

'I'll head up there next, Liz. Thanks for bringing the camera bag, Reuben. Would you take a lot of photos for me?' Meg pointed to an empty wall. 'There's blood splatter in the wallpaper. The camera has several settings including ultraviolet so please take a heap with that as well as infrared and just a normal view.'

'In here?' Liz peered at the wall which had no obvious staining. 'The bodies were located upstairs.'

'And there was no sign of them being moved. Mr Baxter was on the floor at the end of their bed wearing a dressing gown. Mrs Baxter was in the bed. Theory was that the robbers entered the bedroom and Baxter came after them, but only got as far as where he was shot.' Reuben opened the camera bag. 'Three decades is a long time for trace to be left like this. Any chance of identifying it?'

'Good thing we have access to a state of the art lab and my friend there has enjoyed considerable success at doing what seems impossible.' Meg handed Pete a scalpel and several tiny evidence bags. 'You have steady hands so when Reuben has finished photographing, would you take about ten samples from random spots, one for each bag. I've already marked them as being in here, which I assume was a sitting room.'

Pete visibly brightened.

'We'll be upstairs,' Liz said. 'Do you need to bring anything else?'

'Depends. Let's go take a look first.'

Liz avoided looking down to the foyer this time, walking briskly along a wide and long hallway which was at a right angle to the downstairs floorplan. Rooms came off both sides; bedrooms, bathrooms, and another sitting room. At the very end were open double doors.

'This was the master bedroom, according to the info we have.' Liz led the way in. 'There's a huge bathroom through there and a walk in robe large enough for a dozen people over there. From measuring between the marks in the carpet, the bed was king sized.'

There were indents in the thick carpet, even after all this time, not just from the bed but other heavy furniture.

'I've read the reports about the scene of the murder… or whatever those in charge decided to call it, and it doesn't add up.'

'Oh baby, a whole lot doesn't add up, just based on finding the blood on the wall. The photos and analysis of the readings from the nifty tool of mine will show more, but it looked exactly as though someone was shot standing up, about a metre from the wall. So what are you thinking, Liz?'

Back near the window where she'd found herself earlier, Liz

gestured from point to point as she talked. 'The person who found the scene stated the double doors were closed. She remembers tapping a few times and getting concerned because the couple were early risers. I think it was their housekeeper, who we might need to track down. But the point is that if you'd just gone into a room as a thief, unexpectedly come across two people and shot them, would you take the time to shut the door, let alone risk leaving trace? Going back to the report there was blood in the carpet and in the bed which matched the husband and wife but none found anywhere else.'

'If she was shot in the bed, asleep, then it is likely blood would be in and under the bed,' Meg said. 'But Mr Baxter was moving according to reports. If he'd heard intruders he'd got up, put on his dressing gown, and would be heading for the door. I don't know if he had a weapon in the room?'

Liz made a note on her tablet. 'We'll find out.'

'Regardless, he was allegedly shot at the end of the bed and found on his side, facing the door. There would be a considerable amount of blood soaked into and beneath the carpet.'

'But the carpet is intact, Meg. No one has cut and lifted it. I took a good look – without touching.'

Meg grinned. 'Good girl. Trained you well.' She sobered. 'I wish Inspecter Baxter was alive to speak with. This entire case was mishandled from my research and I might need to ask my forensic friend to come take a look. That isn't a problem?'

'Not a problem from me. Will chat to Ben and arrange it. We have a big job ahead.'

A rumble of thunder rattled the window panes.

'Didn't see that coming! Boys won't be happy because the well will have to wait. No outside jobs today.'

It probably isn't even safe to try and climb down it.

The unsettled feeling in her gut was back. She'd never been down a well of any sort but had read enough thrillers to put her off them for life. Knowing Pete, he was itching to climb down. He loved dark and musty and dangerous places.

. . .

After a brief storm the rain settled in for the afternoon, steady and persistent. Reuben had run down and collected the car which was now to one side of the house. The air was still humid but a bit cooler and the house itself hadn't been hot to start with, making it tolerable to keep working.

Meg continued to look for blood and other trace evidence, while Pete and Reuben took more photos and began to build a document of findings. Liz wasn't needed for any of those tasks and kept searching the house, using her observation skills and experience to include or exclude rooms from Meg's attention. At least for now, because the time might come when they'd have to do a second, even more thorough sweep.

The house was huge with eight bedrooms upstairs, including the impressive master. She asked Meg to look into the long hallway which once had been adorned with an imported carpet runner, according to police records. What was missing from the house had her interest. The runner, which might contain blood and possibly trace from the intruders. The master bed, and the furniture in the downstairs sitting room. On their own they were key components into the investigation, yet at some point after the case was closed, they'd been moved or even destroyed.

Liz was making notes as she wandered. Tonight she'd put her thoughts into a proper format and talk to Ben about the next steps. Back at the hub the other team members were just as busy going through old records from the police as well as casting a wider net into the community of the day.

But what about Dad?

She stopped in the kitchen. When Ben first approached Liz to join the new team he'd assured her that he was determined to find the man who'd not only kidnapped at least two children in the past but was responsible for the murder of several people, including Liz's old boss.

And surely was behind the abduction of Lyndall.

It was part of a large and confusing puzzle.

Kyle Moorland had pulled Lyndall out of the sea in Port Phillip Bay and handed her to Liz… not that she'd recognised him behind a clever disguise. Yet much pointed to her father being the mastermind behind Lyndall's kidnapping from her safe room. Saving her and taking credit later was one of his cruel tricks to try and manipulate Liz.

There were so many moving parts right now yet deep down, Liz believed more was interconnected than she'd ever considered.

'Was this part of his work as well?' She spoke aloud then glanced around. Thankfully she was alone.

The idea that Kyle was involved with the murders of the inspector's parents was outrageous in many respects. Yet he'd proved his evilness and ability to form and control human connections in the least expected places. For years she'd unknowingly lived in an apartment building with two of those connections. Then Lyndall's abduction. Trying to unravel how he fitted into the operations of Marcus Bonner, and how much he had to do with the man's death, was still under investigation.

She shook her head to clear her thoughts. This wasn't getting the job done.

The kitchen was a true country affair with black and white checked floor, two huge standalone ovens with gas cooktops, and a wide timber-topped counter. Wearing gloves, she went through each drawer and cupboard, expecting them to be empty. Instead, there was cutlery and crockery, mostly expensive-looking, plus cookware and utensils. Nothing was in the large pantry though and the fridge and freezer were slowly rusting away.

Liz made some notes and took photos.

Everywhere she went it was a similar result. Furniture missing. Personal items gone. But like the items in the kitchen, she found a few other signs that the job had not been completed. In the laundry she opened a washing machine and quickly closed it again. The smell of rotten material was horrendous and she opened a nearby window. If that was thirty years or more of dirty washing… or even clean but not hung out… then what were the chances the contents mattered?

She messaged Meg to come to the laundry next. Had the police search missed this? Or was it something done much later?

'Definitely need masks on for this. Protective clothing even.' Meg wore both after a quick trip to the car. She had the lid of the washing machine open and Liz held a large evidence bag open from as far away as she could be while still being close enough to be useful. Her own mask wasn't helping stop the smell from turning her stomach.

'One bag for each piece. Take your time, Liz. This is gross. Breathe through your mouth.'

'Is this why you are officially a digital analyst?'

'Oh yes. Computers are much easier to deal with, but on the other hand, having the ability to use other skills in this job is neat.'

'Except for right now.'

Meg carefully placed what might once have been socks into the open bag with tongs. 'Except for right now.'

A few minutes later Liz had a pile of sealed bags and Meg was swabbing the washing machine. 'Whoever searched this house after the murders should be fired.'

'Any chance they were put here later?'

'I guess. But why? Everything I've pulled out was just normal washing from both genders. If the inspector was doing his own washing for some reason, it would be boy clothes, surely. No, this isn't a casual wash which was forgotten.'

'What is the smell?' Pete dramatically held his nose between finger and thumb as he peered through the door. 'If I'd known we were doing washing I'd have brought my basket.'

Liz glanced around. The laundry was large with a big dryer, several cupboards, shelving, and a bench. There was an ironing board and a couple of irons, a few folded towels, and an open rack presumably to hang clothes. But no washing basket.

'Has anyone come across a washing basket?'

Reuben was now in the doorway as well and all shook their heads.

'I'm going to be a while in here, guys,' Meg said. 'Might as well check the room for other trace. Liz, can you get the clothes to the car for me please? Or leave them at the front door and we can run them out when we leave."

Pete stepped in and picked up all the bags. 'This was inside the washing machine? I'll put them near the door.'

Liz followed him but stayed in the hallway. 'Meg, anything you need from the rest of us?'

'Not just yet. Although,' she glanced up from swabbing the washing machine. 'I am concerned we might overlook important clues because of the lack of furniture. Which doesn't sound like it even makes sense.'

Reuben nodded. 'It does. A furnished house has a system in place for cops. We work methodically to search from end to end, room to room, ceiling to floor. Here we have open space and no structure. We go into a room which has lights and window covering and either carpet or timber flooring. Not much else. Too easy to overlook something.'

'In that case shall you and I start over and talk through what we see?' Liz asked.

Every set of eyes mattered and for far too long, this case has slipped through the fingers of those who investigated. Well, not now.

FIVE

Pete collected the car and went in search of food for them all. The weather was annoying because he was itching to get down that well. Something had him curious and despite him saying it was best Reuben go in, he didn't really feel that way. Dark places intrigued him and their flashlights hadn't reached the bottom of the stone structure. There could be bones down there, or a secret passage.

The nearest shops were a few kilometres away which gave him a chance to evaluate the area. No doubt there were new homes built in the last thirty years to close in around Heberden House, but at the time of the deaths there'd been mostly small acreages or else empty land.

What had made the property desirable to its owners was a combination of isolation, so they could enjoy a peaceful lifestyle and high degree of privacy, as well as its relatively easy access to Melbourne. The drive out took about an hour and while the location had a rural feel, it was only minutes to a large shopping centre. If the estate was put up for sale it would make a lot of money, but according to the inspector's will, nothing could happen until the case was solved and properly closed.

Pete parked outside a supermarket and grabbed a basket on

his way in. He loved shopping. Loved preparing meals for people but not full-on cooking so much. Stuff he could reheat or put together from several sources was his talent. Once they sniffed out and disposed of the mole – or proved there wasn't one – he'd throw a lavish party and invite the team.

He chose carefully, considering the dietary preferences of the people back at the house. It mattered to treat others with respect… if they deserved it. Liz and Meg and Ben did, for sure. Reuben? Pete hadn't decided but was leaning toward trust and now everyone else had to have the benefit of the doubt.

Back in the car he took a different route. The rain was still steady but in the distance some blue sky was making an effort to show up.

His route brought him behind Heberden House and at one point he was higher than the property and caught snippets of its roof. Pete pulled over and walked back a bit, wet weather gear doing enough to keep him dry. This road was narrow with drive-ways heading off either side every hundred metres or so. He took some photos and made note of where he was by tapping into the app on his phone. Meg had created something quite brilliant and all he needed to do was open the navigation to find himself with better accuracy and data than any regular online map. He sent it to his email for later.

From here he looked over the top of a house, which was set back from the road and lower than where he stood. Behind it was the stone wall belonging to the estate and there was little to see beyond it other than the top of the roof. Glancing around, he couldn't see how there'd be another vantage point as good and he moved to the gate of the nearby house.

It was controlled by a panel and he wasn't about to bother the residents, but took a good look at the home which was partly hidden behind a long hedge. It looked modern. He stepped back enough to take a photo of the number of the property. If this was a paddock at the time of the killings, the perps might have found a way in over the wall. He agreed that they'd need equipment but wasn't ready to rule out a theft gone wrong. Not just yet.

More than anyone on the team, other than Liz, he wanted to find if her dad was involved. For most of the others this was a case to investigate, same as the search for Kyle Moorland. But he knew first-hand the toll that man put on his daughter. Daughters. And grandchild. At least he had no knowledge of a great grandson and would ignore that side of his family in his pursuit of Liz. Kyle was a high functioning sociopath and narcissist if not a hundred other things which Candace was better positioned to diagnose. Pete had the strongest sense the man was somehow involved in the murder of the inspector's parents and he had every intention of proving it.

Liz deserved to find peace.

'This room has ghosts.'

Reuben stood just inside the door of the master bedroom. His eyes slowly roamed the expanse, coming to a stop on Liz, who was back at the window, looking at him.

'Ghosts?'

'Shadows of existence. Remnants of life. Laughter. Tears. Passion. Anger.'

'You feel all of this? Here?'

His face was haunted by something. Drawn. Liz had a strange compulsion to close the distance between them and offer him… what? A hug?

'When I was in here with Pete we were both occupied but now I'm back to look more closely it is quite clear. I must sound mad to you.'

'No. The room is strange and I wouldn't want to be here overnight.'

Reuben joined Liz at the window. 'I noticed you here earlier. Before it rained.'

'I saw the well.' She pointed. 'Through those two oaks.'

'Pete is disappointed about the weather. He did suggest I go down the well but I got the feeling he would quickly take over the job.'

Liz laughed.

'I am curious about what's down there,' Reuben said. 'We couldn't find any sign of use, no windmill or pumps.'

'We'll come back and look. For that matter, I'd like you to get a drone up at some point when it's not raining and give us a better view of the property as it stands today. Even online maps aren't current.' She pulled herself from the window and wandered around the walls. 'What are we missing in here? What do we need to follow up?'

'According to the police files the murders took place between nine and ten in the evening. It was summertime. Seems early to be asleep if you have a couple who loved to entertain and were known for their lavish parties. The staff were gone for the night. I need to check the weather conditions.'

'Yes, and their movements around the time. Had they just come to the house that day?'

Reuben shook his head. 'I read they were here for a longer break. Their other home was used more in winter.'

'I wonder… even though both were officially retired from their respective careers, Ilona still oversaw her business. We might see if there was a diary kept or calendar of events. Records of her involvement in case that leads to anyone of interest.'

'And follow up where any of the staff are today. Although most would be getting on.' He was making notes on his tablet. 'I like the approach of looking into their day to day life because that says more than any interview with onlookers. Possibly even better than forensics.'

'Don't say that in front of Meg.'

He glanced up with a smile and Liz caught her breath. There was something about the man which attracted her. Not just his looks but his intellect and critical thinking and his kindness.

'What's that look for?'

Reuben held the tablet against his chest and closed the distance between them. The room felt smaller when he stopped a couple of feet away, his expression curious.

'Meg. She'll forensically dissect anyone who puts old fashioned investigating above her cutting edge tech.'

He'll believe that. I would.

'I have the greatest respect for Meg and her work. Even more for you, Liz. And as a cohesive team, there's little we can't accomplish.'

A crack of thunder rattled the windows and they each took a step back with a laugh.

They stopped long enough to eat. Pete was many things but at his core was a person with moral strength and a decency he underplayed. His default was clown jester or else full-on ass. The meals might have been an eclectic choice from the supermarket able to be mixed and matched without heating, but they took into account the preferences he'd noticed over time. There was plenty there for Reuben to eat and not enough people bothered to cater for a vegan as a matter of course.

Food consumed, the search continued. With Pete back, he and Reuben continued the room-to-room evaluation and Liz was freed up to check in with Meg who was in the kitchen.

'The laundry is a fantastic place.' Meg grinned and turned her laptop to show Liz a long list on a spreadsheet. 'There's almost fifty groups of samples and that's before the clothes are tested. I'm not into speculation over science but there's a pattern emerging and I think that someone put bloody clothes into that washing machine.'

'We'll take it back to the hub.'

'Hoped you'd say that. Depending on what I find with further testing, we might need a look at the plumbing for any traces of blood. What is happening next?'

'The guys are continuing to check each room. So far there's

nothing demanding your attention so is there anything you want to do or want me to do?'

'Absolutely. I want to look for secret passages.'

Liz smiled, thinking Meg was joking but the serious expression on the other woman's face said otherwise.

'You have my attention.'

Meg slipped her laptop into the bag she usually had slung across a shoulder. 'Can we take a walk?' She didn't wait, immediately leaving the room.

By the time Liz caught up, Meg was at the end of a long hallway, having gone past the laundry and a few doors which were old staff quarters. She had one hand on the wall.

'Here.'

'Looks like a wall. Plastered.'

'Exactly! Ten points, Liz.'

That made Liz take a closer look. The hallway was lined with wallpaper but not the end.

'Did they run out?'

Meg tapped on the plaster.

'That's not hollow. Should it be?'

Liz checked a couple of the hallway walls which sounded hollow.

'Is the house double brick?'

'Nope. And I pulled up the only plans we have which show this as stairs down to a cellar.'

'Isn't the cellar at the other end of the house?'

'It is. Now either somebody messed up the plans or the build, or some renovations were had. Fair enough to close off a staircase to an unused area but to brick it up? I need to have a look behind here.'

Liz stood a few feet back, eyes roaming across the plaster. 'Is it just me or is the job pretty awful? I mean, look at the corner and how it isn't a perfect seal. And...' she knelt and leaned down. 'There's a gap. We might open this up now, Meg. Do you think? Or should we run it past Ben? Get more info.'

'I really want to vote for now but might need some other equipment. My metal detector, as you call it, only has so many uses and I'd rather we open this up once I have the tools to capture any anomalies.'

Well, that's disappointing.

'Alright. Can you sort what you need to do this and then we'll finish off for the day. We have a ton of information to dissect and if Ben agrees, we can return tomorrow with more of the team and a firm plan.'

SIX

Ben was in his office with Hamish sitting across from him. The other man's was the first of the questionnaires to be returned to Candace and with half an hour free, Ben wanted to talk. They'd chatted about the weather and it was clear Hamish was nervous for although he sat with an ankle on his other knee and his arms behind his head, the slight jiggling of the raised foot was constant.

'Candace let me know you were happy to share your thoughts from the questionnaire. I'd like to confirm that before going further.'

'Of course. There's no point working in a team but not being a team player.'

Yet you go out of your way to irritate those around you.

'I appreciate that sentiment. And I expect your background in an Intelligence unit meant having to trust your colleagues. Is there anyone in Operation Nobody you trust as much as those in your past career?'

It was a risky question. Candace had provided a list of subjects and questions for Ben based not only on Hamish's responses but her own method of cutting through lies and deception as well as picking up any weakness or areas requiring more training. Hamish was the least known to Ben but had exceptional skills and references and during the last case – which was the first the team faced – he'd performed well under extreme pressure. More than well. He'd stopped an escaping murderer and kidnapper with a single shot over water from a helicopter at night. Not your average cop.

'Trust is built over time, in my experience,' Hamish said. 'Overall the team has incredible potential.'

'So is that no?'

Hamish smiled slightly. 'If my life was on the line? I trust you. And Liz. And Pete.'

Sorry, what? Pete?

'And you wouldn't be wrong to trust us. Anyone else?'

'May I speak in confidence?'

'Please.'

'I like Reuben but he is very much a straight shooter. He watches people and makes silent judgements and while that's a strong plus with perps, it is unsettling for colleagues.'

'Unsettling?'

'Hard to explain. I find myself guarding what I say in case he misjudges my intent.'

This was interesting. Hamish was a bit like Pete with the way he spoke his mind or failed to filter but Pete didn't care about the opinion of other people for the most part. Obviously Hamish did. He'd certainly toned down his over-the-top way of speaking since the recent case.

'And you care that you are seen accurately.'

Hamish nodded. 'Certainly. I take pride in how I present myself professionally and would be mortified to be viewed in the wrong way.'

Then you need to keep working on how you interact with the team.

Ben made a mental note to discuss this with Candace.

'The others in the team?'

As if relaxing at last, Hamish dropped his arms. 'Meg is the most intelligent person I've ever met. Candace is… well, she's Candace. I like her a lot.'

'Phoebe?'

'Pheebs is a special kind of clever. She seems to have tendrils reaching across the globe with her podcast and team.'

'And Annette?'

Something crossed the other man's face. A shadow of a reaction which immediately disappeared. Hamish shrugged. 'She smokes too much.'

Ben wasn't ready to push Hamish further. He could easily ask if Hamish meant she was using smoking as a way to slack off but the aim wasn't to pitch people against each other. He glanced at his notes.

'Do you have questions for me? Or comments?'

'I'd like to be doing more. Take today for example. Annette and I have trawled through boxes of old police records sorting them into a more logical system. Phoebe isn't here today so we've managed it alone. While the others are exploring the property and doing an actual investigation, I'm left behind shuffling papers.'

At no time did Hamish change the easy going tone of his voice but the words sent a message Ben wouldn't ignore. The other man felt excluded.

'And you'd rather be taking action in a more physical way.'

'I would.' Now, a lopsided smile touched his lips. 'I sound petulant.'

'Not every part of police work is action. You know that. And I've seen just how good you are under pressure and in intense danger. But there was a reason I wanted you working on the old files.'

Hamish leaned forward, interested.

'According to what little we know, those deaths were virtually swept under a metaphorical rug. Only one person believed they were murders yet there is evidence to support his belief which was discarded and I need to know why.'

'So not only the path to the decision to close the case but what went on around it. Read between the line. Gotcha.'

'The other thing, Hamish? Alongside this case I intend to begin investigating Kyle Moorland and I need you to help with that and be able to spot any connections between the two.'

'I can do that. If there's nothing more, I'll go and write my brief for later.'

'Thank you. And believe me… you will get plenty of action in the future. I'm just trying to give each team member the opportunity to work to their strengths, one at a time.'

After Hamish left, Candace wandered in and took the same chair.

'He looked happier leaving than coming in.'

'Might have found one of his positive triggers. Are you around for the next briefing?'

'No dinner party to prepare tonight.' She smiled. 'Liz and co just left the mansion.'

Ben checked the time. 'Would you ask Annette to write her brief? I want to do the memo about my chat with Hamish for you while its fresh in my mind. And I'll order pizzas and get Pete to stop on their way to collect them.'

Liz wrote her report on the way back. They all were, other than Pete who was driving. He complained enough that she'd told him to dictate to his phone and set it up for him. Thank goodness there were noise cancelling headphones in the unit. They stopped long enough to pick up pizzas ordered by the boss at the place they preferred with Reuben running it to grab them. The vehicle smelled of pizza by the time they finally parked beneath the building.

'Can you two take the food and Pete and I will grab the washing machine?' Reuben asked.

'There's a trolley. We don't need to carry.'

'We need to lift it out, mate and I'd rather share the load.'

'The washing load?' Pete quipped.

Everyone groaned.

The afternoon had been long and hunger and tiredness was setting in. Liz wanted to go home. Last night, after the dinner at Candace's apartment, she'd searched for apartments to buy and had a list she looked forward to revisiting. And get some much-needed sleep.

Once upstairs, Hamish took the boxes and set everything out on the round table in the conference room. Phoebe had just arrived after working at home for the day and Annette hurried in and to the bathroom – presumably to freshen up after being on the roof to smoke. She was the only smoker in the team although Hamish would accept one if offered. Liz had never seen the attraction but understood the effects of stress in a job like theirs was dealt with differently by different people. Booze was popular. Liz liked running.

The briefing was done over dinner.

'Who'd like to start?' Ben helped himself to different flavoured pizza from three boxes, piling them onto a plate before taking his seat.

'May I?' This was Candace. 'Not that I have anything to offer than to say thank you to everyone who has already completed and returned the debriefing questionnaire. I'm only waiting on two now. And I want to remind each team member that I'm here not only as a profiler for cases but as a confidential ear should anyone ever want a chat.'

'I knew it,' Pete said.

All eyes turned to him.

'The minute I send in my questionnaire the offer comes for psycho-analysis. I probably broke the form.'

There was a ripple of laughter.

'And my door is especially open for you, Pete.'

'Ta.' Pete grinned at Candace.

Annette cleared her throat. 'Hamish and I made excellent progress on the old files but I couldn't believe the appalling state of most of the boxes. Not the way I'd ever have managed evidence!'

Liz had admired Annette's work ethic for a long time. She'd been a solid patrol officer then as a Senior Constable became expert at overseeing evidence practices before briefly moving into running interview and interrogations rooms in Melbourne's major crimes. Her meticulous and no nonsense approach to accuracy was what brought her to the notice of Ben when he was recruiting for the team.

'Anyway, we wrangled the files into a logical sequence and have found some very interesting things.'

'More accurately,' Hamish said. 'Interesting exclusions.'

'Yes, that's a better description. To explain, there are gaps both in time and information.'

'We think that files are missing, don't we?' Hamish asked.

'We do.'

Ben tried to eat while he made a note and ended up losing half the topping. He sighed and put down the rest of the slice to keep writing. 'I'll email to see if anything was left behind.'

'Except it is within boxes,' Annette said. 'Almost every box has the same issue of either a complete file being gone or else incomplete reports. If this was typical policing from thirty odd years back then no wonder they couldn't solve a murder!'

It was good seeing Annette riled up about procedure. She'd been all over the place with the last case, from disappearing for a smoke or to make childcare arrangements which she should already have had in place, to then performing outstanding field support. That first case had been dropped on a team which wasn't even a day old so no wonder some members had a rocky start.

Growing pains is more logical than having someone planted to watch us.

Reuben sat beside Liz and offered her a slice from the pizza box most people left for him. She happily accepted. The others might think they should leave him an entire vegan pizza but

Reuben didn't offer unless he meant it. And she liked his spicier tastes.

'Great work Annette and Hamish. I saw your briefs come through and will take a look later. Alright, who'd like to speak for the field team?' Ben used his fingers to put everything back on his slice then looked around for a napkin. Candace slid one over.

'Unless anyone else wants to I will.' Meg – who hadn't touched the pizza –didn't bother waiting for approval. 'This case has been grossly mishandled from beginning to end. I'm not surprised files are missing. Whoever ran the case should be fired. Well, I imagine they aren't in the force now but you know what I mean. Tomorrow I will have a full report for each of us but tonight I'll be sorting through a gazillion samples as well as analysing the data from what Liz calls my metal detector.'

'Well, what's is it's real name?'

'I don't actually know, Liz.'

'Shall we ask everyone to offer suggestions?' Ben was amused. 'And for your clever futuristic data table?'

'Sure. Email the suggestions and we'll do a draw or vote. Anyway, the important bits are that there is substantial blood splatter in the lower floor room of the house. The bedroom, which was supposed to be where the couple died is only a secondary scene. And… some person put a load of washing on either before, during, or after the murders and the investigating police did not find it.'

As if satisfied with her appraisal, Meg finally helped herself to food and immediately stuffed it into her mouth.

For the first time, Phoebe spoke up. She was a quiet woman who observed more than joined conversations. Her expertise was unique. She ran a hugely successful true crime podcast and team of trusted staff with a vast network across the world. Like Candace, she wasn't a police officer but a civilian with unusual skills.

'This is a cover-up. What Annette and Hamish have found pointed to the likelihood but Meg's forensic findings confirm it.'

'We're listening, Phoebe,' Ben said.

She nodded slightly. 'Once I have more information I can create a podcast. My listeners love cold cases, the older the better. Last case we focused on Europe with art dealers and art scandals but this one will draw on people's memories of events here in Victoria.'

Ben caught Liz's eye. She was so impressed by the diversity of Operation Nobody. He'd done an exceptional job. If any covert team could solve this cold case, it was them.

SEVEN

The Yarra River was beautiful any time of year but Liz particularly loved it just before the first light of day. She'd run one of her favourite routes around Docklands then down one side of the slow moving waters of the Melbourne icon, following as close as tracks and footpaths allowed before crossing to the other side over the St Kilda Road bridge. For a minute or two she'd sipped water and caught her breath near Hamer Hall, then continued along Southbank Promenade.

She'd left her place in the dark and now the pre-dawn sky was casting a glow across the ripples in the water.

Along here were restaurants, wine bars, and nightspots, which drew locals and visitors alike. The massive Crown Casino complex spanned several blocks and was the home of such famous eateries as Rockpool, Nobu, and Bistro Guillaume.

Beyond this came boardwalks and a more open space to wander and it was here that Liz slowed and finally dropped to a walk. She passed the footbridge which crossed back over the Yarra and taking the path below an overpass she reached her destination. On the other side was a small, almost private marina and she found a spot to warm down and watch the change of colours among the yachts.

This was a quiet part of the river.

A couple of fairly new apartment buildings looked down on several rows of pleasure craft. There was little else here other than shopfronts selling the apartments and boats and one or two cafés. All closed so early in the day. A few apartments were lit but most remained in darkness. Liz remembered hearing many of the owners only visited when they wished to use their boats and it certainly felt barely populated. This was another area she was considering as a permanent home.

The skies were grey as daylight replaced the darkness. With a sudden drop in temperature, a few drops of rain landed on Liz's arms and she got going. As she neared the overpass the oddest sensation raised the hairs on her arms and she stopped to look back.

Nobody was around. No-one walking their dog or on a bicycle or jogging. Not even any watercraft passing. Her eyes scanned the apartment buildings but all was quiet.

So why do I feel I'm being watched?

She knew to trust her instincts and opened her phone, putting it into video mode. Long sweeps of the area might not be visible to her eyesight but once on a large screen and with some enhancing there was a better shot at finding whoever was around.

Or you could stop jumping at shadows.

Liz shoved the phone into a pocket and jogged, following the path to the foot bridge and putting distance between herself and the marina.

On the other side of the river she couldn't help herself and looked across the expanse of water to where she'd been only minutes earlier.

Right on the edge of the water stood a figure. Staring at her.

'I'll see what overhead images might have been taken around that time but the cloud cover won't help.' Meg had Liz's phone plugged into a laptop. 'Let me spend some quality time with this?'

'Thanks. And sorry. I know how much is on your plate right now.'

'That is what a plate is for. Piling stuff on. Coffee, please.'

Liz had no issues being told to make coffee. She'd stopped at home only long enough to change before coming in and hadn't had more than another bottle of water. Finding Meg here was a relief and she'd blurted everything out.

She set the coffee machine up for the day, using the familiar task to settle stupid nerves and an over-stimulated imagination. Ben and Pete arrived as she made the first cup and she called over the half-wall between the rooms that she'd make more. Carrying two in each hand she stopped with them at Meg's desk, where the other two were watching the video over her shoulder.

'Was it Kyle?' Pete asked. He took his and Ben's coffees, his eyes concerned. Of everyone, he knew what the criminal master-mind had put Liz through over the years.

'It was too far to tell and by the time I ran back over the bridge they'd gone. I should have checked the area more thor-oughly.' She placed Meg's cup down. The video was far clearer but again, there was no movement. No sign of her father.

Of course it was him.

The couple of photographs she'd attempted were useless thanks to the distance.

'I'm going to run all of this through a program which might assist a bit and I've got the co-ordinations and data so this is yours once again.' Meg unplugged the phone and handed it back. 'Next I'll put in a request with our special friends who are kind enough to share satellite images.'

'Appreciate this, Meg. Liz, come and fill us in.' Ben headed to his office.

Once Liz sat she drank half the coffee in one go. She had to keep her emotions in check and look at this logically. As an expe-rienced police officer.

'Start at the beginning.'

She began from the time she left her building until reaching Riverside Marina. 'The place was dead quiet. I go there once or twice a week at that time and usually there's at least some movement as people start their day. Occasionally a couple of yachts are coming or going, but not today. I felt some rain drops and then a sense of being watched.'

Pete and Ben nodded. Both were like her and let their natural instincts alert them to danger.

'After I couldn't see anything while videoing the area, I crossed the footbridge.'

'And he was just standing there.'

'Almost exactly where I'd stood a few minutes before. He didn't move and I couldn't clearly see his face plus he wore a wide brimmed hat and a long coat. A raincoat I think.'

'What makes you think it's Kyle?' Ben asked.

Pete shot him a look. 'Of course this is Kyle.'

Ben ignored him, waiting patiently for Liz to respond.

'I don't know if it is. I mean he talked to me face to face recently and I had no idea it was him so I'm going to be second-guessing myself for a long time.' She shrugged. 'My attempt to photograph the person was dismal and I sprinted back along the same path. He'd gone, of course and I spent way too long searching the area. For all I know this was a resident or by-passer looking at the river, not at me.'

'He's clever, Lizzie. Someone able to kill to steal an identity and not be found out for decades has to be, let alone all the other crap he pulls,' Pete said. 'He warned you to stop looking for him.'

'So how would he know we are?'

'He may be watching you. Time to move you somewhere safer.' Ben reached for his phone.

'Absolutely not. Thanks, but Kyle has had plenty of chances to hurt me and hasn't. There's some kind of unfinished business with us that he wants to pan out a certain way and if I suddenly drop out of sight then he'll put things in motion before we've had time to corner him.'

Ben's hand left the phone and he nodded. 'Okay. But I'll arrange surveillance. Meg and Reuben can set things up and between them there'll be no trace of it. Are you prepared to keep doing what you normally do? Run that route?'

Her heart was going a little too fast. 'Yes. Maybe not alone though.'

'You won't be. Give me a bit of time to work on some ideas.'

'Liz, move in with me,' Pete said. 'If not with me, then Candace. She's got room and her apartment is as secure as any I've seen.'

'Nah. You'd hate me as a housemate. I'm messy.'

'You are not.'

'I could be.'

His eyes dropped to the empty coffee cup in his hands, his lips tight.

I've offended you.

'Hey, I appreciate the suggestion. The offer. But Pete, if it was Kyle then he's revealed himself for a reason. Me suddenly moving anywhere will likely tell him I'm using the team to find him. I don't want anyone hurt. I don't want you hurt.'

He looked at her. 'It goes both ways.'

Ben's phone rang. 'The aim is to avoid anyone being hurt other than the bad guys. I need to answer this.'

Ben waited until the others left and answered, spirits lifting at the thought of speaking to the one person in the world who made his life complete.

'I was about to hang up! I even checked the clock to make sure I'd not phoned you on Ellie time.'

'Ellie time is always the right time. Just finished a short meeting.'

'At seven-something in the morning?'

Hearing Ellie's voice lowered Ben's blood pressure on the spot. He was sure of it. Being away from her so often and the life they'd built in a small coastal town, well, it sucked.

'This is a team of early-birds. Like you. What's on the agenda today?'

'Last night I created a new menu for autumn and want to test it on the staff and Michael before going much further. So I've been to the markets and just arrived in the restaurant. I like it when we're closed and quiet.'

Ben laughed. 'And you like it even more when it is open and noisy.'

'This is true.'

Michael was Ellie's older brother who'd suffered life-changing brain injuries a few years ago. He lived with Ben and Ellie, and since the move was becoming more mobile and coherent than in all the time in expensive and exclusive residential care. He'd never walk again unaided nor hold a job, but he was speaking in proper sentences and getting pretty good at swimming in the surf down the road from their home. Ellie had moved to the town with Michael to open her little restaurant and Ben followed in the hope they'd create a life together.

They had.

'Are you okay, honey? You sound a bit worried. Distracted.'

He leaned back in his chair and swivelled it away from the desk, his eyes closing briefly. If anyone could pick up on his mood, it was Ellie.

'Liz had an odd encounter this morning. We believe her father may have tracked her down.'

'Oh no. She's alright?'

'Yes. Sorry, should have led with that. It was all from a distance where she goes running.'

'From what you've told me he is a terrible person so the sooner you find him the better.'

There was a slight sound behind Ben and he turned his chair

to find Hamish in the doorway. The man's hand whipped up as though to tap on the open door.

How long have you been standing there?

Ben gestured for him to come in.

'Sweetheart, I have to go for now. Will you give Michael my love?'

'Always. And lots for you.'

'Same, Ellie.'

Trying to push away the irritation at being interrupted, Ben ended the call and looked at Hamish.

He stood just inside the door and was obviously uncomfortable. 'Sorry, Ben. Hadn't seen you were on the phone.'

'No problem. What's up?'

'Annette got an email about your query regarding any missing files from the cold case. We've been invited to go and search for ourselves.'

'Invited?'

Hamish grinned. 'I'm being polite. Do you mind if we do?'

'Please. Shall I have a word with whoever wrote the email?'

'I believe Annette knows them and is presently formulating the appropriate response for when we arrive. Or potentially, leave. Just in case we are kicked out.'

'Alright but keep notes. Are you going now?'

'Unless you need us for something more pressing?'

'This is important, so see what you can find. Phone if there's any pushback.'

Ben watched Hamish speak to Annette at her desk then she turned and nodded. In a moment they were leaving. Good for them. Hamish would enjoy being out of the building and Annette wouldn't mince words with anyone who stopped their progress. Putting them together was working better than he'd hoped.

EIGHT

Pete sat in Candace's office with Reuben and Meg. Liz had been given the job of going shopping to restock the fridge and pantry which she'd complained about and told everyone she knew she was being got rid of and wouldn't buy anything delicious.

Candace was unhappy about the events at Riverside Marina and had insisted on talking without Liz. 'Given how little we understand about Kyle's network it's best Liz doesn't know most of what you're planning. Not the fine details.'

Reuben and Hamish were both experts in the field of operation intelligence. Pete wasn't half bad himself but didn't have the technical skills they had and his approach was less finessed. Years of working undercover – often with the absolute bottom of the pit of wrongdoers – had taught him a thing or two. Even now he had contacts to call upon for just about any situation. And if this team couldn't protect Liz and find her damned father, then he'd look elsewhere for protection.

'Pete? Did you hear the question?'

'Sorry, Candace.'

'I wanted to know if you have anything specific about Kyle which might help us put together the best surveillance.'

'He has ears everywhere.'

'Anything less sweeping?' The corners of Candace's lips flicked up for an instant.

'You saw what he was like when we were hunting that little girl's abductor. Kyle Moorland had at least two people in his pocket living in the same apartment building as the child *and* Liz.'

'We're having a briefing on him later today and I'll be taking notes. This man is far from the average perp.'

'Don't admire him, Reuben. He's evil.'

'Admiration is not the word I'd use.'

For once Meg didn't have a tablet or other device attached to her. 'We can't risk anyone going in to bug Liz's apartment.'

'Then the building its in,' Pete said.

She shook her head. 'If it was Kyle at the marina do you really think it was random? He'll know her recent habits which could well include visitors at home, and she doesn't have them.'

'She doesn't? Nobody?' Reuben asked.

'Not since moving to her current address. Unless you know something I don't?' Meg trained a steady gaze on Reuben, who merely raised an eyebrow. 'The point is that we risk alerting Kyle if we do anything.'

Pete got to his feet, too frustrated to sit still. 'She won't move somewhere secure. We can't add surveillance to her apartment. Tell me what we *can* do?'

'We can sit and brainstorm, Pete.'

Candace waited for him to take his chair again.

'Liz knows her father better than we do so until we've done the full briefing and made a plan of action to capture him, I believe we need to trust her instincts.'

Meg nodded. 'And if we are going to add surveillance then it can be on Liz.'

'Sorry, what?' Pete asked. This didn't sound right.

But Rueben agreed. 'I can add the tiniest of trackers to anything she uses. Car. Phone. Clothes.'

'And I've already put something into place to alert me if her mobile devices have unusual activity,' Meg added.

Pete was back on his feet, facing the others. 'Does she know?'

'She does not,' Meg said.

'Then take it all off.'

'Not happening. Liz needs us.'

'But not this way.'

Candace leaned forward. 'Yes, this way. The terms of the contract to work here are clear about the rights to use surveillance, technology of all kinds, human or otherwise, to protect or observe all aspects of a team member's life. Within reason.'

'And you think this is within reason?' Pete didn't remember reading any such clause. Right now he didn't remember even reading the contract before signing it. Probably too keen to move on to a new adventure than check the fine print.

'We all want to protect Liz,' Reuben said. 'If she doesn't know what we are doing then she won't accidentally give any signs which Kyle might pick up.'

'Do you have another suggestion, Pete?' Candace asked.

'Yes. You get her to place some surveillance in her own apartment. That's doable.' He looked at Reuben. 'Just run her through how to install your high-tech cameras or whatever and she'll do it. Has to be better than nothing.'

'Unless there are existing bugs in there,' Meg said. 'Actually, I can send her a program to run on her phone which should indicate the presence of anything. I agree with Pete.'

Ben nodded. 'Reuben and Meg, can I leave this with you both? Just keep the personal tracking to ourselves for now.'

'Hang on—'

'Pete, you've got a win here. End of discussion.'

I hate this. It isn't right.

He wouldn't let anyone harm Liz, and if the team wasn't prepared to protect her, then he would.

* * *

Liz had no doubt about what was happening and while the part of her which was self-sufficient and used to protecting herself didn't like it one bit, there was another side of her personality able to see the logic behind it.

I just need to know what Dad's up to.

She'd brought her father into the spotlight of Operation Nobody. The man's wickedness and her determination to stop him was part of the reason Ben recruited her. Ben was ex-Missing Persons and a shrewd detective, who by taking on the senior role in this covert unit, had his own masters to please. If that meant he'd pour resources into finding and stopping Kyle Moorland then so be it. She'd been around long enough to understand the politics behind policing.

More than long enough.

The shopping completed, she returned to the old brick building hidden in plain sight within a mostly-forgotten inner suburb. There were no homes in this part, only abandoned buildings dotted among new offices and many potentially shady businesses. With the coming of Operation Nobody, local police had reduced their normal drive-throughs. The crime rate hadn't suddenly soared with the lower presence – not yet anyway. But it was allowing the team to be a little less obvious when they moved in and out with any of the more obvious vehicles. No amount of trying to hide them was completely foolproof. The less other law enforcement saw the better.

Back inside the hub, Pete hurried to take some of the bags and carried them to the kitchen. 'I'll help unpack.'

'What's wrong?'

'Wrong?'

'You never help.'

'Changed man. In fact I'll do it all and bring you a coffee. Go and prep for the briefing.'

He was pulling food from bags with an intensity it didn't warrant. In all the years she'd known him and worked with him, he'd rarely been as anxious.

'Dude?'

He shook his head.

Out in the main room, everyone was busy. Ben was in Candace's office with the door closed. Meg had the usual managed chaos at her desk. Reuben and Phoebe were in discussion.

'Where are Hamish and Annette?'

'Huh? Oh, gone to records. According to the sergeant there we have everything and if we don't believe her, go and look. So they have.'

Liz chuckled. 'Annette would be ropeable.'

'Dunno.'

As Pete put both hands into a bag, Liz grabbed his arm. 'Stop. Change rooms.'

He nodded and followed.

The change rooms were unisex and had private showers with space to dry, hang clothes, and get dressed. She waited inside one cubicle until he joined her then locked the door and turned on the water. Crossing her arms, she leaned against the door with one eyebrow raised.

'I can't tell you.'

'Well you kinda just did, Pete. Something has got up your nose so spill.'

'Surveillance.'

'And nobody can come in and install it where I'm staying without the risk of alerting Kyle. Except I could. Or some.' Liz had a fair working knowledge of different kinds of bugs, but lately she'd seen new types whose technology was beyond her experience. 'Then bug my car. Computer. Whatever it takes.'

Pete's face gave it away. That was exactly what they were doing but without telling her.

'I trust the team. I trust you, mate. And you need to believe that Ben and Candace and the rest want the best chance of catching my dreadful father.'

He didn't look convinced but the tension had left his expression. 'Reuben and Meg are going to talk you through doing a sweep of your apartment and planting some bugs. I wasn't going to leave you with nothing.'

'Thank you. Out of everyone, I know who has my back no matter what.'

'Ditto. Just doesn't sit right with me.'

'I hear you.' She turned off the tap. 'This is a strange new world we've got ourselves into.'

While Hamish and Annette were out, Liz reviewed the reports from everyone who'd visited the mansion with her. Ben had printed them, adding handwritten notes, and he expected her to do the same.

The different writing styles were interesting, with Reuben keeping to the facts while Pete made random complaints about the weather and the well. He really hadn't enjoyed the day. Meg's was the most detailed, with a list of what she'd done in each room and the timeframe for the tests she was running and some she'd sent away. She also mentioned wanting to bring her forensics friend in at some point and Ben's comment matched how Liz felt – 'absolutely'.

She pulled up an aerial map of the property. It wasn't current but Reuben would remedy that once he got his drone up in the next few days. Pete's report included his thoughts about access to the wall from a road he'd been on and Liz zoomed in to the co-ordinates he'd noted. This part of the boundary wall was the only one with residential land against it. The others had natural bushland against two and the street on the last. The ground looked a bit higher where the houses were so perhaps getting over the wall was easier from there. She made notes about checking when back at the mansion. Pete might enjoy getting his hands dirty.

The well wasn't visible, and a close zoom became too fuzzy. She switched to the plans of the property. These were among the inspector's records and included an overall map of the land as well as another of the house. Both were very old, probably from when the place was originally built.

As Meg had pointed out yesterday, there was a cellar or similar underground room down steps from what was now a wall. It actually ran a long way beneath the house. Why would it be bricked up rather than the door locked? They'd not got into the cellar through the other end of the house yet, nor a decent look at the half dozen buildings scattered around the grounds. The list was growing of things to do and the priority had to be finishing a search and accessing whatever was behind those bricks.

Is there another way in? Could the killers have come from under the building?

Liz noticed her hands were clenched and slowly released the pressure. There was something about this case which felt familiar and yet how? She'd never met the inspector. Never heard about the murders of his parents until well after they happened. And never stepped foot in the mansion until yesterday.

Even Reuben had expressed his sense of being unsettled there so that was all it was.

It had to be.

NINE

The full team gathered around the table in the main room, waiting for Meg to finish setting up her presentation.

'While Meg's occupied, update us all on the visit to records?' Ben directed this to Annette.

'Humph. Double humph,' Annette said. She looked as irritated as she sounded. 'The sergeant thinks she owns the place. Put us through the third degree why we even wanted to check, because her staff never make mistakes when it comes to evidence.'

'Funny how we located an entire box,' Hamish said.

'You did?' Phoebe's eyes widened. 'Was it mis-labelled?'

'Not at all. And it was exactly where it was meant to be.'

'But how can that happen?'

'Good question, Phoebe,' Ben said. 'And one I'll be asking at my next meeting with the powers-that-be. The box went straight to Meg's lab and she'll take a look for signs of tampering, prints and so on before it's opened. We want to know who has handled it and the contents. The fact that the other boxes were missing items and now you have another box which might contain them concerns me.'

'Good thing we didn't open it.' Hamish was staring at Annette, who shrugged without looking at him.

The table suddenly lit from within.

'Sorry about taking so long. I'm testing a new program which should make it easier for us to access any data specific to our individual tasks.' Meg touched the screen. 'Until now a presentation such as this one would then be sent as a whole to every device, whereas if I have it right, you'll be able to ask it for just what you need.'

There was a murmur of appreciation from the team. Data was at their fingertips thanks to Meg's talent. Each had a personal tablet which accessed a series of apps as well as information specific to their roles. The apps were also on their phones and computers but the tablets were individualised.

The vertical screen came to life, displaying a 3D image of a man. His body slowly rotated so everyone got a good look. Liz drew in a sharp breath.

Meg gestured at the figure. 'Meet Kyle Moorland, also known as Garry Ford. His stats will be on your devices now and we have a fair amount of good intel to share.'

Liz gazed at the image as it turned. It was a good likeness. Strong facial features, muscular lean body, arms, and legs, white hair cropped short.

'First of all… do not expect him to look like this. He is an expert at disguising himself. Excellent at changing his voice and speech patterns.'

'And don't try to outrun him if he gets a head start.' Pete looked glum. 'He's fast.'

'He's what… late sixties?' Hamish asked. 'I'd catch him.'

'Be my guest. Last person who said that choked on his dust.'

Hamish grinned. 'You?'

Pete snorted. 'Nah. Another young, fit man who overestimated his abilities. Bit like you, mate.'

Except Pete hadn't caught Kyle either that night. It was Pete who'd been closest to Kyle to begin with and was quickly overtaken by Andy Montebello. But he'd never let Andy forget that a man more than twice as old left the cocky young detective in his wake on a foot chase through Brimbank Park.

He glanced at Liz as if it occurred to him she could set the record straight with a few words. She winked. That would keep him on his toes.

I'll let him retain his dignity this time.

'Speed aside,' Meg continued. 'Kyle has a keen intellect and dangerous traits. Candace?'

'Yes, he is complex man. A narcissist, most certainly. High functioning sociopath, without a doubt. He is fuelled by the need to achieve certain outcomes and it is only recently we're learning what they are. Kyle is charming. Profoundly intelligent and calculating. Patient. Cruel.' Candace gazed at Liz, her eyes kind. 'Somewhere inside this man is despair. He longs for the perfect life he believes was taken from him and has tried at least twice to reconstruct it. He succeeded once for a while.'

'And it drives him to keep trying.' This was Annette, who spoke quietly.

Reuben pointed at Kyle's image. 'I've read everything I've been able to find on him and will study the new data as well, but I'm missing something. He built a network of criminals then discarded them, probably more than once. He kidnapped at least two young girls with the intention of raising them as his own children. And he's faked his death more than once. If what drives him, as Annette so aptly put it, is to recreate a lost family, then why be so covert and dishonest?'

'Because re-creation isn't going to give him what he wants. Me, Reuben,' Liz said. 'At least, I think so.'

Candace nodded in agreement.

'Which is the conclusion I formed as well, Liz. Yet his path might have been different. Better and certainly easier on those in his life. Something stopped him from reaching out to you and your family in a way which was open and true. That's the bit I'm missing. Are his beliefs strong enough to do that?'

Meg changed the screen to a symbol.

'Kyle has this tattooed on his arm. See the three-headed snake and the sword? His obsession with Aryan doctrines is underpinned by a superiority complex.'

Reuben looked at Liz. 'Yet your mother didn't fit his idea of a suitable genetic match.'

'I don't know if he genuinely loved her, at least at the beginning, or if it was a way to hide his dreadful allegiances from the world. Or did he find this way of life later, as if discovering religion. None of this was obvious when I was a child. I just thought he was always angry and hated us.'

'He didn't hate you, Lizzie,' Pete said.

'Then how *does* he feel about me? He told me I gave up the right to be his daughter because I'm a police officer. Time and again he's found ways to blame me for his actions and I understand it is part of his various personality defects, but at no time have I seen love.'

And I shouldn't have said any of that.

Giving away her feelings wasn't comfortable, let alone among a team she was still getting to know.

'Sometimes love is too hard to show, Liz. For some people.' Annette's words were delivered gently. 'If he is a sociopath and narcissist then wouldn't it be almost impossible to reveal whatever good emotions might be deep in his soul?'

'He doesn't have any good anything.' Pete crossed his arm. 'Kyle's a cold-blooded killer and devious human. Sorry, Lizzie.'

Ben cleared his throat. 'Okay, now we've dissected the man, let's focus on what we know concerning his movements in the last few months.'

Liz excused herself for a minute to reply to a text message from her sister, Anna. It was an invitation to dinner tonight.

Would love it but I'm working until late.

We should catch up for a chat next week.

All okay?

Sure is. Just sisterly stuff.

That was one of the codes they'd made a few months ago. They had several in case they wanted to communicate without fear of a message being seen by the wrong person. Sisterly stuff wasn't one to panic about but Anna did want to talk and not on the phone. She checked the time.

How about next Wednesday at the café?

Sounds good. Love you.

Liz sent back a love heart. Wednesday was five days away and the code meant they'd meet in five hours. The café was code for Melbourne Central, a huge shopping complex in the city. They'd meet by accident, laugh about the coincidence, and find an open place to talk. It was ridiculous that her sister's life was still impacted this way by the man who'd been abusive to Anna and eventually stolen her little girl to raise as his own child.

Not for much longer, Kyle. I'm coming for you.

Back at the table the image of her father was shrunk to just a few centimetres height and as Ben spoke, other images appeared on the screen.

'Ah, Liz. To recap, this is a visual of what we know about Kyle,' Ben said. 'Your family – including your mother, sister and her deceased husband, their daughter and grandson. What we know is he left the family when you were a young child and later faked his own death.' He pointed to the image of a man similar to Kyle although a couple of decades younger. 'This is Garry Ford. The real one.'

Phoebe peered at his image then Kyle's and back again. 'This is the man whose identity he stole?'

'And his life. Befriended him and gained his trust then pushed him over the rail on a cruise ship. Poor bloke went into the water dead, wearing another man's clothes and with their I.D. By the time he washed up there was enough deterioration to hide his real identity and no DNA testing done. No point, when it was obvious he was Kyle Moorland.' Ben glanced at Liz. 'You didn't even know he was allegedly dead and buried until a few months ago.'

Liz nodded. 'Anna found out by accident ages after and decided not to raise it with me. Old wounds and all that. And then we were estranged for a long time after Ellen was abducted. She rightly blamed me. When the second child was taken a few months ago, the M.O. was strikingly familiar and when I spoke to her, she told me she knew it couldn't be him because he'd died.'

Hamish stared at her from the other side of the table, his face set. Was he being disapproving? She didn't break eye contact and after a few seconds, he did. He could judge her all he wanted. It was nothing she'd not thought a thousand times. No criticism from another person would match the internal dialogue and nightmares that had haunted her for eighteen years, after she took her eyes off her niece long enough for her to be stolen.

Nobody else seemed to notice the moment. Ben was talking about the network Kyle built of people who would do his bidding.

'One part of the man we still know too little about is his affiliations with different hate groups.' Candace enlarged the image of the tattoo. 'This leads nowhere, really. To date the main reason we're looking at it is its appearance on at least one other person who we know worked for him. I've sent it to a religious anthropologist in London who specialises in symbols so hopefully we'll get some intel on it shortly. We're aware of a couple of groups who expelled him decades ago, but so far no current allegiances have come to light.'

'Most people in his employment don't know him personally.' Meg zoomed in on a new group, all male. 'Great example here where Kyle spent years setting up several men with specific roles to play in the second abduction. Two lived in the same apartment building as Liz and were able to watch her more effectively than putting surveillance cameras inside.'

'And gather information cameras wouldn't see,' Pete said. 'I remember phoning Liz about the missing kid – Eliza – and she already knew.'

'One of my neighbours told me. This man.' Liz pointed to a scruffy type in the group. 'He never knew who was pulling his strings.'

A second group appeared on the screen and Pete took over. 'And we all know this little shit called Tony Shaw was involved in the kidnapping of Lyndall Smith. He provided stolen surveillance and grunt and boats and dealt closely with this moron—' he stabbed his finger in the direction of a suave man in a designer suit. 'Marcus Bonner, who we strongly believe worked directly with or for Kyle Moorland.'

Hamish dramatically took a stance as if propping his body to shoot, then held up an imaginary rifle, primed and aimed it at the image of Marcus, and fired an invisible bullet, complete with sound effects. Then he lowered the pretend weapon and blew away smoke which didn't exist. 'And that is how I dealt with that scum of the earth.'

TEN

The minute the briefing was finished Phoebe hurried to her desk and began packing up to go. Her face was flushed and she didn't look up when Liz approached.

'Before you leave, could I ask a couple of questions about the podcast?'

Phoebe nodded then shook her head and reached for her phone, almost knocking a coffee cup over as she did.

Liz steadied it. 'Shall we have a word with Candace?' She kept her voice soft. 'She's gone up to the roof for some air so we'll be alone with her.'

After hesitating for a moment, Phoebe glanced around the room. 'Just the three of us?'

'Yes, come on. Fresh air sounds good to me.'

They used the stairwell and at the second landing, Phoebe stopped and leaned against the brick wall, looking pale.

'Are you ill?'

'No. Yes.'

'Do you need medical attention?'

Phoebe sucked in a long breath and started back up the steps. 'No. No, just some distance from Hamish.'

Ah… I thought that was the issue.

There'd been an uneasy silence after Hamish did his little pretend shooting but he'd been pleased with himself and was oblivious as he added commentary.

'Put the perp in the cross-hairs of my sight. Steady hands. One job. Bang and the job is done.'

It was insensitive and distasteful. Everyone wanted Marcus Bonner stopped but shooting him had been the only option when the man had fired on the helicopter.

They reached the top floor and pushed open the heavy door to the roof. The building was only a few floors high and Operation Nobody worked on the third floor as well as a couple of random parts of other floors. Otherwise it was empty. Around them were lower buildings and quiet, narrow streets. The roof was little more than an open area with a couple of vents and other services and a metre and a half high brick barrier on the parameter. No pool or bar like some modern apartment blocks and inner city business buildings.

Candace stood near a corner, tapping on her phone. As they approached she noticed them and slid the phone into her pocket.

'Are we interrupting?' Liz asked.

'Never. Just catching up on work while I breath air that isn't cycled through filters.'

Phoebe went straight to the barrier and rested her arms on the top layer of bricks to stare out at the city. 'Except out here we have to deal with pollution. Poison everywhere.'

Her tone was despondent and Candace frowned, then glanced at Liz.

As Liz tried to find an opening, Phoebe turned to lean her back against the brick and gazed at Candace.

'What Hamish did has upset me and I don't know why.'

'Ah… his little dramatic replaying of shooting a gun. I saw Pete and Reuben head off with him toward the elevator, so imagine they are having a quiet word with him. It wasn't appropriate and neither of them are slow to speak their minds.'

'And if they don't, I will,' Liz said.

'No, no don't. Not on my account.' Phoebe spoke so quietly it was hard to hear and her eyes were huge and worried. 'I shouldn't have said a word.'

Candace looked around, presumably to make sure they were still alone. Liz had been doing that anyway because if Phoebe was this upset, she needed privacy.

'You should always speak up,' Candace said. 'I take your safety, both physical and emotional, seriously. Everyone's safety. I'd like to sit down in a private space with you at your convenience. If you'd like to talk?'

'I don't want to let… well, let the team down.'

'Your work is so important to Operation Nobody.' Liz sought the right words. 'You are highly valued, Phoebe. We know you aren't a police officer. You aren't jaded by dealing with criminals as most of us are. And that makes you unique. A bit like Meg and a bit like Candace.' She snuck a look at Candace who nodded slightly. 'What we are trying to do with Operation Nobody is meld civilians with unique talents and qualities with cops from a range of backgrounds. It is a work in progress.'

'I understand that,' Phoebe said. 'I don't know why this bothers me so much.'

'Then let's make a time and come and see me at home, if you like.' Candace offered an encouraging smile.

Phoebe nodded. 'Yes. I would like the chance to sort this out. I'm used to dealing with people of all types and Hamish doesn't normally bother me but that action…' she shuddered.

'He shouldn't have done that.'

Liz hadn't liked it but she understood his need to act out after such a difficult event. Taking a kill shot might be necessary, but no amount of training prepared a person for the fallout. He also needed time with Candace and if Hamish wouldn't initiate it, then she'd talk to Ben and make it happen.

'I'll leave the two of you to work out the details.'

. . .

'Are you an idiot, mate?' Pete's arms were crossed and he stood, legs apart, a couple of metres away from Hamish. The body language was deliberate and crossed arms made it a fraction less likely he'd smack the other man across the back of his head.

They were in the basement carpark where Pete and Reuben "invited" Hamish to go after Pete saw Phoebe's expression. It was obvious she was upset and why wouldn't she be? She was a podcaster not a frigging detective or intelligence officer. He and Reuben had the same response and approached Hamish together.

'I'll have you know my intelligence quotient is high and a far cry from the standard 25 points assigned to those considered idiots.'

Reuben laughed. It wasn't a happy laugh but one which resonated with Pete. Hamish was on a whole different plane from the rest of the team in more ways than one way.

'Poor choice of words. I should have asked what the fuck were you thinking back there?' Pete asked.

'No need for such crass language.'

'Dunno. Let's take a vote. Who thinks it is appropriate language in the current context?'

Reuben raised his hand and Pete joined him.

'Outnumbered. And waiting for an answer.'

Hamish glanced at Reuben then back at Pete. 'What is this?'

'Question time. What were you thinking with that little display of how to prep and shoot a gun? Let alone the following rhetoric about what it was like to kill someone. In front of civilians.'

'You are overreacting.'

'Mate, I couldn't care what you do or say. I ignore you most of the time. But this team includes a podcaster who has no up-close-and-personal experience with cops other than through helping rid the world of criminals with her words. Meg and Candace are accustomed to the crap but Phoebe isn't.'

The cogs were turning. Hamish was silent but his face told the story. He'd not given any thought to his audience.

'Pete and I and Liz and Ben and maybe Annette… we know you were blowing off a bit of steam after the stress of taking down Bonner,' Reuben said. 'It still wasn't pretty to watch. Imagine the impact on someone who has never seen active duty.'

Hamish opened his mouth and shut it again.

Time to press it home.

'See, we need Phoebe. She gives us a completely fresh look at things and has a network at her fingertips the bad guys could only dream about. Losing her would be devastating whereas losing you?' He paused for dramatic effect. 'Not so bad. Life without Hamish would go on and possibly thrive.'

'Wait… thrive? Am I not a valuable member of this team?'

Good, we're getting through.

Reuben took over. 'Valuable is an interesting word. You are one of the best shooters I've come across. Tick. Your strategic thinking is brilliant. Tick. And you are brave and relentless. Tick.'

'O-kay.'

'But Hamish, you are oblivious to other people. To their sensitivities.'

Hamish snorted. 'Coming from the man who told Tony Shaw he'd make certain he was in solitary for twenty-three hours a day for the rest of his life.'

'You forgot the bit about only serving him food which he hated.' Pete admired Reuben's calm but deadly interrogation style. 'And never seeing the sun again.'

'Except I knew exactly what kind of scum I was dealing with. And I'd never expose someone with Phoebe's background to it. You have to filter stuff. Take a moment to check if what you're about to say or do, or for that matter, *how* you say it, will make someone uncomfortable.'

'You're making me uncomfortable, Reuben.'

'And it is intentional. I don't believe for a minute you are trying to upset other members of the team. But you have.'

Hamish walked a few steps away then turned back. His forehead was lined with worry.

'I'm really not wanting to cause any harm. Phoebe is such a sweetheart.'

'And that's another thing,' Pete said. 'Check how you talk about and to the women in the team. Liz is not Lizzie-beth and she's told you that enough times. None of our team members are your potential romantic partners. Not even Reuben.'

Reuben chuckled.

'No one is looking for terms of endearment or special consideration. And I guarantee that you playing Romeo is only holding you back. We're all here because Ben wants a strong, coherent team and right now, anyone who undermines that has to deal with me. Got it?'

This was a dangerous approach. Hamish could easily arc up and go running to Ben to complain about harassment. Or resign. Or turn into an enemy. With the question mark already over his head, any mis-steps were like a spotlight on Hamish. Not that Reuben knew about it. Reuben was just a decent copper who was not yet privy to the concerns about a mole in the team.

For a moment, Hamish gazed at the ceiling as if expecting to find answers above. Then he offered his hand to Pete to shake.

'I'll apologise to Phoebe. And I'll pull my head in.'

A more relaxed Phoebe had spent a few minutes talking to Liz about the podcast before picking up her bags to leave. Much of her work was done at home where she had a custom-built studio and she intended to work on a teaser to send out about the cold case murder.

As she headed for the door, Hamish, followed by Pete and Reuben, let themselves in and Phoebe stepped right out of the way, suddenly grabbing her phone to check and turning her back.

Hamish paused and Pete put a hand on his shoulder, encouraging him forward.

So what has gone on with you three?

Reuben passed them both and lifted his eyebrows at Liz as he went to his desk.

Liz needed to meet Anna and slid her laptop and tablet into her bag as Hamish and Pete walked in the direction of the offices. She watched them. Hamish wasn't exactly under duress but Pete was wielding some kind of influence. They stopped at Candace's office and she met them at the doorway, had a short conversation, then ushered Hamish in.

Pete closed the door and came to talk to Liz, his eyes on her bag.

'Going home?'

'Not yet. Meeting my sister.'

'Need company?'

'I'm just catching up with Anna.'

'Yeah. Okay. How about a drink later?'

'Maybe. Can I let you know?'

Pete was watching Candace's office.

'What's going on?'

'Secret men's business.'

'I see.'

He suddenly flashed a smile her way. 'But I'll tell you everything over a drink.'

ELEVEN

Melbourne Central was built around Coop's Shot Tower, built in the late nineteenth century of red brick and supplying not only shot pellets but all manner of lead items including pipes which housed the city's first electricity system. Heritage listed in the 1970s, it was eventually encased in a twenty-storey glass dome, and now housed more than three hundred shops and businesses. As a bustling and popular shopping complex, it was an excellent choice of location for Liz to meet Anna.

She was there a few minutes before seven and waited on level two, not far from the packed food court where she could lean on the balcony railing and have a decent view of escalators and people on lower levels.

There was a man over the other side of the level whose height and build fitted Kyle's. His hair was short and white. And he was scanning his surrounds the way she had. Heart racing, Liz took a few steps. If she walked quickly she might reach him before he could get to an exit. But then their eyes met and it wasn't Kyle. A moment later a woman around his age waved and he went to meet her.

He isn't here. Even if he intercepted our call, he doesn't know our code.

Her relationship with her older sister was better than ever. The years of estrangement were regrettable, but firmly in the past, and Anna's life was now filled with happiness instead of deep-seated grief and despair. No more anti-depressants or drinking too much. But getting back her daughter – and delightful grandson – had come with its own difficulties.

To protect the three of them from Kyle, Anna had moved from her home of three decades in Keilor. Their names had been changed, thanks to assistance from connections of Operation Nobody. It was taking time to adjust but Anna was determined to make it work. She hated Kyle with a passion and had every right to do so.

As Anna came up on an escalator, Liz couldn't help checking the area again for signs of their father. Expert in disguise he might be, but there were ways to spot someone following or watching.

Once confident he wasn't around, she began window-shopping, Anna's reflection getting closer and then passing her to go inside a popular clothing store. A moment later, Liz followed and selected a couple of items to try on. She was in the changing rooms first and left her door ajar as she hung the clothes on a hook.

Anna peeked in, almost threw herself through the door and locked it. 'I wasn't followed.'

'I know.'

They looked at each other for a split second, then embraced in a warm, generous hug.

Some of the stress of the day drained away. Holding her sister, knowing she was safe, was enough for now.

'You've lost more weight!'

Anna did a little twirl. 'Grandchildren are the best invention ever as I never seem to stop chasing after that little dynamo. Another four kilos gone for good, thank you very much.'

She looked amazing. Once-red hair was its natural dark brown and in a soft cut above her shoulders. She'd dropped the excess weight which had crept on after the death of her husband a few years ago. And her eyes shone with happiness.

'What is that smile for, Lizzie?'

'You look so well. So content.'

'I'll be more content once you catch our mongrel father.' Anna hung her large handbag over a hook and pulled out a big envelope. 'I found these among Mum's stuff. No idea if any of it is useful, but there's a diary. And photos.'

'Mum's diary?'

'It was the year my father left. And yes, I did read a bit but it is pretty confronting, so keep that in mind. She went through so much more than I ever knew.' Anna's face dropped. 'I wouldn't give it to you but I hope there's some clues about him. Anything to help you and your team.'

The thought of reading her deceased mother's private diary didn't sit well, but she accepted the envelope Anna pressed into her hands.

'Okay, thanks. I'll go through everything and return them as soon as I can.'

'These are yours as much as mine, Lizzie. Once he's behind bars I want you to come and choose more of her jewellery and stuff, and we'll make copies of all the photos.'

About to say she couldn't possibly do that, Liz found herself nodding. She had so little of her mother's, only some photographs and a pendant.

'I'm going to find him, Anna. Today the team has been briefed and the investigation is underway. I want to be able to drop by and have you all over for dinner without worrying about Kyle creating more chaos. I want us all to have our lives again.'

'I trust you. And Pete. I'll never forget what he did to find my Ellie.'

Other people came into the changing areas, a staff member loudly trying to talk someone into a colour they didn't like. Time was up for today. Liz hugged Anna again and whispered, 'I'll go first and make sure the coast is clear.'

'Love you, Liz.'

'Same. Lots.'

Liz took the clothes with her, making a few comments aloud about not being the right colour. As expected, the sales assistant immediately followed her which would give Anna a chance to emerge without being noticed. As soon as she was clear of the store, having left the clothes on the counter, Liz took up her earlier position at the railing. A few minutes later, Anna wandered out with a purchase in a branded carry bag and made her way through other shoppers to reach the food court.

Liz sat at an outside table at one of the upmarket bars lining the Yarra River. Pete was inside ordering drinks after muttering something about this being above his pay grade and next time he'd choose the location. She'd been home to put the envelope into her safe, not ready to open it. Tomorrow would do once she'd slept on the idea.

More likely worry all night about the contents.

The night was still warm, although it was close to nine and those wandering past were a mix of late diners and early clubbers. She was neither. Liz had never been one to party or socialise other than with close friends. They'd dwindled over the years as her work took over much of her life but it was all in response to the abduction of her little niece. That day changed everything. Ellie's life most of all. Anna's... whose husband eventually drank himself to death over their loss. And hers.

Except I should have protected her.

Old emotions bubbled beneath the surface. It didn't matter that Ellie was safe and back where she belonged. Liz had let her family down.

She was trusted with Ellie. Five years old, funny, smart little Ellie. She'd stayed with her aunt on many occasions when Anna and Sav were taking short breaks. They had their routine of park time, ice creams, and lots of fun. Every day, unless it was raining. Predictable. Kids liked that.

So did perps.

And one had watched and waited until Liz took her eyes off Ellie in the park long enough to steal her away.

'Stop. I know that look.'

Pete had returned, carrying a tray. He sat opposite and leaned forward. 'Ellie, right?'

Liz nodded.

'Ellie is home.' He pushed a glass of wine in front of her. Then another.

'Two?'

'The line up to order is out of control, so yes. And if you hadn't noticed, there's chips. I'm starving.'

She was suddenly hungry.

'Those are fancy .'

'There's three dipping sauces. Aioli, sweet chilli, and some weird kind of avocado thing which Reuben would like. Should have brought him along.'

'Why?'

'He's the new kid in town so would have to pay.'

'Do you want some money or are you complaining for the sake of it?'

'The latter. Cheers.'

The wine was exactly what Liz needed to relax and the chips filled her empty stomach. First glass finished and plate empty, she was ready to talk.

'Come on, tell me what you and Reuben did to Hamish.'

'Less than I'd have liked. He seriously needed a smack across the back of his head but we settled for a stern lecture.'

'Glad you opted for no violence.'

'Had to be a good example to Reuben. Anyway, I reckon Hamish just doesn't think. Whatever is in his mind comes out, so

I've suggested he work on his filters, but some people don't have them and it's not their fault as such.'

'Whose idea was it for him to see Candace?'

'Joint effort.'

Except you had your hand on his shoulder.

'I'm glad you two spoke to Hamish.'

'Phoebe doesn't need to see that kind of crap. How's Anna?'

'She's well. Happy, other than the obvious stress from Kyle.' Liz picked up the second glass of wine.

'The family has ongoing surveillance. I'm more concerned about your safety.'

'Me? Kyle won't hurt me.' She glanced around, then leaned a bit closer. 'Anna gave me an envelope full of stuff.'

'Stuff?'

'She says there's old photos and one of Mum's diaries.'

'You haven't opened it?'

'It's in my safe for the night.'

Pete gave her a searching look.

'What?'

'We can take it into the hub now if you prefer.'

'I don't prefer. I just have no idea what to expect. Anna said she started reading the diary but it upset her. Most likely this is nothing more than some sad memorabilia from the past.'

'Or it might help the investigation.' Pete nodded. 'Why don't you leave the mansion to the three of us tomorrow and you go through that envelope at work?'

That had merit. She could make sure the contents were tagged and copied and she wanted to take a look at the records Annette and Hamish were dealing with.

'Alright. Do you want to take someone in my place?'

'Nobody can take your place.'

'What nonsense.' But she smiled.

'I'll ask Meg tomorrow if she needs someone else, but Reuben and I have a date with a well.' Pete suddenly grinned. 'Unless we take Hamish. Might be good for him to get his hands dirty.'

TWELVE

Meg, Pete, and Reuben had already left when Liz arrived at the hub. Annette and Hamish had got hold of the last box after Meg took fingerprints. She'd wanted a record of who had handled it in case questions were raised about the chain of access although she'd only run a search if absolutely necessary. How many people would have touched it in all those years? Rather than go to the conference room and interrupt Annette, who was working with Hamish at the round table, Liz settled at her desk and made some space.

The contents of the envelope slid out and she sorted them into small piles.

A handful of photographs inside a clear plastic bag.

A small, worn diary.

A sealed envelope in her mother's handwriting with 'Liz' on the front.

Liz held that in both hands.

In her heart she knew this wasn't about Kyle, but a personal letter from a mother who was dying of cancer to her younger child. It was a degree of separation which felt profoundly personal. Her chest tightened. Not yet. Not until this is done.

Picking up the diary, Liz sighed deeply. To read this felt like a betrayal of trust, and yet it might offer a clue to some part of Kyle's history which would lead to his arrest.

What would Mum have wanted?

Her mother was a kind, gentle woman who'd deserved better than Kyle. Even now Liz could hear her voice and visualise her smile. Losing her when she was in her teens had impacted her life in so many ways and while Anna, being older, had stepped up and taken Liz into her own home, it wasn't the same.

For now she put it aside.

This left the photographs and Liz donned gloves to slip them from their bag. She spread them out in two rows of seven. All were old and none were familiar… although the subjects were.

Of the fourteen, several included Liz at different ages but all before her fifth birthday, she was certain. After then, Kyle had left and she had no recollection of her mother taking photos again. Yet these weren't all taken by her mother because there was one when Liz was a baby and in her mother's arms. Tears welled at the wide smile on her mum's beautiful face. All the gold hair on the baby's head gave away the identity. Her hair was much darker now but it started golden, unlike Anna who'd been dark growing up, before dyeing it red.

It was the only one with Mum.

Three more were the two sisters together. Splashing in the pool Liz remembered from their Geelong home. Under the tree in the backyard. And one with Kyle.

She drew in a quick breath.

He looked so young. And he was smiling, which wasn't something she remembered.

Smiling at me.

Liz felt sick. The man was a monster. And her father. Reconciling the two was an ongoing battle between terrible memories, the knowledge of his more recent past, and a persistent curiosity about him.

She forced herself to look at the remaining photos. All but one were of her. Different backgrounds, different ages, different clothes. Liz estimated she was between four and five and all were strikingly similar in pose. And in every one, the little girl smiled with an utterly cheeky grin, directly at whoever was behind the camera.

Who am I, really? How could I have loved a madman?

This wasn't useful, the endless circling of thoughts. Self-blame over Ellen. Loathing about her need to know more about her father as a person, instead of as a dangerous killer. Last night waiting for Pete she'd spiralled and here she was doing it again.

Picking up the photos, she went in search of Candace.

While Reuben set up the winch and safety equipment, Pete helped Meg carry in what seemed like a ton of her own gear. The largest was a metal box on wheels.

'So this does x-rays?'

'Kinda. Nah, something a bit different. Do you want the technical explanation?'

'Not even if you paid me. This spot okay?'

They were in the long hallway at the back of the mansion where the laundry and all the service rooms were, along with the staff bedrooms.

'I can adjust it from here, so yes.' Meg stared at the wall at the end of the hallway. 'Hopefully this will let me see what is behind the plaster.'

'Happy to grab a sledgehammer and shortcut the process.'

'Later. Once we know what we're dealing with.'

'Do you need a hand with it?'

'Not for this but I'll message if I need it moved upstairs. Go and play in the well.'

'What if I get stuck?'

Meg turned around and levelled one of her stares at Pete, which always made him feel like he was back at school being assessed by his Maths teacher.

'Fine. I won't call you. I'll just stay stuck. Forever.'

She shook her head a little but a small smile made him grin.

'Right. Reuben probably can't work out how to set up the winch. Better go and help.'

'Thanks, Pete.'

At the far end of the hallway he glanced back. The top of the box was open and Meg was sliding cameras or similar up a pole she'd raised. She was the cleverest person he'd ever met.

Outside he jogged toward the well.

The weather today was better than the last visit, with no chance of rain and not overly warm. Being here so early in the day helped and with a bit of luck they'd be back at base before lunch with decent intel to go on with.

Reuben had everything set to go and was prepping one of his drones.

'Aren't we doing drones later?'

'This one will fit down the well shaft.'

'So we send it for a look-see first?'

'How deep do you think that is?' Reuben gestured to the structure.

It wasn't a wishing well style but a hole in the ground surrounded by a square made of bricks, two rows high. When they'd found it there was a metal covering beneath a ton of old branches. If someone wasn't trying to conceal it from above, then Pete wasn't a detective.

'Can't see the bottom unless we turn on the lights.' Pete reached for one of two floodlights on stands.

'Leave it off for now. The drone has a spotlight. Can you finish this and I'll sort the controls?'

A couple of minutes later the soft whirr of the drone began to echo as the small unit descended beyond the brickwork. A laptop was open on top of the drone's case and Reuben sat on the ground watching the screen, using controls reminiscent of a games controller. Pete gazed down the well.

'Estimate it's about five metres down. Did you stop it on purpose?'

'Having it do a slow 360 turn. There's no sign of a ladder but there are what might be slight indentations in the walls.'

'Hand and footholds?'

'Maybe.'

Pete itched to follow the path of the drone. He might not be ten years old anymore but he still had the heart of an explorer and curiosity of someone who hadn't experienced the worst of life. No way was Reuben going down there first.

The drone dropped further and now only its spotlight gave an idea of its whereabouts. He'd never answered Reuben's question about the depth of the well but it had to be at least ten metres. Again it seemed to stall and turn before moving again. He gave up watching and joined Reuben.

'Look at this, Pete.' Reuben focused the camera on the internal walls of the well. 'We're near the bottom and just here is a change in the structure.'

Pete peered at the screen. 'Reinforcement. Extra supports.'

'Yup. So what is it supporting.'

Reuben manoeuvred the craft right to the bottom, letting it hover and slowly rotate again. Then he tilted it to face down. The bottom was hard dirt. Level again, he zoomed on a crack and followed it. Up. Across. Down.

'A door.' Excitement pulsed through Pete's veins.

'With no obvious opening mechanism.'

'You are recording this?'

'Even our words, mate.'

'Didn't agree to that.'

'Sue me.'

'Can you go up and then tilt down?' Pete moved a bit closer to the screen as Reuben did so. 'What is that?'

On the floor, against the wall away from the apparent door was a piece of something. Fabric possibly. A soft layer of dirt rose as the drone closed in and Reuben lifted it. 'Can't see.'

'Guess I'll have to take a look myself.'

. . .

Meg had packed up the box and wheeled it to inside the front door. Until she downloaded the data it had captured – to a more powerful computer than the devices she carried today – there was no way to know what was behind the plaster.

When her phone rang she expected it was Pete pretending to be stuck in the well.

But the number was anonymous and she almost declined it. Despite her number being unlisted she still received spam calls, and if it was one then she'd quickly end it.

She tapped "accept" and said nothing.

And the caller did the same.

'Speak or I'll hang up,' she said, not having patience for prank calls.

'I thought you were the clever one.'

Kyle Moorland?

Even as Meg's heart lurched she was tapping her phone to set a location seeker into action.

'Oh, I'm not really clever at all. I take samples and run tests and look at data. Nothing special.'

His laugh was friendly and that on its own was unsettling.

What the hell do you want?

'Modesty is underrated, don't you agree? Particularly in women. So many believe they have an entitlement to take the place of men. As if they'd ever be on the same plane as even the worst of us. Except perhaps one woman. An exceptional one. But I mustn't go on. I wondered if you'd do me a small favour?'

Still processing his nonsensical comment about women, Meg wanted to tell him where to shove his small favour.

'Which is?'

'To pass on a short message. For Elizabeth.'

'I'm sure you have her number, Kyle.'

He laughed again but there was a bitter tone to it. Sinister.

'Risky. I might hang up and Elizabeth will miss hearing the message.'

Narcissistic, misogynist killer he might be but Meg quieted her voice.

'Alright. I'll pass it on. What is the message?'

'Tell Elizabeth she shouldn't stop her usual run along the river. The early mornings bore me without her brief appearance as a reminder.'

'Reminder?'

His sigh was heavy. 'Of her rightful place in my life. The time is closer.'

'Time for what?'

'Ah… if only I trusted you, Meg. Deliver my message and perhaps a suggestion that if Elizabeth wishes to know then she can ask me next time we meet.'

The end of the line went dead.

Meg opened the app she'd built to identify locations and came up with a hit on the Mornington Peninsula. She phoned Ben.

THIRTEEN

'Do you recognise any of the other backgrounds?' Candace had the photographs spread out over her desk. 'You said this one was the back garden, and this.' She slid two further away. 'We'll scan them all and enlarge but are there any clues? Any memories stirring?'

'Not from the photos but I was so young. And they are all different. A beach, rooms, parks, but no, nothing familiar.'

Candace picked up the one with Kyle and his daughters. 'He is half-turned away from Anna. And she's looking solemnly at the camera, not him nor you. His full attention is on you. Your sister is a strong woman. She had to be.'

Liz nodded. She'd been in here for a while but hadn't found the words to ask for help sorting out her thoughts. Controlling her emotions. It just wasn't in her nature to seek or accept the kindness of others. Not even when it was from a mental health professional she trusted. Pete was the closest to a confidante.

As ever, Candace was uncannily perceptive. Her gaze settled on Liz. 'And so are you.'

'Except I only witnessed the abuse. Kyle never directed it my way. Nothing I remember, and Anna said he never raised his voice to me, let alone a hand.'

'It was still trauma, Liz. Terrible trauma at an age when you had no ability to understand what was going on in your family. Our caregivers are meant to nurture and guide, not traumatise and mislead. Your mother was the former and your father… very much the latter.'

Yet I want to know him.

'Not only that, but he abandoned you.'

'Mum divorced him. There's a difference.'

'She divorced him after he'd left one of many times. I spoke to Anna at length when we were searching for little Eliza, using the disappearance of her Ellen as comparison, and she filled in a lot of blanks. None of it was confidential… have the two of you not talked about that part of your lives?'

'Some. But the priority has been around catching him so all of us can have normal lives. After what he put her through, she deserves that.'

'As do you, Liz. Let me reassure you that Kyle abandoned you in ways beyond simply leaving the family home. It left you with a lot of unfinished business.'

That was the perfect way to describe it.

'There's a diary as well. Anna said it is confronting. Upsetting. I know I should read it to see if there's anything useful to the team but I'm…'

She swallowed down a lump in her throat.

'Would you trust me with it? I'll extract only anything pertinent to finding your father.'

'Candace, yes. Yes please. I feel I need some—'

A sharp tap on the glass door made them both turn as Ben flung the door open.

'Sorry to interrupt. We have a fix on Kyle's location.'

Liz was on her feet immediately. 'Where?'

'Close to the art gallery in Mornington.'

'Bonner Gallery?'

He nodded.

'How?'

'I'll explain on the way. We need to leave now.'

Candace rose. 'Should Liz go? Isn't that what he wants?'

Ben looked at Liz, then Candace. 'Probably is. But, yes.'

Ben drove with Liz still catching up on the reason behind this. Candace had followed her to the door out of the hub and promised to collect and lock up the items from Anna. Right now nothing mattered other than finding Kyle.

'Why would he phone Meg?'

Ben took the turn-off to the Western Freeway and turned on the sirens and lights, accelerating as traffic obediently parted.

'Probably wants us to know he can reach everyone at his whim. And there's more. Not been time to tell you.'

The last ten minutes were a rush of collecting phones and tablets, stopping at the armoury for personal weapons, and the regulation check of the BearCats, the armoured response vehicles, before leaving the building. Annette and Hamish were behind them, almost on their tail.

'Tell me what, Ben?'

'He asked Meg to pass on a message for you.'

'Why not just phone me? Okay, ignore the questions and tell me.'

Her heart hadn't stopped pounding since Ben had spoken Kyle's name.

'She has a recording but the gist is that he misses seeing you run that route along the river.'

Of course. It was a strong message that he'd been watching her for long enough to establish her routines.

'Okay. Anything else?'

'Not the exact words and it was a short call. But he's trying to tempt you into making yourself visible for some kind of approach. At least that's my take on it.'

'So what is he doing at the art gallery? Isn't it under surveillance?'

The Bonner Gallery just outside Mount Martha was an important part of their investigation into the abduction of Lyndall Smith a few weeks ago. Marcus Bonner was eventually shot dead by Hamish. While no proof existed of a connection between Bonner and Kyle, the latter had fished Lyndall out of the bay in such deep disguise Liz hadn't recognised him.

'Not as such.' Ben's face was set. 'We have a security firm monitoring it and doing regular walks through the grounds but we're limited to that. Funds aren't stretching far enough and until next of kin is located there's only so much we're able to do unless there's a situation.'

'But that's ridiculous! Kyle might be camped there.' Liz checked the app on her phone for the screenshot from Meg. 'I know these things aren't one hundred percent accurate but Meg's tracker shows the phone was within the grounds. No guard walking around is going to find someone like my father who probably knows the place inside out, and laughs every time they visit.'

'Or he could simply have phoned from the street outside to see if he got a response such as this.'

'So we're wasting our time?'

Aware how sharp and angry she sounded, Liz closed her eyes for a moment and told herself to get a grip. This wasn't anyone's fault and her attitude wasn't helping. She opened her eyes and glanced at Ben.

'Sorry. I'm really angry with Kyle.'

'Liz, one way or another this is adding valuable information. If all it was is a prank to see if we are able to track a phone call, then that helps us. If he's trying to see what our response time is, then again, it tells us just as much.'

'What if he wants to draw us away from the hub? What about Candace?' A sudden dart of panic shot through Liz.

'Even if he finds the building he's not getting in. And

Candace is on alert to watch for anything unusual.' Ben slowed as they headed into the Burnley Tunnel. 'Meg is heading back to the hub to download data from her machine as well as work on the call she got, so Candace won't be alone.'

Liz stared out of the window. Whatever Kyle was up to, he had a plan.

The vehicles parked a block away and leaving Annette behind as a driver, should one of them need urgent back up, the other three approached the Bonner Gallery on foot, each with an earpiece in. Hamish sprinted off to find a way along the back of the property and Liz and Ben split up to cover the rest. The sirens had been off for minutes which had slowed their progress a little but announcing their arrival would ensure Kyle vanished... if he was even still in the area.

This part of the area was secluded. Set into the hillside with glimpses across the bay, the grounds were protected by a high brick wall and wrought iron gates. For the first time, Liz was struck by the similarity to Heberden House. This had also been renovated about fifty years ago, to accommodate the needs of artwork exposed to the public. She'd circle back to that comparison later.

The street was quiet. While there were houses along here – all set behind electric gates and hedges – nothing stirred. Liz waited a hundred metres or so from the closest corner of the grounds, her senses reaching out for information. But the only movement was from Ben, who'd reached the far end of the long wall and was doing his own observing.

'Nothing along the back of the property other than dense bushland. Ouch.' Hamish didn't sound happy through the ear piece. 'Why are there so many spikey plants in this country? At least in England we grow up avoiding poison ivy.'

'Liz, let's approach the gate while Hamish catches up with us.'

She was a bit closer than Ben when the ringing started. It sounded like a mobile phone but the ground was clear, so it wasn't one accidentally dropped by a pedestrian. It abruptly stopped.

'Ben? You heard that?'

The ringing began again and now she could see a phone duct-taped to one of the iron uprights. The caller ID was one word.

Dad.

Even as her blood ran cold, Liz was reaching to touch the screen, to accept the call.

'Liz, stop!'

Ben's directive barely made it to her brain but she must have hesitated for he got there first, almost throwing himself between the gate and Liz.

'It's Kyle.'

'Take a step back. A few.'

They both did, watching the lit screen until the caller hung up. Ben's hand was on Liz's arm. Whether it was to prevent her answering the phone or offering support she didn't care. She'd almost made a basic error thanks to the unthinking reaction.

'Sorry,' she murmured.

'No need. Just want to be sure it isn't dangerous.' He dropped his arm.

Hamish jogged up the road as the phone started yet again.

'Persistent,' Ben said. 'Annette, please drive to the front gate. Sirens not required.'

'Good grief, is that Kyle Moorland calling?' Hamish was panting slightly and made a show of brushing invisible leaves or something off his clothes.

'We need Meg.' Liz's eyes were fixed on the phone.

'Hamish can manage it but I want you to phone Meg and tell her what's happening.' Ben turned away. 'Mate, under no circumstances answer the caller. Get the testing kit and do your stuff with photos, notes about the tape. Everything. Then take get it into an evidence bag. I'll help if you need extra hands.'

Annette drove up the street and behind her was a car with the name of a security firm across its doors.

Where were you lot when my father was taping a phone to a gate?

Liz considered asking them but Ben was already heading their way, so she dialled Meg instead.

FOURTEEN

The inside of the well was worse than the drone's camera had indicated. First was the smell. Dank, almost rotten. Like old compost and waterlogged boots left in the sun too long.

Getting a bit poetic, old boy.

Pete was about halfway down the shaft and the rope had a bit of a swing to it. He kept his knees up to use his boots to push away from the walls, glad about the quality of the harness which gave him more freedom to manage his descent than those he'd used in the past.

'Hold again.'

The winch stopped and the sky darkened as Reuben peered down.

'Still okay?'

'Loving it. Just want to check out some of these indents.'

He planted his boots apart against the walls to steady himself and focused on the closest indent. It was just wide enough for an adult shoe and a few centimetres deep, and was cut roughly. Pete held it and looked around. The next one up was easily within his reach as was one below.

'Definitely for climbing. Let's get to the bottom.'

Pete kept his eyes on the floor as he descended, careful to

stop Reuben again when he was close enough to stand. He didn't yet, surveying the rough surface using his headlight and taking photos. The ground looked firm and was covered with a mix of dirt and debris which had fallen in. Using a pair of thin tongs from his harness, he collected a selection for an evidence bag then carefully did the same in a new bag for a tiny piece of fabric. Those in a pouch, he moved more of the surface debris around until he was close to what they thought was a door. Something was odd about dirt here.

'What have you found?'

Reuben's voice echoed slightly.

'Have we got some of that powder? For a cast?' Pete couldn't believe his eyes. 'Think we have a shoe print.'

Meg got off the phone and dropped her head into her hands. Liz had tried to keep her voice calm but Meg knew her well enough to hear the strain. She felt enough herself. Things were happening fast and it was becoming too much to manage. As soon as she got one job done another came. And another. Some took minutes while many were intricate and required ongoing attention, yet she was one person with only two hands.

And many computers.

This was true. Being part of Operation Nobody had opened up a new world where money was less of an object than working as a normal forensics investigator. Ben was the only person she had to ask instead of submitting forms and often attending meetings to beg for finance. He'd make things happen. At least most of the time. But right now, with two cases and one developing fast which required her constant attention, she'd make a mistake without some help.

Ben had agreed a while ago she could second her very talented friend to help with the cold case murders. With everything going on she hadn't pinned him down on exactly how to start the process.

Well, Candace was here and surely she'd be able to get things underway.

Ignoring the pile of work awaiting her urgent attention, Meg went in search of Candace. She wasn't in the main part of the hub nor the conference area or the kitchen. Not in the bathrooms or any of the overnight rooms. It was procedure to let another team member know if they were the last person inside. A quick check with her locator app indicated Candace was in the building and likely on the roof.

She could wait. Candace was as entitled to a break as anyone. More than some.

Back at her desk, Meg set up a search for the phone found at the mansion. Once she had it here it was just a matter of downloading its data to look at a history more detailed than most people would expect was possible. Being able to connect it to the phone Kyle was currently calling from would help her algorithm plot a pattern but in her experience he was exceptionally clever about being found. After all, he'd lived in plain sight for almost twenty years without detection.

'Why do the bad guys have to be so smart?' she muttered.

That done, she began the process of downloading the data from her work at the mansion. This would take a while, possibly hours, and didn't need her attention. What she needed to do was get into her lab to pull the washing machine apart and start on the remnants of clothing. And continue with the hundreds of samples from the mansion, and…

'Aargh!' Frustration burst out before she could stop it.

'Meg? What's wrong?'

How did I not hear you come back?

'Not a thing, Candace. Stretching my throat. Practicing a song. Summoning a forensics demon to take over the stuff I can't get to.'

Try as she might to smile, it wasn't happening.

'Actually, something is wrong. I can't seem to work at the capacity I'm accustomed to.' She gestured at her desk, then stood and waved at the room. 'All these computers and devices and my very fancy table all make me happy. Very happy. The lovely people who work here do as well. And the pay rise was delightful. But…' she was sounding whiny to her ears.

Candace crossed the distance between them. '*But*, there's far too much happening right now for one person to cover all the bases. Let alone the one person who makes the data sing.'

'Better than me singing.'

Against her will, the back of her eyes prickled. She wouldn't cry. That was for dudes who got hit in the groin.

'What do you need, Meg? Other than a vacation?'

'Coffee.'

'We'll get one together.'

The act of making coffee stopped the need to keep babbling about how hard her life was. Candace put two cupcakes onto a plate and led the way to the round table.

'Who bought cupcakes?'

'I made them.'

'Are they as good as your dessert the other night?'

Not waiting for an answer, Meg helped herself. Biting into soft caramel and slightly spicy apple inside a vanilla cupcake was enough to keep her mouth full and settle her thoughts. That and the coffee finished, she sighed.

'Is this how you used to treat your patients?'

Candace smiled. 'Still is.'

'Good strategy. Shut them up with food and drink and spike the dopamine at the same time. But thank you. It helped.'

'That aside, what do you need to spread the load a bit?'

Only one thing would make a difference. One person. 'I can handle the digital forensics or the physical forensics. With one case I can do both but there's a backlog of samples to process and a washing machine to dismantle, let alone me tracking Kyle.' Before she could get worked up again, Meg made a show of finishing her coffee which was already gone. This wasn't her at all.

Candace opened her phone. 'Communication is something we need to improve. As in, Ben and I with you and probably Liz.' She turned the screen to show an email. 'This was sent yesterday to confirm details from a conversation Ben had arranging for Jeff Scott to spend three months here and—'

'Yes!'

Meg leapt to her feet and hugged Candace then quickly sat again.

'Um… sorry.' She couldn't get the smile off her face.

'Perfectly fine. I take it you are happy with that arrangement?'

'Jeff is the most brilliant forensic scientist I've met. You'll love him. Everyone will. When is he arriving?'

'Tomorrow. We'll allocate team members for orientation and hopefully by lunch time he'll be in your lab working.' Candace got a message and frowned, swiping it away and turning her phone face down on the table.

'Are you okay?' Meg asked.

'Me? Certainly.'

Yet your worry lines are all on show.

'Thanks again, Candace. For telling me about Jeff and definitely for the cupcakes.' Meg stood. 'Liz called from the gallery.'

Candace collected the plates and Meg the coffee cups and took them to the kitchen.

'Hamish was about to remove the phone from the gate but all of them seemed a bit freaked out that it just kept ringing. Well, it would stop then start over.'

'Poor Liz,' Candace said. 'Her instinct would be to answer it. And there's no sign of her father?'

Meg shook her head. 'The security firm had just arrived when we spoke and there was a rather heated conversation in the background between them and Ben. Sounded like they want to see a warrant to let the team in because of the state of limbo the property is in.'

Both their phones dinged and they checked.

'From Pete. Better not be sending selfies. Do you know that he wanted me to rescue him if he got stuck down the well?'

They checked the message at the same time. It was a photo but not a selfie. A familiar thrill of discovery filled Meg.

'What am I looking at?' Candace asked.

Meg was already hurrying to her desk and spoke over her shoulder.

'A partial shoe print, and if I'm not mistaken this is from the bottom of the well.'

While the rest of the team continued searching the gallery, Liz returned outside. The security people were at the gate, still on their phones to whoever Ben had told them to call. Kyle's phone was locked in the vehicle Annette drove and it was still going through its cycle of ringing out then starting over when the doors were closed on it.

The image of her father furiously hitting redial over and over was mildly amusing.

Once through the gates, all four had done a brief sweep of the grounds. It was clear Kyle wasn't hiding behind a tree or under a bush so they'd moved inside. But after helping clear the first floor, Liz knew her time was better spent checking the outer walls of the building. Her mind was back to comparing Bonner Gallery to the mansion once belonging to the Baxters. She had to return to the mansion soon. No matter what games Kyle was playing, Liz knew in her gut she had to solve the double murders. There was a connection and it was likely this diversion to the gallery was meant to disrupt the team's efforts.

The building was externally different in style to Heberden House but inside, the staircase and mezzanine and a number of other rooms were eerily alike. Both were built from stone but while the mansion was white, this was painted dark grey. The window shapes were nothing alike nor the roofline and entrances. It had to be coincidental similarities she was seeing.

Liz walked along each wall, as close as she could. Some parts were difficult with established garden beds abutting the stone but she still climbed through to check behind without having a clear idea what to look for. The front of the building was pristine, which made sense, being where visitors came in. And the first side had nothing out of the ordinary. Around the back the structure changed shape, splitting into two single level wings, the first with its own entrance.

She messaged Annette and asked her to come to where she was then took a series of photographs. A wide driveway made with bricks – similar to those from the mansion – included parking bays and a huge turning area.

A message arrived from Pete. Just a photograph which she pinched out to better see. A shoe print. Part of one which was surrounded by dirt and debris and an artificial light. So he was down the well. What on earth would a person have been doing down there to leave a print? And how long ago?

'I'm here.' Annette was puffing. 'What's up?'

'After intel. You've been here before.'

'Well, sure. You and I interviewed Marcus Bonner.'

'No, when you were a student.'

Annette held up a hand and took a long breath, then nodded. 'Sorry. I have to stop smoking because my fitness is crap. But yes. On a high school excursion.'

'Would you take a minute to look around and tell me what you remember?'

'Okay.' Annette stared at the ground for a minute. 'Um… we were all in the school bus.' She straightened. 'Did a turnaround there and stopped for us to alight. There were twenty or so of us. Art students. I never considered it before, but should we track down the ones who attended?'

'We should.'

'I can help with that. Anyway, there was someone who greeted us. A woman. She gave us a little spiel about the gallery, told us not to touch anything or wander off, then led us through that door.'

They walked to the entrance in question, a weathered, solid

timber door which was wider than standard. It was locked, of course. Liz quickly texted Hamish to find the door and unlock it from inside. She wanted Annette to retrace her steps from all those years ago. 'What do you recall about the woman?'

'Not an awful lot, I'm afraid. I remember being in awe of her though. She was elegant. Not pretty at all with a stern face but her hair was silvery and beautiful and almost shimmered in the light and her makeup perfect and she wore a lot of jewellery and a straight skirt and jacket. Funny how that stuck in my mind.'

'Would you prioritise obtaining employment records for the gallery going back as far as possible? It should have happened when Marcus Bonner first came to our attention but everything moved so fast between our meeting with him and his death that we didn't have a chance.'

Annette tapped notes on her tablet. 'Actually, I believe they were taken to the hub. At least, I remember several boxes of files going there and being put in the unprocessed holding section of storage.'

The lock squeaked as it was turned from inside and the door didn't sound much better as Hamish opened it. 'Well, hello there. Are you making a special delivery?'

Annette went inside with a, 'we're both pretty special.'

Hamish grinned at Liz and closed the door behind them all.

FIFTEEN

Hamish relocked the door then sprinted away to catch up with Ben upstairs. Liz waited for Annette, who'd stopped a few metres along a very straight hallway and seemed to be deep in thought.

There were a dozen or so doorways along here and the hall was quite narrow.

'Yes, this is where we all came in. The doors were closed then.'

They began to walk, peering inside each of the now-open doorways. The first half were staff quarters, quite basic with a bed, side table, and wardrobe. Two were larger and also had small desks so likely belonged to past housekeepers or butlers.

'This has all been left as it must have been at the early part of last century,' Liz said. 'Other than the beds being stripped and all personal items removed. I wonder if that is part of the heritage listing terms?' She was taking photos as they continued. This reminded her of the hallway in the mansion with the odd wall at the end.

'Oh, I was right. This is the kitchen I mentioned.' Annette went into a huge space. 'And it is also preserved in its earlier state.' She checked the double sink and opened cupboards and even peeked inside one of the ovens. 'How odd though to bring a group of teenagers through the part of the building kept exactly as it was for decades. I wonder where the most recent staff had meals and stuff. Particularly with all the fundraising balls which were held here.'

Liz put her tablet onto a long wooden counter and searched for the documentation on the gallery. During the hunt to find Lyndall, a lot of information was collected with the expectation of raiding the gallery. It hadn't come to that.

'Okay, so here's the original house plans from when it was sold in 1971. Apparently the building was originally a house, then a private school, and then left empty for a dozen years. It was purchased by a company then resold to Marcus in 1985. He must have been about thirty years old yet paid almost half a million dollars back then.' Liz enlarged the plans. 'Interesting. The other wing isn't on the plans from 1971.'

Annette peered at the tablet. 'I honestly can't recall if I saw the other wing and that would have been in 1995. So did he add it later?'

'Is that even possible?' Liz picked up the tablet and they headed back to the hallway. 'Aren't heritage listed properties meant to stay intact? I guess they had changed the main room to facilitate the gallery so perhaps there were exemptions. Just odd there isn't an updated plan.'

'I'll try and track down more about it.'

Beyond the kitchen was another heavy wooden door, which was open. They stepped into a room which appeared to be an addition. It had a long, curved wall to the left which ended at another hallway, and to their right was the start of the gallery.

'We came in here and there were seats,' Annette said. 'All of us waited for what seemed like ages before the elegant lady returned. And that's about as much as I remember because the rest is a bit of a blur. I know we were shown several of the gallery rooms but the details are hazy. Sorry, Liz.'

'Goodness, don't be. You were sixteen.'

Liz wandered around the room. There was nothing on the walls and the floor was concrete. The ceiling wasn't high like the rest of the gallery.

'I think this was built to accommodate the wings. When you look at the wing we were in, both ends have heavy wooden doors.'

'Oh… it would have been its own separate building once.'

'Lots of old homes had staff quarters away from the house but this had the kitchen away as well. Must have been interesting bringing meals across in wet weather.'

Ben and Hamish came in from the gallery.

'We've checked the surveillance cameras and can see Kyle taping the phone to the gate,' Ben said. 'Before that, he made a phone call.'

Liz felt sick. 'To Meg. More games.'

'I'd like to return to the hub. We've sent the recording to Meg and she's keen to get the phone.' Ben turned to Hamish. 'Would you go and get the other vehicle?'

'On it, boss.'

Hamish was sprinting again. Where he got such energy was beyond Liz. She was fit and loved to run, but not around a building.

'Have you been down the other wing?' she asked.

'Twice. Hamish more than that because he was here with Reuben when we were looking for Bonner.' Ben gestured toward the doorway to the wing in question. 'That has accommodation which is now empty but has been used in recent times, a small kitchen, bathrooms, and offices. And it has the security room. The whole thing looks purpose built with reinforced walls and windows.'

'Kyle has to be involved.'

'Agree. Let's get the phone to Meg and we'll go through the video together.'

· · ·

'Love this new plaster stuff.'

Pete had swapped places, leaving Reuben to set the evidence cast. Now they were both up on the ground again. The cast had dried incredibly fast, thanks to new technology, and they were carefully packing it into a box.

'The last few years have given us so many advances. But nothing beats sharp eyes and good instincts. You did well, Pete.'

Unused to compliments, he didn't reply. Reuben was a talent and he was beginning to see why Ben recruited the ex-intelligence cop. Smart and a thinker.

'I want to prise open that door,' Pete said.

'Might need to wait in case Meg wants anything else from down there. But we can take a good look from above.'

The cast packed, Reuben opened another box, this one holding a large drone.

'Yeah, but it can't see ten metres or more underground.'

'Perhaps not. It may reveal old signs of digging. And I want to map all the buildings, or at least get a good start.'

Pete's phone dinged. 'Liz is heading up. Okay, so they have footage of Kyle leaving the phone on the gate. The others are going to the hub to work on what they've found. She'll give us a lift back.'

'I need a couple of hours.'

'It'll take her an hour to get here and there's enough work to keep her occupied.'

Leaving Reuben to play with his drone, Pete headed to the outbuildings. He had his tablet and a digital camera and one of three sets of keys to give him access to anywhere on the property. The other two were in a safe at the hub.

The first shed was set up for garden maintenance. About the size of two double garages, it had a row of hand mowers, half a wall for every kind of gardening tool known to humankind, wheelbarrows, and heavy duty shelving. These held an array of garden-centric items. Pots of all sizes. Propagating materials. Labelled seeds in brown paper had seen better days.

A second door opened to an outdoor area formerly used for composting, the remains barely more than dirt now. A path took Pete to a huge wind-tunnel. Much of it was shredded, pieces of heavy-duty plastic flapping in the breeze, but it must have once been impressive. Inside were overgrown vegetable gardens and a surprising number of plants still growing. There was a pumpkin vine intruding on other beds and covered with healthy green-grey fruit. With the torn covering, rain would have gotten in, enough to keep the plants growing, and some would have broken down with viable seeds and simply continued their circle of life.

Life always finds a way.

For the first time in decades, a memory inserted itself. His mother digging over rich black soil while he, as a little kid, proudly carried a bucket of seeds to plant, chatting non-stop.

Pete was smiling. Back then life was simple. Good. And one day he'd buy his own place miles from nowhere and grow food and read books and drink wine. Perhaps he'd even grow the grapes. No neighbours. No annoying people. Except Liz. Meg. Lyndall even.

He shook his head to clear the thoughts and moved to the next building.

The gates to the mansion were open and after she drove in, Liz closed and locked them. All the way here she'd checked her rear vision mirrors and taken a few detours. It didn't mean Kyle wasn't tracking her anyway. She'd given up wondering how he knew her every move. Or what felt like it.

A drone was skyborne and rather than interrupt Reuben, Liz parked close to the main house. Before texting Pete she took a close look at the driveway and took photos. The brick seemed identical to that at the gallery, so was this yet another weird coincidence. Except there was a fine line between coincidences and deliberate moves.

Pete returned her message and she headed to the back of the building.

Behind it were stables. Or what was once stables. Now it was a garage with five double tilting doors plus a couple of passenger doors. Everything was wide open and there was a hammering sound coming from its depths.

She stepped inside, pausing to let her eyes adjust to the darkness.

'Oh good. Come and see this.'

'Whatever are you doing?'

At the back of the building was a remaining horse stall, filled with musty old straw. Except much of it was raked to one side, exposing a metal plate in the floor. Pete was breathing heavily and sweaty and somehow his T-shirt had ended up hung over a hook.

'Why are you topless?'

He grinned and posed. 'Hot work.'

'Do you see me stripping off because I get overheated? Or Meg? Phoebe? Annette? Candace?'

'But women don't do that.'

'Why?'

'Okay, okay, okay.' He pulled the top back on. 'Ever consider being a lawyer? You make a good argument.'

'Why are you attacking the floor? Is it a trapdoor?'

She shone the flashlight from her phone onto the plate which looked old and heavy. It was about a metre square and had no obvious sign of a handle. It was slightly below the cobbled bricks which lined the floor in here.

'Door of some kind. Just can't work out how to open it.'

For the first time Liz noticed a selection of tools leaning against a wall. Pete picked up a huge sledgehammer.

'This might work.'

'Or hit it further into the ground. What else have you tried?'

'Crowbar. Small sledgehammer. The shovel. Something else I have no idea about.'

'No explosives?' She smiled.

'Thought I should ask first.'

'Why doesn't the crowbar work?'

Pete returned the sledgehammer. 'Can't get it under the metal or find a large enough crack to slide the sharp end into.' Back at the plate he knelt and used his own flashlight to go around the edges. 'I've looked already and because its recessed there's no room. Unless...' He muttered something uncomplimentary about his inability to see properly. 'Maybe take some steps back, Liz.'

Once he'd picked up the sledgehammer again, he picked a spot and raised the tool, bringing it down against the bricks lining one side of the plate. They exploded with chips and dust going everywhere and Liz retreated a bit further. He whacked a few more until there was a clear space then donned some huge gardening gloves he'd found somewhere and cleaned up the area. A defined crack was now obvious between the floor and metal plate and he looked at Liz with a big grin.

'What do they say about wills and ways? Shall we take a look?'

SIXTEEN

Liz walked away from the building, needing a moment to think. Pete was waiting for the go ahead and she should just say yes but her years as a street cop and then in Homicide kicked in hard when he'd reached for the long crowbar.

She'd always followed rules. Done what was expected. Never stepped outside the lines. Unlike Pete – who had no qualms about doing what he deemed necessary – Liz had never questioned authority. Not until the day her father had tried to escape on a boat with someone else's little girl.

And I got you safely back to your mother, Eliza, just like I promised.

But a good man had died. And Kyle still escaped.

She stopped by a tree and leaned against its thick trunk watching the drone work its way along one side of Heberden House. What would Reuben do about the metal plate in the stable? So far he'd been as by-the-book as she used to be. She couldn't factor him into this decision because it was hers to make.

A quick call to Ben would get his okay. Unless he said to wait.

'Why am I second-guessing myself?' she whispered. But she

knew why. Kyle was messing with her head again. Worse than ever before.

Liz sent Ben a text message, attaching a photo she'd taken of the metal plate.

Pete found this in a stable. We're going to remove it and see if it leads anywhere. Update you soon.

The phone went into a pocket and she strode back to the old stables. When it vibrated, she ignored it.

Pete was on the phone and he raised both eyebrows at Liz as he spoke.

'Yes, boss. Not a problem. Sure.'

After ending the call he put the phone on a post.

'Was that Ben?'

'Are we going to lift this thing?' Pete put one hand on the crowbar. 'We only need to take a look. Might just be more dirt under there.'

Neither believed that.

'We are.'

He nodded and offered her his gloves.

'Keep them. Too big for me.'

'I'll leverage it until it cracks, then if you can put your weight on the crowbar, I'll lift.'

Pete inserted the curved, sharp end into the gap he'd made. Liz moved closer as he put downward pressure on his end, grunting as the plate slightly moved before releasing it.

'Heavy. And has been there a while.'

'We can wait for Reuben to finish. Get some more equipment.' Except Liz wanted to know now. 'Can I do something?'

'Grab the shovel.'

'Then what?'

'Go round the outside using a corner of the blade. See if we can loosen it.'

As Liz did that, Pete again worked the crowbar and as a small gap appeared, Liz pushed the shovel further in, preventing the plate from resettling once he took a break.

'Good thinking. This time I'll try and slide the crowbar under so it keeps a bit of space free for my fingers. Leave the shovel and come and help.'

Between them, the metal plate gave in, raising enough for Pete to do exactly as planned. 'Keep the pressure on because I'd like to have all my fingers at the end of this.'

While Liz put all her weight on the crowbar, he forced gloved hands under the plate and with a guttural groan, lifted the plate. He got it upright then Liz helped push it away from the hole. No longer held in place, the crowbar and the shovel disappeared into darkness.

'What's wrong? You look half worried and half... proud? Is that even a thing?' Candace had turned from the whiteboard she favoured when Ben joined her near the round table.

You really can read me like a book.

'Liz sent me a message. Here, let me read it. Pete found this in a stable. We're going to remove it and see if it leads anywhere. Update you soon.' He turned his phone to show her the screen. 'With this image.'

'You might need to tell me what I'm looking at.'

'My guess is the covering of a tunnel. Or something similar.'

'Oh.'

'Yes.'

'And you are worried because Liz simply told you what she was doing rather than asking if she should wait for more information on it?'

He nodded.

Candace chuckled.

'What?'

'And you are proud because she didn't ask. I see your dilemma.'

'It gets worse. I called her straight back with no response so phoned Pete. He agreed not to do anything further until I can get there, which is tomorrow.'

Trying to hide a smile, Candace picked up her marker again. 'Did he really agree?'

Ben thought about it. He'd told Pete to lock the building until tomorrow and the other man said he would.

'He agreed to lock the building. I guess I wasn't crystal clear.'

'Pete knew what you were saying. But he'll back Liz. Always. Doubt if he even told her you called.'

'Thing is, I want Liz to take charge and make decisions in the field. She didn't need to tell me they were removing the metal plate.' Ben settled on a chair. 'When she takes command stuff happens. Good stuff for us and terrible for the bad guys. Yet she loses faith in herself sometimes so what am I doing wrong?'

'Not a thing. Liz is here because at heart, she's fearless. Strong. And a thinker. Thanks to Kyle she's lost some confidence but it will return.'

'Can I help her?'

Candace pulled out a chair and sat, still holding the marker, which she waggled at Ben.

'Don't hover.'

'Hover? I don't. Do I?'

She didn't answer but simply leaned back in her seat.

He ran through the sequence of events. Liz messaged him. He'd called her straight back.

'Oh.'

Candace tilted her head with the smallest of smiles.

'Right. I should have left her to it. Good grief. Then I doubled down and phoned Pete.'

'Gold star for working it out.'

All I wanted was for Liz to know I had her back.

'Okay, Doctor. How do I fix this?'

'You know how.'

As much as Ben respected and admired Candace, there were times he wished she would be more forthcoming. Tell him what to do. How to act. Help him be the best leader of this fledgling team possible.

Or is that what she's doing right now by making me connect the dots?

Ben had been so busy creating the perfect team that he'd forgotten his roots. As head of Missing Persons, he'd not only managed a team but overseen difficult and sometimes heart-breaking cases. Over the years he'd honed his people skills to a point where he was good at reading others... at least for the most part. His most difficult case was also his last in the role after the woman he'd loved for more than a decade – losing her for a long time before they'd found each other again – was hunted by a killer. Now she was his wife and safe. And he'd swapped his high pressure role for one where the worst crime was local vandalism.

By the time he'd been offered this job he'd come to the conclusion he still had more to give and that there was only so much surfing he could do. Ellie had already told him he needed to go back to something more challenging. Well, this was more challenging and it was clear he was only just beginning to understand how much.

Pete and Liz made a trip to the BearCat for supplies and were back in the old stable. They worked together to tie a couple of ropes to solid posts and set up floodlights directed into the hole.

'I don't have the physical strength to haul you up if something goes wrong,' Liz said. She'd taken the harness from Pete before he could put it on and was adjusting it around her waist. 'Either that or we wait for Reuben.'

'Spoilsport. Whichever way.'

But Pete grinned and unrolled a rope ladder. According to him, this hole wasn't as deep as the well and the five metre ladder should easily reach the bottom, avoiding the need for the winch.

Liz had no intention of doing more than climbing to the lowest rung and getting some video. The harness secure, she activated the small camera on its front.

'Okay, all good?' Pete attached another rope to her with a climbing clip. 'The ladder is secured with the other ropes but will feel unstable.'

Ready to remind him she was an experienced mountain climber, Liz bit her tongue. He was saying the same stuff she would. She nodded and sat on the edge, feeling for the rung closest to her feet. That done, she supported her weight with the guide ropes and turned her body until she was facing the ladder. Liz glanced at Pete and almost giggled at how intense his expression was as he stared back. Was he afraid she'd fall and leave him to explain?

'Hey, dude? If I drop like a stone and go splat, just retrieve the harness and ladder and cover the hole again. Nobody will come looking.'

'Yeah, sure. I'll say you ran away.'

'Where? Like, where did I run too?'

He screwed his face up. 'Nah, it is more that you ran *off* with a cowboy to live in the countryside.'

'A good looking cowboy?'

'If you like skinny-as-all-hell, down on their luck losers with thin moustaches. Has seven kids under ten.'

'Seven? Where's the mum?'

'She fell down a hole.'

Now Liz did laugh. But Pete was right into his story.

'She was looking for a way off the farm. You know… one of those dusty, parched farms with cow skulls and tumbleweeds?'

'Are we in the United States?'

'Yes. He was a long distance boyfriend of yours who lured you over the sea with the promise of a brave new world.'

'Just so you know, I already started recording the video.'

Pete shrugged. 'Better make sure you don't fall then. Otherwise the team will be fruitlessly searching overseas.'

Before the conversation became even more nonsensical, Liz took a step down, moving her hands one at a time from rope to ladder. Then another. The hole was well lit by the floodlights but her heart was pounding regardless. She loved climbing and abseiling and orienteering for the rush which accompanied each. This was a little different. Uncovering the truth about the dreadful night the Baxters were killed in their own home was her job. One mistake might set them back.

Step by careful step, Liz descended. The sides of the hole were compacted soil. This had been dug through existing earth without any reinforcement.

'Going okay?'

The smell of the soil and eons of decomposition was fresh and also dank. A weird mix.

'Another couple of rungs.'

Periodically, she stopped and turned to allow the camera to view the sides but to her eyes, there was nothing to record. Pete had told her there were hand and footholds in the well. No such things existed here.

She was as far down as the rope ladder allowed. Liz gazed at the bottom, hooking an arm through a rung and using her phone to record video where she felt the camera on her front wouldn't see. Below her the ground was rough. The floodlights weren't penetrating all the way here so she turned on the flashlight on her phone...

'Pete? Looks like someone started digging a tunnel.'

'Started?'

His voice echoed.

'It goes a couple of metres. Or maybe more. We're going to need a proper look.'

'So can you see further?'

She'd have to stand on the bottom. Protocol was to avoid contact with surfaces until there was either samples taken or no other choice.

Liz lowered herself until she was on the firm base of the shaft.

'We need to put some resources into this.'

Her light flickered further into the tunnel.

'I think this heads under the house.'

SEVENTEEN

On the way back to the hub, Liz made phone calls then wrote a brief on their discovery. They were in the Domain Tunnel when she finally slid the tablet into its sleeve.

'Done?' Pete asked.

'As much as I can think of. I downloaded the video from my phone but Meg will have to do the one from the harness camera. Reuben, I'm so sorry not to have said a word to you yet.' She turned in her seat to look at Reuben in the back. 'How did the drone go?'

'Lots of data to analyse. There's definite signs of hollows underground in several places around the building. Mostly straight lines from it to the well, to the stables, and two other spots on the grounds which we've yet to look at.'

'Tunnels?' Pete asked.

'There's not enough clarity to show that. But long, straight gaps.'

Reuben was being cautious and rightly so. He could only comment on what he'd seen through the screen as he flew the drone and wasn't one to speculate.

'Ben is arranging a specialist team who will explore both the shaft in the stables and have a go at opening the door in the well,' Liz said. 'We don't have the expertise nor people power for what might be time consuming and dangerous.'

'I like dangerous,' Pete muttered.

'We know. And what *we* will do… you both with me and Ben, is break down the wall at the end of the hallway inside the house.'

'That's more like it.'

Even Reuben looked pleased, and he and Pete started a conversation about how to approach the problem of getting through the wall.

Liz leaned back in her seat and closed her eyes for a moment.

The day was moving too fast. And too slow. She needed to be in multiple places at once yet couldn't even focus on one issue at a time before another arose. This was part of policing, and she'd dealt with heavy workloads and competing cases for years. Never had so much been at stake all at the same time.

As the vehicle slowed and turned off the ring road, Liz drew in a long, slow breath and opened her eyes. She had to be on her game. No more letting Kyle into her head.

'Pete, go the third way.'

'Not being tailed.'

'Please.'

There were four routes the team used at random once a kilometre out from their building. It wasn't about being tailed as much as whether Kyle had surveillance operating. Liz didn't put it past him to have people working or living in the suburb and watching out for the units or her own car. And while there was a chance he already knew the location of Operation Nobody, the less intel he could gather, the better.

Except if we have one of his informants working for us, then he'll know more than we can imagine.

The thought was uncomfortable.

Yet the longer she worked in the team, the less she believed

anyone was bent. Annette had settled into being her usual self –
the solid cop Liz had known for so long. And although Hamish
still needed some lessons in being a decent co-worker, he no
longer gave off any red flag vibes. She made a note on her phone
to talk to Candace and Ben about the questionnaire results so far
which reminded her she'd not done hers. Another note, this time
to bring her paperwork up to date asap. Because she didn't have
anything else to do. At least that made her smile, even if it was
rueful rather than happy.

Phoebe was in Ben's office with the door closed when Liz
followed Pete and Reuben into the main room. She only noticed
because Hamish was in the kitchen, staring over the part-wall in
the direction of the offices. After putting down her gear at her
desk, she went in search of coffee.

'Liz… would you like me to make you some late lunch?'

Hamish had nothing to show why he was in the kitchen. No
cup or glass or plate and nothing being cooked.

'Thanks but no. I'll eat once I get home.'

'Okay.'

His eyes drifted back to the office.

'Do you want a coffee, Hamish? I need one.'

'Um, tea. Tea would be good but I'll do that.' He collected the
kettle and filled it. 'I can make tea for you?'

He was trying. Or panicking. Both, even. Liz stepped away
from the coffee machine.

'Tea sounds good.'

'Excellent.' Hamish put on the kettle to boil and ran his finger
down a list on the wall where everyone's preferences were written. 'Liz, tea. No sugar. Dash of milk. Not black with lemon?'

'Not very adventurous with tea.'

'Missing something special.' He went through the motions of
making tea but kept checking the object of his attention.

'How long have they been in their meeting, Hamish?'

He finally turned and gave her his full attention, a cup in one hand and teaspoon in the other.

'Too long.'

'And you think….?'

He sighed. 'I think I need a personality overhaul. Liz, I've made so many mistakes since joining the team and I'm unsure how to fix things without making it worse.'

Poor Hamish looked so woeful that Liz almost offered him a hug. Almost. She hadn't forgotten their first meeting when he'd been crawling under a house and thinking he was a bad guy, she had dragged him out and they'd rolled down a hill together. While he'd taken it as an opportunity to come on to her, Liz had been scathing.

'Just be yourself, mate. Don't try to act like you think others expect you to. If you believe Phoebe is in there complaining about you then don't.'

His eyes shot to hers. 'Do you know something?'

'I know that Phoebe has confidential sources which even I'm not privy to so if she needs Ben's attention to discuss the podcast then let her have it without second-guessing the reasons. The world doesn't rotate around you.' Liz smiled to soften the words.

He nodded and finished making the tea.

'I like you, Liz. You are strong and sensible and smart. Anyway, I hope the tea is good. And thanks.'

After handing her a cup, he wandered back to his desk, his body language more relaxed and not even one glance toward the offices.

Now to be strong and sensible and smart about myself.

Written on a sticky note in Candace's hand was a message.

Vince rang on the landline and would like to catch up. He said it isn't urgent.

There was one landline phone in the building whose number was given to trusted allies and family members of the team. Vince and Lyndall both had it, as did Anna. Liz checked her mobile phone and saw a missed call from Vince from earlier in the day. She collected the landline handset and let herself into one of the overnight rooms, dialling as she sank onto an armchair.

'Vince Carter.'

Hearing his gruff voice was good.

'Just me. Sorry I didn't pick up your call earlier.'

'Hi, Lizzie. It occurred to me the landline is better anyway, if Kyle's snooping around.'

'Meg keeps running some kind of check on my mobile but I agree, talk on the landline unless you urgently need me.' She'd briefly spoken to Vince after seeing Kyle the other morning. 'Is everything okay?'

'We're all good. Melanie is up with Lyndall cooking something for dinner. You know how those two are. But that's why I called.'

'About dinner?'

He chuckled. 'No, about Lyndall. Or at least a comment she made earlier. She didn't want to bother you with it but we were talking about the case your team is on. The double murder. You know I'd met Inspector Baxter a number of times. Decent man.'

Were those murders the same year Lyndall fled France to hide from Marcus Bonner?

'Still there, Liz?'

'Yes, what did Lyndall say?'

'She remembered them. She'd met the Baxters once at a dinner.'

'Oh my goodness. In Europe?'

'No. In Melbourne. A couple of years earlier, when she and Alain were here briefly.'

'Where? What does she recall? Who else was there?'

'Easy on. I've told you the extent of the conversation. Melanie interrupted and Lyndall muttered something about it all being in the past and not worth mentioning. You know this is hard for her.'

'I do. Sorry. But about dinner?'

His voice brightened. 'Would you like to come up? I know they'll both love to see you.'

'I wish. Not until we work out what Kyle's up to. But I would like to send someone in my place. If that's okay?'

Vince groaned. 'Don't even tell me. But sure. Why not. I'll go warn Lyndall and set a place for shithead.'

Pete idled his car at the bottom of Lyndall's long driveway. He was just inside the electric gate, which was a new feature, and had spoken to the security guard who kept an eye on both houses. This wasn't where he'd expected to be for dinner but the second Liz told him about her conversation with Vince, he'd volunteered to come. She didn't want to be near here, thanks to the risk of drawing the attention of her damned father to her friends again, and he was the only other person Lyndall was likely to feel at ease with discussing her past.

Lyndall mattered to him. As strangers, they'd saved Vince's life and dispatched a bad guy. Covering up her part in it was a natural response. They'd forged a friendship when he'd once mentioned a childhood yearning to paint. She'd been endlessly patient with his early attempts and they'd shared many a meal and decent bottle of wine. Nobody else knew how close they'd become – unlikely friends from very different backgrounds – not even Vince who'd kept an emotional distance from his neighbour for decades until her kidnapping.

Now he needed to draw on the trust they'd found. He'd seen her distress after escaping from Bonner and his people. Her past was profoundly heartbreaking and to a degree, still was. Although she now knew her second son was alive, she wasn't prepared to risk his life again by seeing him until Kyle Moorland was finally caught and a terrible organisation fell.

He slowly drove up the hill, glancing to his left as he passed the almost new cottage Vince shared with his little grandkid, Melanie. Despite the show of dislike between the men, Pete had forgiven Vince for reporting him all those years ago. If anything, it was a wakeup call that the then-young detective was walking too fine a line.

Not that I'll ever tell him that.

To the other side, a herd of maybe twenty cows raised their heads from grazing to watch him. Each of them was a rescue job… just like the dozen donkeys which treated Lyndall like their leader.

At the top of the climb he parked and got out, happy to stretch his legs. Too much of his time was spent driving or sitting lately. He fancied some time on a surf board.

'Peeet!'

A child raced at him, throwing herself against his waist before he could respond.

'Melaneeeee!'

She giggled and let go. 'I made lasagne all by myself.'

'No way.'

'Yes. Way.' Now, she grabbed one of his hands. 'Come on. I need to check the oven.'

'Why? Is it trying to escape.'

'You are silly. Do you like ricotta cheese?'

'I sure do.'

'And pumpkin and spinach?'

'More of the first and less of the second.'

'Excellent. And there's brooo… um, breee… anyway, bread with tomatoes and stuff.'

'Bruschetta?'

'Oh that's it! And salad. And Grandad said he might open a bottle of wine except…'

'Except? Did he say after I leave?'

Melanie nodded.

'He loves teasing me. Do you know that we are old friends?'

'I dunno. I've heard him call you shi—'

'Nope. You never have. He calls me shiphead. Because I like the water.'

Melanie gave him a weird look as if trying to work out if he was telling the truth.

'Did you know I have a PWC?'

'Does it hurt?'

He burst into laughter.

'Well what is it then?'

'A personal water craft. A jet ski. Like a motorcycle you ride on the water.'

'Lyndall told me all about them. Liz and she rode one together.'

'They sure did.'

They stepped onto the back deck and while Melanie rushed through the open sliding door, Pete slipped off his shoes.

'Come in, Peter.'

Lyndall met him halfway to the kitchen and they hugged. She gripped him tightly and he squeezed back, surprised how much he'd missed her.

'Would you like a beer or glass of wine?'

She released him and led the way to the kitchen, where Melanie was peering into the oven. Vince was at the fridge and nodded. 'Pete.'

'Vince. Beer thanks. Light, if you have it?'

'Did you know Pete has a jet ski?' Melanie asked.

'Can't say I did,' Vince opened a beer and handed it to Pete. 'Shall I get that lasagne out?'

Pete stayed out of the way as the other three worked together to finish everything for the meal. It was obvious how much they'd become a family, even if Lyndall still lived here alone and there was no talk of marriage or co-habitation. Vince had mellowed in the past year and little Melanie was no longer the withdrawn and frightened child she'd been after losing her parents.

'Right, shall we get this all on the dining table and then later, Pete and I can have a quiet talk.' Lyndall glanced at him. 'I imagine that's why you're here.'

EIGHTEEN

An hour after Pete left, most of the team had also gone for the day. Only Ben, Phoebe, and Liz remained. Meg was in the building but had disappeared to the lab to prepare it for the arrival of their new forensics scientist. Before going she'd downloaded the drone's imagery and was running it through a program to analyse the data. It was an overnight job.

Liz reviewed the work Annette and Hamish had completed. The files and notes and evidence from the Baxter killings were carefully itemised and recorded digitally and she was able to use the table to have multiple images open at the same time.

Annette truly was meticulous and even though Hamish preferred action over the grunt work, he'd contributed with short but informative notes. Now it was up to Liz and whoever she decided to use to help, to make observations and conclusions. She'd excluded Annette and Hamish as they'd already spent so long with the material. Reuben was her first choice. He had an analytical mind as well as having a good eye for connections.

'Sorry to interrupt you, Liz.' Phoebe spoke softly from just behind her. 'I wonder if you'd have a moment to listen to something?'

'Of course. And you're not interrupting. I'm just trying to make sense of a whole lot of random information.'

Phoebe gazed at the vertical display. There was the open report Annette wrote, several images of evidence, and a crime scene photograph, without the bodies but with the blood and markers.

'Meg is so happy about her friend coming to work here,' Phoebe said. 'She told me if anyone can process the washing machine and the clothes and find old evidence, then it is him. And then she can concentrate on the digital stuff again. She's so talented.'

'She is. And so are you.'

For once, the younger woman smiled rather than dropping her eyes. 'Would you listen to the teaser I've recorded for the podcast tonight? Ben likes it and I'd like your take as well.'

They went into the other room where Phoebe had set up a small speaker and tablet on the round table. After they sat, she turned to Liz. 'The podcast goes out at around ten tonight. My intention is to finish mastering this and send it out to our subscribers no later than eight which will encourage a larger audience.'

'How many subscribers do you have?'

'Globally about six million. In Australia it is about a quarter of a million. They subscribe directly and there are heaps more who listen through other channels.'

'I had no idea it was so big!'

'People love true crime.'

She tapped the screen of the tablet and Liz leaned her arms on the table to listen as music led into an announcement that this was tonight's subject and some details about time and name of the podcast and Phoebe's name.

'I have a special assignment, my lovely sleuths. Soon we will go back in time to a most dreadful and puzzling double murder. A cold case so cold that our friends at Victoria Police froze the investigation. What I need is for you to cast your minds back to

1995. For those who are too young, I am sure you have the skills, my blossoms, to do some digital digging for me. So… who is in? Not sure yet? What if I leave you with some clues. A mansion. A successful and well-loved older couple. And to add some intrigue… their own son was a prominent member of the police force at the time of their deaths. This is Phoebe Renshaw. I'll talk to you soon.'

There was more music and the recording ended.

'Oh, Phoebe! That's fabulous and you sound so good.'

'I do? Thanks.'

'And it is perfect. I'm going to subscribe and listen and I don't know why I haven't already. No wonder you have so many people listening.'

The colour rose in Phoebe's cheeks. 'I'll send you an invite with a code which gives you free access forever. Actually, I should do that for the whole team.' She picked up her phone. 'I'll do that before the episode airs and it allows you unlimited listens. Oh and of any past episodes.'

'I really am happy to pay though. You shouldn't have to miss income because we're on the same team.'

'Missing income isn't on the cards as long as the current subscribers stay entertained. My team is well paid and that matters more to me than anything I make. Well, that and looking after our charities.'

Liz's phone dinged.

'That's the link, so just follow it when you want and the rest is pretty intuitive. Anyway, you think this teaser is interesting enough?'

'Absolutely. What else needs doing to it?'

'I'll shoot it off to my sound person who'll make it perfect. And it will go to my European team to translate into several languages so people have a choice of my voice in English or someone else's in theirs. The podcast just needs finishing touches and then it is out of my hands.'

'Well I'm incredibly impressed, Phoebe. Do you need me for

anything else? I don't want to hold you up with all my questions.'

Phoebe's smile was wide. 'I love talking about the podcast but yes, I should get this finished. And I'm so happy you liked it.'

At the door, Liz glanced back. Phoebe now wore headphones and was intent on her tablet. What a difference seeing her so confident and even proud talking about her work. Ben's decision to bring her into the team was becoming more and more logical.

Ben was at his office door as Liz headed back to the table. They'd spoken on her return but only to discuss Pete going to see Lyndall. He stepped back and invited her in.

'Phoebe is amazing.' She needed to say something.

He gestured for her to take one of the tub chairs on a far side of the office and he joined her once she'd sat. With no desk between them, Liz knew this was more than a normal conversation or even the half-expected lecture about answering her phone.

'She is amazing. I take it she played the teaser?'

'Her voice is perfect for the podcast and she has this way with words... no wonder she's successful.'

'I think we need a chance to talk and with almost an empty building, figured we'd be less likely to be interrupted.' Ben's phone beeped and he glanced at the screen then put it face-down on a round coffee table. 'Case in point.'

'This is about earlier.'

'This is about me not giving you space to lead.'

Sorry, what?

Her face must have reflected her thought because Ben grinned. 'Not what you thought I'd say?'

She shook her head.

'We've had a roller coaster of a start. Our little team. Thrown straight into Lyndall's abduction before you'd even met everyone, yet look at the outcome. Lyndall safely home, a European crime organisation now being investigated, and several criminals off the streets.'

'All in a matter of days.'

Looking back, what they'd accomplished did seem unbelievable.

'What you did by making the decision to go to Rye... I support that. A bit more communication would be good but when you follow your instincts, results follow.'

'I had to go. All the evidence was there that something was going on in the region yet I had no logical way of explaining it. Same as when I disobeyed orders not to approach my father when he was preparing to leave with Eliza. It went against all of my experience and training, but I had to do it.' Her heart sped up.

'You saved Eliza.'

'But Terry died.'

'And he might have anyway. If you are still beating yourself up over it, then I want you to do some sessions with Candace.'

His phone beeped again and he glanced toward it but didn't check the message.

'Why did you tell me what you and Pete were up to?'

Liz had thought about this a lot.

'You are right that I need to see Candace. I spoke to her this morning and was interrupted by the call Meg received.' Liz's shoulders ached and she forced them to relax. 'All this interference, all the games my father is playing, are getting to me. Even though my intention is to catch him, there are times I second-guess myself. I don't want another Terry situation. I don't want anyone else harmed because he sees them as either a means to control me or an obstacle to his ambition.'

Just hold it together, Liz. This is Ben. He's safe.

'I can't imagine how hard this is. He was out of your life for decades, then you thought him dead, and then he has turned his full attention on you, without actually saying what he wants.'

'He's like quicksilver. Just when he's surrounded, he changes shape. And his network is so hard to uncover.'

'I have some good news in that regard. There's been major steps forward in Europe concerning the ring which Bonner, and potentially Kyle, were part of. And our friend from the last case, Tony Shaw? He's talking at last.'

Good news indeed. Tony Shaw was Bonner's right hand man and shared a similar tattoo to both him and Kyle.

'Can I see him?'

'No. At this point we'll let him keep spilling his guts. Maybe later.'

There were so many things Liz wanted to ask Shaw.

'Meg told me she finally processed and answered the phone. That it was a recorded message rigged somehow to play once answered and keep dialling until someone did.' Hearing Kyle's voice again was yet another reminder of his inherent evil. 'I guess you heard the message?'

'Yeah. He wants to take you to a posh restaurant for dinner. I know he's your father but he's a nut job.'

That made her laugh. A proper laugh and Ben joined in. The idea of meeting Kyle, both in black tie, at an exclusive Melbourne restaurant, had to be laughed at. It was either that or crawl into a hole and cry.

Dinner had been exceptional. Actually, any meal he didn't need to make was good, but Melanie – under the guidance of Lyndall – had made a lasagne to rival some he'd had in Lygon Street. The kid was talented. She drew really well. Could sing, from the occasional song he'd heard, and now this. Obviously didn't take after her grandfather.

'Another beer?' Vince asked.

'Nah. Thanks. Some of that apple cider though?'

Pete had settled in the sunken lounge room after being told by Lyndall to make himself comfortable. The sun had set but the sky was still light enough for him to make out the hills on the opposite side of the road. He'd spent far too much time up there after she'd been abducted from the house. There and along the ridge behind her paddocks. Hours of searching – not for Lyndall as he was convinced she'd been removed forcibly – but for signs of whoever must have watched her property, possibly for weeks.

"I wish Liz had been able to come as well,' Lyndall said. She put two glasses of apple cider on the coffee table and took the armchair closest to him. 'Always love seeing you but I miss her.'

'She feels the same. Once we catch Kyle I reckon we need to throw a huge party. Music. Dancing. More of Melanie's lasagne.'

The last bit brought a smile to Lyndall's face but it quickly dropped. 'Sounds nice. I just look forward to a time we are safe. And maybe I can finally see…'

Pete reached across to squeeze her hand. 'It will happen. You'll be reunited with your son. It is one of our driving motivations to catch Kyle and destroy the organisation he's tied up with.'

She nodded and settled back in her chair. 'I don't know if I ever met Kyle Moorland, not until he fished me out of Port Phillip Bay in disguise recently. But I knew Marcus very well, and for the longest time we'd meet at gallery openings or special events, along with private dinners for just a handful of people. And it was at one such dinner I was introduced to the most intriguing couple.'

'Joseph and Ilona Baxter.'

'Yes. Joseph was charming and had such a smile and way of making one feel important. And Ilona… quieter but her eyes missed nothing. I felt she was very intelligent but gave little away. There were a dozen or so guests and the dinner was held at their home and—'

'Wait. Sorry, but which home? The mansion?'

Lyndall shook her head. 'No. Close to the city.'

'Go on.'

'There was much talk of art and Marcus went on about his

vision to open a gallery in Melbourne. Ilona said they owned a property which would be perfect.'

Pete took out his phone. 'Do you mind me making notes?'

'Please.'

'Do you remember the year?'

'It was 1991.'

'What else was said about the property?'

'That's where my memory fails me, Pete. I don't recall anything more about it but the conversation was always moving fast. Changing subjects and so on as happens when there's plenty of drinks and egos involved.' She smiled to herself. 'People wanted to ask about my paintings which was flattering.'

'And deserved. Anything at all else you recall?'

'Only that... and it was such a strange thing to remember... toward the end of the night I overheard Joseph tell Marcus that Ilona was going to involve him in arrangements which would open new doors.'

'New doors?'

'I wish I'd asked questions but it made no sense then and doesn't now other than knowing what evil lived inside Marcus. It sounded like a business plan and they were business people. I'm sorry.'

'Don't be. This shows a connection we've been trying to find. You've done well, Lyndall. Really well.'

NINETEEN

Liz longed to go for a run along the river. She stood at the window in her bedroom gazing at the street awash with run-off from hours of rain, and there was no sign the weather would lighten up anytime soon. It wasn't that she wouldn't run in the wet. If anything, it might protect her from Kyle's relentless shadowing of her every move.

Don't be melodramatic. He can't be everywhere you go.

And that was the problem. While he'd had a network for decades, had removing Marcus Bonner and his cronies decimated it? The only indicator Kyle still had people out there was the unsettling way he'd made contact… such as at the marina and by phoning Meg. For all the team knew, he was working alone now. Yet how could they risk relaxing their protocols? Following Rupert's instructions to the letter, she'd placed several surveillance devices inside the apartment the other day. So far there'd been nothing out of the ordinary.

Last night she'd listened to Phoebe's podcast, headphones on and a glass of wine taking the place of a meal.

What a clever and talented woman Phoebe was. As reserved as she was at work, once behind her microphone a whole different side emerged. Polished and precise as well as amusing at times, Phoebe outlined the Baxter case without resorting to shock tactics or speculation. Every bit of information was in the public domain already but Phoebe's words made it sound like a brand new story. If even one person's memory was prodded then they might have another piece of the puzzle.

She turned from the window and collected her laptop case which included her tablet, and small handbag. Liz didn't know why she bothered with the latter as she normally wore clothing with pockets, but some old convention kept her carrying one. Her mother always had one, a huge one, filled with everything under the sun. The little purse where she carefully carried coins and notes was always buried under bandaids and tissues and spare socks. Not for herself, but for her children.

What a peculiar thing to remember. Liz hated wearing wet socks. Wet feet were fine but soggy socks? Yuck.

The rain slowed her drive into work thanks to commuters forgetting to adjust to the conditions and having to detour past two accidents in the space of a couple of kilometres. She was still first into the hub and made coffee while bread was toasting. There was something peaceful about being here alone. All the lights off other than one in the kitchen and one over her desk. The coffee smelled oh-so-good and the toast too, when it popped. After slathering the pieces with butter, Liz headed to her desk. Today was about the mansion. Whatever was behind that wall would give up its secrets.

She booted her computer, leaving the laptop in her bag to take later. The toast was perfect because her one glass of wine so late last night had turned into three. Nothing as good as carbs the next morning.

There were several memos from different members of the team. The only one which mattered right now was from Pete and she opened it while eating, quickly scanning his words.

Last night he'd sent a text when he was leaving Lyndall's house. He had some intel and would talk to everyone tomorrow. It wasn't urgent.

'Everything is urgent, dude.' The words had just left her lips as Reuben wandered in.

'Mmm…. Coffee. And toast.'

'Nope. No toast here.' Liz quickly pushed the last bite into her mouth.

'And yet I smell it.' He stopped near her desk and did a dramatic sigh. 'Just a few minutes earlier…'

'Soz. I ate all the bread.'

'Right.'

'I need more coffee, so shall I make two while you find an alternate breakfast?'

'I think that's only fair.'

It didn't take long for Reuben to find a frozen loaf and slide a knife between pieces to separate it.

'Actually… would you do some more? I'm so hungry this morning.'

'Already have. You look hungry.'

'Huh? How do I look hungry?'

Reuben didn't answer but filled the toaster with bread.

She dug around in the fridge for the vegan butter he used along with a jam she'd found while shopping. Nothing in it but fruit and sugar. She put both on the counter and pushed her plate over, then returned to making coffee.

'Happy to put butter on yours, Liz.'

'I want to try yours. And lots of jam please.'

'Yes, ma'am.' He had a smile on his lips as he opened the jam.

'Am I being bossy?'

'You are being happy. You look happier today.'

'I'm looking forward to going to Heberden House. And Pete sent a memo about his dinner with Lyndall.'

'He did?'

'Was just about to read it.'

Plates and cup in hand, Liz returned to her desk with Reuben close behind so he could read the memo with her.

'Okay, so Lyndall attended a small dinner party at the

Melbourne home of the Baxters in 1991. Marcus spoke about wanting to have a gallery in Victoria. Ilona said they had the perfect property.' Liz glanced up at Reuben. 'We need to find out who was behind the company that sold the gallery to Marcus.'

'Agree. Shall I do a search?'

'Let Annette. She'll be staying here today and has some other things to follow up.'

Like every connection to the Baxters. The evidence boxes had provided a fair amount of information but clearly not everything.

'I want to track down whoever worked for them, no matter when and whether in the various homes or their businesses. Reuben? Who is talking to Tony Shaw?'

He looked surprised. 'News travels fast. There's two detectives from Australian Federal Police he's dealing with. Some cross-border charges are pending and I guess he's realised nobody is coming to his rescue and his only hope is a deal.'

'Which Ben had already offered him.'

'Shaw is arrogant and believed himself untouchable.'

'Would you be allowed to speak with him? You did an amazing job with his interrogation and I want to know if he'll turn on Kyle.'

'Doubtful. At least not until AFP are done with him, but I'll talk to someone and try. Now, I'm going to go eat before Pete arrives and steals my toast.'

This was Ben's first time at Heberden House and he didn't know how he felt. The cloud of gloominess hanging over the property was to do with more than the rain, yet the building must have once been grand. Back in his time in Missing Persons, he'd trust his gut about places. Some just gave off an air of tragedy. Despair even. This had both in spades.

Pete was voted best person for the job of unlocking the heavy chain around the front gates and Reuben drove through and waited for them to be relocked.

'You know he'll complain all day now about being forced into the rain,' Liz said.

'Only until I hand him a sledgehammer.'

Ben had no issues with Pete and his moods. All it took was some activity or a specific role to fulfil and he'd put one hundred percent in. Boredom was Pete's biggest enemy. Not unlike Hamish.

The door opened and Pete threw himself in. 'I'll have you know I spent an hour styling my hair this morning.' He brushed himself off as the vehicle started up the driveway, splashing raindrops over Liz.

She didn't seem to notice. Her eyes were off to the left and Ben followed the direction. From viewing aerial maps and some of the drone data he knew the well was over there. Why was it so interesting to Liz? As far as he knew she'd not been near the well... although after the discovery of the other shaft in the stables, it made sense she'd have it on her radar. At least once Meg had Jeff Scott settled in, she'd have more time to focus on the digital side of her job again, including the apparent tunnels beneath parts of the grounds.

Reuben went past the main house, following the driveway along the side and then parking as close as he could to a plain door at the back.

'There's no covered areas?'

'I can park in the old stables, after Pete opens them,' Reuben said. He glanced in the rear vision mirror at Pete's unamused face. 'Means we'll have fifty or more metres each way carrying equipment. Here we can grab it out pretty quick.'

'Fair call. Who has the house keys?'

'Well, me of course,' Pete said. 'Am I not the keeper of all locks? The faithful one who risks his own health and wellbeing to protect properties from perps and our team from... actually, what am I protecting you from?'

'A dull existence.'

Liz climbed out before Pete could answer. Ben and Reuben laughed and in a moment were helping her unpack an assortment of tools and equipment while Pete opened the house.

The door led to what Ben would consider a mud room. A place to leave shoes and coats, get dry if needed, and tidy up enough to enter the main part of the house. There were hooks along a wall with shoe racks below. A sink. A handful of old lockers. He opened them one by one. Each empty until the last.

He pulled out a black apron and showed the others.

'Bit fancy for you, boss,' Pete said. 'Frills are more Reuben's style.'

But Liz was quiet. She gazed at the apron, her forehead wrinkled in thought.

'Anyone have an evidence bag?' Ben asked. 'How old would you think this is? Liz?'

'Hmm? Oh. No idea. Never owned one. But Pete's right – there are frills so I'd think it belonged to a bygone era. Not really one from only thirty or forty years go.'

She had a point. It reminded Ben of paintings he'd seen from far longer ago than then. A bag provided, he slid it inside, sealed it and wrote where he found it. 'Do you know if Meg has been through here? Forensically?'

'Not if you just found an apron,' Liz said. 'She's been here twice but had to cover a lot of ground. Should we arrange for Jeff to come out?'

'Yes. Yes, once he settles in, he and Meg can come back.'

They went through another plain door. It was solid timber and had a broken lock. It opened partway along the hallway they needed.

'I remember Meg and I passing this room and we tried the handle but couldn't open it,' Liz said. 'It's somewhere in my notes to try with other keys if there are any – there's a few doors we couldn't unlock.' She inspected the inside of the door. 'This is clearly broken now. We'd have noticed.'

Pete and Reuben glanced at each other and put their equipment on the floor. As one, they moved into the main part of the house, side arms drawn. Ben and Liz did the same but in the other direction, checking a room at a time to clear the area. No intruders. Nothing obviously damaged.

They met up with the others at the bottom of the staircase.

'Clear upstairs. Haven't checked down here.' Pete whispered. 'Shall we spread out?'

Ben nodded and each chose a direction. He and Liz started in the large foyer then she disappeared into one of the formal rooms. He checked a large room at the front of the house. This was where Meg found blood splatter and believed the Baxters were killed. It was empty of everything other than some wall lamps and small side tables. The room overlooked the gardens to the gate. It would be easy to see a visitor, or potentially an intruder, if they came from that direction.

If Meg was correct and they'd been in here when shot, where had the killer come from? Were they entertaining and the guest turned murderous? The police report from the time said no. They were in bed. This appeared to be a sitting room. Somewhere once comfortably furnished with an open fireplace. Probably bookshelves and a drinks cabinet. Rugs.

Liz had questioned the whereabouts of the furniture and other contents, and he had requested that information from the solicitor handling the estate of Inspector Ronald Baxter. So far no response had been forthcoming.

'Whoever was here is gone, boss.' Pete appeared in the doorway. 'Reuben and I are going to run out and check the outbuildings.'

'Okay. Liz and I will set up the gear.'

Alone again, Ben messaged Candace to ask her to follow up with the solicitor. Why the contents were removed was a mystery. Nothing in the evidence boxes indicated that had happened, so it had to be well after the murders. But was it while the inspector was still living?

Liz caught up with him in the foyer with a shrug. 'Kind of weird. No other indication of a break-in plus the outside door was locked.'

'So someone has one key but not the other?'

'Or I'm remembering wrong.'

Ben doubted that.

'When we're back, would you ask Meg what she recalls?' Liz asked. 'I don't want to accidentally influence her.'

'Sure. And I'd like to take a look at any parts of the property you want me to see. After we get through the wall of course. Anywhere not yet visited.'

'Like the lockers? Can't believe we didn't get in there the first two times. And there's the cellar.'

'Love a good cellar.'

'I'd just love to find some evidence, Ben. That way we can put this place into the solved file and never have to return.'

With that odd remark, Liz led the way back to the equipment.

TWENTY

Reuben and Pete reappeared while Liz was setting up a tripod with a camera to record what they were about to do to the wall. It was the final step of preparations and Ben had just said he'd have to go searching for them if they weren't back in a minute.

'We left the wet weather gear hanging in that room. And although there's no-one on the property, we know someone was.' Pete's hair was drenched, making it curly rather than its usual beach-waves. 'Footprints.'

'What? Where?'

'Behind the stables the grass has died off and the rain made for perfect conditions to leave several shoe prints in the mud.' Reuben might never have been in the wet. He must have found a towel somewhere. 'Sorry we took so long but I made a cast while Pete followed the prints.'

Ben looked from one to the other. 'You have been gone twenty minutes and have made an evidence cast and followed an intruder's footsteps?'

Reuben grinned. 'No messing around. We wanted to be here, smashing a wall.'

Liz burst into laughter. She couldn't help it. Every time she stepped onto this property her emotions rose. And humour was far better than tears.

'Anyway, I feel vindicated by my observations from the other day,' Pete said. 'Reckon the perp moved pretty fast but tried to be careful. They kept to firm surfaces until they couldn't. There's slide marks from skidding or losing traction up an incline which ends at the wall. And it is about where I took pics of the house which backs the property. Lowest part of the wall to climb from both sides and there were some mud marks on it.'

'We should go and visit that house,' Liz said. She looked from Pete to Ben, who made no sign of moving. 'What if the perp's still on their property? In their back garden or even in the house? Someone might be in danger. We can checked the streets. Or at least look for cameras.'

Maybe she should have led with the last bit. It sounded less panicked.

'I should have been clearer, Liz. At the bottom of the wall were a couple of old wooden boxes stacked on top of each other which I think came from the stables, which was unlocked. High enough for me to climb to the top of the wall. The other side is only about two metres high so I dropped down and took a look. Nobody was home. And no bad guys in sight.'

Yes, why not tell us that first?

'Cameras?'

'Yeah, but only at the front so I left a card under their front door.'

Reuben looked thoughtful. 'So someone has a key for stables and for the back door yet had to break through the second door. Why not open the front door?'

Pete pulled the set of keys out and searched through. 'All different apart from the stables and back door. Must only have a copy of that one.'

Ben got on the phone and wandered away.

'How good is the evidence cast?' Liz asked.

'Considering how wet the ground is, I'm happy with it,'

Reuben said. 'Because this mix of Meg's sets so fast it actually is better. Less time for movement to mess it up. But I'm going to teach Pete how to do them because I can run faster.'

'You cannot.' Pete began inspecting the tools.

'Did he tell you he doesn't know how to do an evidence cast?' Liz grinned. 'Because he does. We all do.'

'We all do what?' Ben was back. 'Never mind. There's a locksmith coming to put new locks on all three doors in question, all different. I've asked for a couple of patrol cars to discreetly look around the area but short of them coming across someone acting suspiciously, they've got next to no chance of finding our friend. And, yes before you ask, Liz, I did send them a photo of Kyle.'

She did a zipping motion across her lips. It was precisely what she'd been about to ask.

'Locksmith is a couple of hours away so how about we do what we came for?' Ben suggested. 'I'm in the mood to smash something.'

Liz went upstairs after a while. Getting through the wall was taking longer than expected. Meg's clever machine had shown at least two rows of bricks with reinforced steel mesh and while the equipment was up to the job they had to stop to remove debris every few minutes. At the point where they'd found a third row of bricks, Liz excused herself. The video could manage without her and so could they.

Starting at one end of the upper floor she rechecked each room, opening the doors of any build-in cupboards and then peering out of each window. The rain had turned into mist which didn't help visibility.

At the open doors to the master bedroom, Liz hesitated. This was a sad room. Even Reuben felt it. What had he said?

Shadows of existence. Remnants of life. Laughter. Tears. Passion. Anger.

That was what he'd called ghosts and there was something

evocative about his description. Liz didn't believe in ghosts any more than she believed in deities. Almost everything in life had a logical explanation. Even the hairs which sometimes rose on her arms if she felt she was being watched must have a biological basis although the instinctive sensation was far from understood.

Dogs saw things which weren't there, and cats even more so. Not visible to the human eye.

Liz went straight to the bedroom window. Last time she'd stood here a storm approached. Perhaps it always rained here in sympathy with the terrible events which took place more than three decades ago.

More esoteric musings?

Shaking her head at herself, Liz looked across to the well. That was an interesting find – a partial shoeprint at the base of a long-unused well. Poor Pete was itching to get back down there and prise open the door. Or blow it open if it wouldn't concede quietly. She smiled. He was having fun now, using a sledge-hammer and bolt cutters downstairs.

About to go back to the team she had a thought. What if that shoeprint somehow matched those Reuben just took? Might it be the same person? Someone who knew more than one way in or out of the home? She leaned her forehead against the window to think.

The well had been closed up when found but not with a sealed lid. It was likely some water had got in over a period of time and probably Meg would be able to analyse the soil samples to determine that. Or the new guy would. Either way, someone had left evidence of their presence and the question was how long ago?

She sighed and lifted her head.

The mist parted.

Someone stood on the other side of the gate.

Someone who was staring back at Liz.

· · ·

The first obstacle was getting out of the building. The front door had a dead lock and Liz didn't have any keys.

She raced past the staircase and a series of random rooms until hurtling into the hallway.

'Hey Liz. Come and see.'

Pete's words barely registered as she ran through the mud room and flung the back door open.

Misty it might be but the rain was still here.

She slid along the bricks, then moved onto the grass along the side to maintain traction. As she rounded the corner of the house she looked for the figure. It was too misty and too far to see.

'Lizzie! Wait up!'

'Kyle's here.'

Somehow she got the words out.

Somehow she kept her feet.

Her face was wet. She brushed a hand across her eyes to better see. Kyle wasn't getting away this time. Although she didn't have the key to the chain around the gate, she had a gun. She wouldn't hesitate to use it on him. He had to be stopped.

The last few metres were a blur.

A man on the other side of the gate.

His hand held up.

Liz reached for her side arm.

'Lizzie, stop! It isn't Kyle.'

Of course it was.

She'd seen him from the bedroom.

But Pete's voice was persistent and she forced her legs to stop.

Pete touched her shoulder. 'Locksmith. Stand down.'

It wasn't possible. Kyle was tracking her every move. Following her. *Taunting* her. She couldn't visit her sister or niece or great-nephew. Her friends couldn't come to her apartment.

He knows my every move.

She stumbled away.

Into the white misty rain.

Away from the gate where Pete was chatting to some dude who was apologising for upsetting the lady.

Liz found herself at the old stables, her legs dangling into the shaft as she sat on its edge staring into the darkness below.

What am I doing? What have I become?

She'd had her hand on her holster.

That poor man must have wondered what on earth was going on as some deranged woman ran toward him.

Her hands shook. Her whole body ached. The shame was overwhelming.

'Oh, Lizzie.'

Pete was there. He draped a blanket from the vehicle over her shoulders and settled beside her. For a while they just sat. His phone beeped and he sent a message. Then again.

'Ben and Reuben are taking a break while the locksmith works. He did the stables lock first up. Been looking all over for you.'

'Did I… did I upset him?'

'Nah. He thought he'd given you a scare because he was staring at you. He'd messaged Ben to be let in and didn't get an answer then saw you at a window. He's cool though.'

'I was almost touching my holster.'

'And would you have shot him?'

Her eyes finally turned to look at him. 'No.'

'Exactly.'

I wouldn't even have shot Dad. Not unless there was no alternative.

What was the point of any of this? The closer she got to the truth, the more her head was being messed with. Find Kyle she might, but what would the ultimate cost be?

'Hey, you're shivering. Good thing I grabbed this when I took the blanket.' Pete reached behind himself. 'Coffee. Should still be hot in the thermos. Do you think we can sit somewhere less dangerous? Rather not have to explain to the others why we're at the bottom of a hole.'

Once on his feet, Pete grabbed Liz's hand and pretty much hauled her up. Did he think she was planning on deliberately falling in? Her legs were a bit unsteady so she didn't fuss. They found a spot near the open door, perching on wooden crates.

'These are the same as the ones at the wall,' Pete said. 'Just enough height for me to scramble up but anyone shorter might struggle. Reckon the perp grabbed them as they bolted which means they knew the landscape well enough to pinpoint the one spot they could scramble over. That and having a key is a powerful lead.'

He poured a cup of steaming coffee into the first lid and handed it to Liz before using the smaller inner lid for himself.

The aroma seemed to kick her brain into gear and a couple of sips warmed her insides.

From here they could see the back of the mansion across grass and the bricked ground. A white van was parked behind their vehicle and the man from the gate worked on the door. Ben was talking to him.

'Oh, crap.' She hadn't meant to say it aloud.

'They don't know.'

'How though? I must have looked like I'd lost my mind flying into the hallway then out the door.'

'You did.' He grinned. 'But then Ben realised he'd missed the message from the locksmith and I said something about you must have seen the dude at the gate but I still had the keys. They just thought I was following you to unlock the gate. If a bit fast.'

She sipped to avoid talking.

'I've got your back, Lizzie. You know that.'

His voice was soft and his eyes intense.

Liz nodded.

'And we're going to take him down. Kyle. Just stay close to one of us, please.'

Again, a small nod.

'Good. Soon as the locksmith goes I want to show you what we found. We've got through to another room but haven't gone into it yet.'

His phone beeped and after checking it, Pete stood. 'Ben needs me. Finish your coffee and dry off.'

As soon as Pete was out of earshot, Liz found her phone and dialled Candace.

TWENTY-ONE

There was no way anyone would know from him that Liz had almost lost it. Pete meant it when he said he had her back. She was the best cop he'd ever known. The only one he completely trusted. And until her damned father had interfered in her life, she was the most stable and sensible one.

When I get my hands on him—

'Pete? New set of keys to swap for the others.' Ben held out three. 'I've got three copies of them.'

Taking the keys, Pete spent a minute getting each onto the ring with the rest. Ben could worry about the ones back at work.

They were in the kitchen with two more thermos on the table and an open plastic container with a selection of muffins, courtesy of Candace who seemed to be bringing in baked goods every morning. Reuben was letting the locksmith out through the gate and hopefully Liz would come in soon. The less anyone noticed her absence, the less to explain.

'Liz okay?' Ben asked.

Great.

'Liz? Sure. She had to make a couple of phone calls and had got drenched going to let the dude in. Took her some coffee.'

Ben gave him a searching look but rather than reply, helped himself to a muffin.

'At least the rain stopped.' Pete eyed off a muffin but his stomach was still churning from seeing Liz so upset. He decided to take a chance anyway and selected one with nuts poking out of the top. Stuffing food in his mouth made it harder to answer questions. He wandered to the windows which faced the back of the property.

Liz was crossing the grass, her head down but at the driveway she suddenly looked to her left and stopped. Reuben came into view. They talked. Her back straightened and something he said made her smile. Then he touched her arm and she nodded and leaned toward him. Just a fraction.

Pete turned away and collected another muffin.

It was good she felt safe around Reuben. Pete had noticed the easy friendship which began almost the minute they'd met. Liz needed more good people in her corner and Reuben was a good man.

But hurt her and I'll kill you, mate.

Liz had never been involved with a colleague, not romantically. It kept life simple. Avoided the inevitable messiness of a break-up in full view of other cops. He wandered to the other side of the large kitchen table and took a bite, eyes on the door as Liz and then Reuben came in. Nothing seemed unusual. Just two colleagues passing the time of day.

'What on earth am I looking at?' Liz peered into the darkness of a void behind what was once plaster and brick.

'Step back a second and I'll add some light,' Pete said.

She did, giving him room to manipulate one of the stands holding a floodlight into place. For a demolition of this size, the area was surprisingly clean. Outside was a pile of old bricks, plaster, and the rigid metal mesh. A wide broom leaned against a wall further down the hallway.

When the floodlight turned on, swirling fine dust was the first thing Liz saw.

And then the crates.

On one side were half a dozen, each wooden and similar to those in the stables.

On the other were two long metal cases.

The space itself was no bigger than a large walk in robe and a quick glance showed nothing else of interest.

'There looks like another bricked up wall behind here,' Ben said. 'Even though this is designated on the plans as the way to the cellar, someone had other ideas.'

All four of them stared at the boxes.

'Shall I start opening them?' Pete offered.

'Carefully. Run a detector over them first in case of radiation.'

'Right. I'll go get one and a small crow bar.'

'Liz, shall we take a look at the other way into the cellar?'

Although she was curious about the contents of the boxes, she nodded. There was limited room in the space they'd opened. After collecting a flashlight, Liz followed Ben down the hallway.

Her heart rate was normal again, at last. First Pete and then Candace had reassured her she was safe and protected, and although logic said if Kyle wanted to harm her he'd find a way, Liz was again able to look at the big picture. Bringing her father to justice would solve the problems of a lot of people and that was what she'd hold onto. Not the moments of panic and anxiety about the fine details.

'Ben?' She caught up to walk beside him. 'I got a bit upset earlier.'

'You okay now?'

'Better.'

'Do you want to talk about it? Or are you good.'

Typical Ben. He'd known she'd stuffed up but trusted her to deal with it or else come and ask for help. How different from the last person who'd been her boss – although briefly – when the little girl was kidnapped. Andy Montebello was a decent cop but very ambitious and she'd been close to being removed from the case multiple times for pushing that fine line too much.

'I'm good. And I'm going to start seeing Candace profession-ally for a bit. Get some advice on staying focused about my dad.'

They turned a corner and continued down a different hallway and Ben glanced at her.

'Not a bad idea. She's responsible for keeping me from driving home every night.'

'Oh… home to Ellie?'

'Miss her so hard.'

They reached the end of the hallway and stopped, Ben sighing deeply.

'Sometimes I'm between a rock and a hard place. Ellie is my world. Ellie and Michael. We were apart for so many years and now I've gone and put distance back into the equation. But I was bored silly with my job.'

'And somewhere along the way you'll find the balance you need. Ellie's really busy with her restaurant. And Michael is doing well. You're only a couple of hours away… less with a helicopter.' Liz smiled.

'Yup. Wouldn't be the first time I borrow one to get to her.'

Ellie had once been in terrible danger, stalked by a killer and alone in the bushland in Gippsland. A police helicopter with Ben and Andy inside was one of the reasons Ellie survived. That, and her own courage and initiative.

This wall included a door. It was quite grand really. Wider than normal in dark timber with an ornate pattern and an old-fashioned brass lock.

'Yet another key. Did the Baxters trust no-one?' Ben had a set of keys and began going through them.

'Turns out they were correct not to be trusting.'

'You're not wrong. Ah, this one looks right.' He inserted a key which turned easily. Too easily.

'O-kay. Not locked. Did Meg take prints?'

Liz opened her tablet, searching for the list from the day

they'd first come here. 'Um… yes. Oh listen! Digital prints recorded. Door was locked. Opened with our key then closed and locked again.'

They looked at each other.

'What if the intruder had this key as well?'

Ben opened his phone and dialled with it on speaker, his eyes on Liz as it was answered. 'What's up, boss?'

'Hey, Meg. Are you alone?'

'In ten seconds. Enjoying the rain?'

'More like fog now. Liz is here with me.'

'Hiya, Liz. I was just telling Jeff all about you.'

'Oh dear,' Liz said.

'Only the bad bits. Right, not only am I alone but also in a room I just checked for bugs, so please let me in why I'm here?'

'Two things. Do you remember the door to the cellar?'

'Wide. Dark. Had a different kind of key.'

'And you left it locked?'

'I did. I took prints, unlocked and opened the door – and even resisted a quick look inside which is remarkable given how delicious it smelled – then closed and relocked. Checked the handle as I do with every door to make sure.'

'Great. Second thing. Can you create a list of any phone calls or messages which have gone in or out of the building since we left this morning?'

Meg took a few seconds to reply. This was tricky territory.

'I can. But I'm limited to those belonging to Operation Nobody. Not personal phones.'

'That will do as a start. And I'll need footage from all cameras in and around the building for the same time, let's say from half an hour before we left to two hours ago. Make the phone call range the same.'

'How fast do you want this?'

'Just for once we're back. That's a few hours away.'

'Consider it done, Ben.'

The call terminated, Ben put the phone away and glanced at Liz. 'I'm worried.'

'Either the intruder was very lucky and heard us drive up, or someone warned them.'

He nodded. 'Might have had a lookout.'

'In which case was it my father?' The thought was sickening. If they'd missed catching Kyle by minutes… 'He has a network.'

'Or *had* a network.' Ben opened the door. 'We've taken Marcus Bonner and Tony Shaw from him plus a dozen people involved with them. If Shaw co-operates we will know more but let's not assume Kyle has hundreds of minions. Although we keep talking about an organisation, there'd be more evidence of its existence if it was wide spread. It might just be him now.'

Meg was right about the smell. As they went down a stone staircase the unmistakable aromas of oak and tannin and old wine intensified. The steps were narrow and steep so they took their time descending what felt like a long way, with only their hand held flashlights as guides.

At the bottom was a small space with two doorways, both without doors. The first was a small room with a long and narrow table against a wall, and shelves with glasses and utensils almost unrecognisable beneath decades of dust. Cobwebs were draped over almost everything and in here, the mustiness overwhelmed the nicer smells.

'Some kind of tasting room?' Ben asked. 'Brings important guests down to feel they're special, perhaps. There's some stools pushed right under the table.'

The second doorway opened to a cavernous space. The roof was double the normal height and a row of huge wine barrels made the room feel narrow and accentuated the feeling of space above.

'How on earth did they get these down here? The stairs seem far too small.' Liz stopped at a barrel which towered over her. 'Do you think it is full?'

'I can't imagine why they even have them. This isn't a

winery… unless, perhaps before the building was here? I'm trying to remember what is quite sketchy knowledge about the early wine industry in Australia.' Ben took a couple of photos. 'We might put this to the team over the next briefing. Most likely there's nothing which impacts our investigation.'

'Unless there's bodies in there.'

Ben shot her a surprised look and she chuckled.

'Now I want to open one.' Ben continued through the cellar. 'Later.'

Next were row upon row of wine racks which were about half filled. It was cold so far below the house, so probably ideal for the wine. Liz pulled out a bottle and blew the dust away. 'The label is hard to read. Something estate.' She returned it to its spot and sneezed. 'Sorry. I wonder how long since anyone was down here.' Liz turned her flashlight to the floor. 'Actually, pretty recently.'

With both of them illuminating the dirt beneath them, faint scuff marks appeared. Not proper footprints as the ground was so hard it resembled black concrete, but spots where the layers of dust were disturbed. And something else. Liz couldn't believe it and held her hand up then gestured where she focussed her light. Ben squatted and peered at the object then back at Liz. Without a word passing between them, she dug an evidence bag from a pocket and he took it. A moment later he held it up.

'It is an earring. Right?'

'Yes, Liz. And I've never understood how someone loses one when all they're doing is walking.'

'I'm sure Pete would happily pierce your ears so you can find out.'

Ben straightened. 'I'll pass. This is good. It looks untouched by dust.'

For some reason, Liz's mind went to Annette's description of the woman who'd been at Bonner Gallery. Elegant. As was this jewellery despite its odd design.

They spent a few minutes searching the ground and taking photos but no more lost pieces appeared.

'Let's see how far this cellar goes.'

There was no sign of radiation or any of several other nasty things the detector was designed to find, so Pete and Reuben had carefully moved each box until there was a long row along one side of the hallway. They then began the job of opening them.

Two lids were on the ground. Both boxes were empty.

'This one felt heavy,' Pete said. He was going to be furious if none of them provided anything of substance. 'Or do you think we should open a long one?'

'Let's finish these.' Reuben had the short crowbar and was adept at popping nails. He grinned at Pete. 'Want to bet on what's inside?'

'Hm. Yes. But what shall we wager?'

'Dinner? You, me, Liz, Meg? Winner chooses where. Loser buys.'

'Good grief. I have to win then because I'm not eating at some fancy vegan place.'

'Stop denying it, mate. You love the stuff I cook.'

Pete had to give him that. And he wasn't anti anything but loved to tease. Food was food. 'I reckon this one contains something valuable.'

'That's a bit too vague.'

Reuben began to pop nails.

'Wait, what's that?' Pete wandered back to the cavity they'd opened. 'Can you hear it?'

Reuben held the crowbar aloft as he joined Pete. There was a tapping. A long, squealing creak.

In the brick wall they'd not yet destroyed, a crack opened.

Wider.

And then Liz's face appeared.

'Hi, guys!'

TWENTY-TWO

Until Ben's phone call, Meg's mood had been buoyant. Positive. With Jeff here and already settling in, she was seeing much needed light at the end of the proverbial tunnel, and maybe this time the light was from something other than a train hurtling toward her. But if Ben had a new reason to suspect a member of the team was playing for the opposition then she'd do what he needed and hope the day didn't dissolve into a train wreck.

She left Jeff working with samples from the mansion and headed to the hub. So far he'd met Candace and had a very quick walk around the main rooms. Jeff was keen to get started and Meg knew there'd be plenty of opportunities for him to meet and greet, so spent a couple of hours with him in the lab. Happy hours. Having someone who understood her work was a gift.

Annette and Hamish were again working together and Meg watched them from the kitchen as the kettle boiled. She knew Liz wanted more information about the history of Bonner Gallery as well as a list of anyone – including their current whereabouts – who ever worked for the Baxter couple. It was a big job and presumably Hamish was assisting.

They'd both been here early. Meg arrived last, for once, after being in the lab late last night to prepare for Jeff's arrival. The only person missing at that point was Phoebe, which was normal, and Jeff, who was due in mid-morning.

None of you are spies. Surely not!

She was confident about the senior team. Ben, Candace, Liz, Pete. Not that anything in life was certain but these were people she'd trust with her life.

Yet some bad guys were good guys once.

Meg pushed away the glimmer of a thought reminding her everyone has secrets. She made her tea and kept watching, stirring long after the sugar was dissolved.

Phoebe was an interesting person. Smart. Eloquent and elegant. An introvert who kept her thoughts to herself most of the time and was a brilliant business woman. Her true crime podcast and its subsidiary offshoots such as a popular digital magazine and newsletters was perfect for Operation Nobody. But it also might be an inspired cover if Phoebe was aligned to someone like Kyle.

She shook her head. It didn't sit well.

Same with Reuben. He was exactly what you saw... which was a pretty nice view. If you liked tall, muscular, good looking dudes who cared about the planet and were handy in a gun fight. The man was rare and had an element of kindness about him which was at odds with his career choice. But he wasn't deceitful. Of that she was certain.

So, that leaves two.

Hamish said something which made Annette laugh. Not just laugh but throw her head back and make her shoulders shake. Since when was he funny?

The man was irritating. Well, he *was* improving and that had a lot to do with other people telling him to pull his head in. He was an exceptional operator. His history made it difficult to see him as unfaithful to his masters. He'd worked his way quickly up the ranks in British Intelligence and been instrumental in bringing down a particularly nasty leader of a para-military group, as well as taking out Marcus Bonner who was in a speed-boat. From a moving helicopter. In the dark.

His credentials were impeccable but his communication skills were awful and he had no track record in Australia other than a few months with a covert team in another state.

And then there was Annette.

Previously their paths had crossed on cases, including the one where the child was kidnapped from the park near Liz's old apartment. And Liz had worked with Annette a fair bit over the years and considered her to be a solid police officer with a good critical mind. The problem was that out of everyone, Annette had left herself open to speculation. Things like disappearing to smoke might be no more than mismanagement of a bad habit, or could be a chance to make phone calls outside the building. And there were different recollections of events between Annette and Hamish.

I think it was all settling-in nerves with them both.

With a sigh, Meg found a bottle of water and returned to her desk. She had to get the list and footage for Ben and while she was at it, would write a little program to alert her when either Annette or Hamish left the building today. Just in case.

The rain had completely gone, leaving mostly blue skies and fresher air, when the team had packed the last of the gear into the BearCat.

'I'd like to take a quick look at both the well and the shaft in the stables,' Ben said. 'Pete, can you come with me, and the both of you go back through the house to make sure we haven't missed anything? Or left anything unlocked?'

Liz would have preferred to go for a walk but Reuben was already on his way back inside while Pete was crossing the driveway, whistling some annoying tune. Ben rolled his eyes and followed Pete.

Reuben had gone down the hallway to the demolished wall.

Several empty crates were piled up and one metal box open and also empty.

'Much as I enjoyed playing with the sledgehammer when I could wrest it from Pete, I wish we'd known there was an easier way in.' Reuben rotated a shoulder and grimaced. 'Might miss gym tonight.'

About to suggest he needed a massage, Liz bit her lip. No matter how she'd say it, there was a chance it would sound wrong. As though she was offering to do it. Maybe it was just her equilibrium being out of kilter. Pete would laugh at her if she told him he needed a massage. Ben would probably nod and agree then make an appointment with someone. With Reuben it was too early to know how he'd respond.

'It is just a bit of a muscle ache, Liz. No need to look so worried.'

Reuben smiled and she managed one back.

'Even if we'd gone through the cellar first, we'd probably have ended up pulling down the wall because it was put there for a reason.' Liz stepped into the space they'd opened and touched the door. 'Someone has gone to a lot of trouble to build this into a false wall and hide boxes in what, from the hallway, appears to be a dead end.'

'I'll be interested to know what Meg finds… or Jeff, I imagine. He may be able to date some of the debris we removed.'

'And I'm interested in seeing what's on those video tapes!' Liz returned to the hallway and nudged one of the crates with a toe. 'Whatever was in these is long gone but we now have some new leads. Possibly new ways to connect Kyle with all of this.'

One crate had been filled with VHS video tapes, neatly lined up and all with a typed title on their side. Another held a random assortment of items which presumably were from the house. Candlesticks and crystal vases and ornaments, all carefully wrapped and packed. And a third crate contained an original gold cutlery set and a selection of what looked like collector's pieces of porcelain. One of the metal boxes was packed with a range of firearms and other weapons.

'Actually, I thought the guns would be your first pick. They were to Pete and Ben.'

Reuben shook his head. 'Hate the things, if I'm honest. If they lead us to those responsible for the deaths of the Baxters then I'll be happy. But they're old. Possibly collector-value old.'

Such a curious man, aren't you? Crack shot but hate guns. Capable of killing yet want to save the world.

At the foot of the staircase they each chose a direction, Liz going up. She worked methodically from the furthest room – the main bedroom – checking windows were locked and nothing had been left behind by anyone on the team.

It was only as she approached the landing that the music started.

Soft and pretty. Music to dance to… a waltz perhaps. Liz stopped, her hands on the ornate timber railing, smiling at the scene below. The furniture all pushed against the walls made a dance floor where couples moved in elegant and precise time to the music. One day she might dance like that. Wear a beautiful gown like some of the women. There was one couple who danced especially well, their bodies in harmony and the other dancers retreated to allow them the space.

The music stopped. The dancing stopped. The man looked up at Liz.

'No!'

She stumbled backwards, hitting something solid.

'Lizzie, hey, it's just me.' Reuben's arms went around her, holding her firmly. 'Breathe. You are safe.'

Tears streamed down her face.

'My father… he was there. Just then.'

'He isn't here.'

'But he looked at me. Oh my god. Reuben, I've been here before. I was here as a child.'

• • •

This changed everything. As frustrated with herself as she was for crying – let alone sobbing in a colleague's arms like a baby – a weight had lifted. Pieces were falling into place.

Reuben had held her against his chest after turning her in his arms. He'd said nothing other than making some soothing sounds and when she'd pulled herself together and stepped back, had only concern in his eyes. No scorn or disdain. Liz had dried her eyes and softly apologised. He'd nodded. And that was that.

On the way back to the hub, Liz calmly explained what she'd seen to the others. A flashback to her childhood. Her father being a guest. She left out the part when he'd looked directly up at her because that was her imagination working overtime.

'Do you remember anything else? Other guests? The Baxters?' Ben asked.

'Nothing. And you should know I experienced something similar last time I was in the house. Pretty much the same spot as well, so it must be an important memory.'

Pete hadn't taken his eyes off her the entire time she'd spoken. No doubt he was thinking of questions to ask when they were alone because he could read her face. Reuben had taken the wheel and said nothing at all. Poor man was probably embarrassed.

'I'd like you and Candace to debrief please. The rest of us will unpack and bring up what we need but I want you to talk to her immediately. Okay?'

Ben was right. The team would need a meeting to discuss this new information, as well as all the findings from Heberden House. He wanted her to be in a position to speak about this without falling apart. Not that he knew she had. She snuck a look at Reuben and his lips curled up for a second as their eyes met. For the rest of the drive back, her mind searched for other glimpses of her childhood but as usual, only came up with the same few moments. Playing in a pool with Anna. Parents yelling at each other. Doors slamming. Crying. Except now there was a new one. But why on earth would she have ever been at the mansion?

Candace was waiting at the door when Liz let herself into the hub. She held two coffees and led the way to one of the overnight rooms.

'Chair or bed?'

Liz almost burst into laughter. 'Don't therapists usually offer a sofa?'

'You watch too much television.'

'Never, really. But I read a lot. I'll sit on the bed. And thanks for the coffee.' Liz dropped her bags on the bed and perched beside them. 'So, the boss messaged you?'

'The boss did.' Candace took the chair, crossing her legs with an intent expression. 'What happened?'

'I'd finished checking the floor and as I approached the landing heard music. For a second I thought someone was playing music on a phone or something but then when I looked down to the room below, there was a party in progress. People dancing.'

Candace asked a few questions about the kind of music, the clothing, the look of the room and Liz answered the best she could but the details weren't clear.

'Was this what you experienced today? Or the previous time?'

Ben really did tell you a lot.

'Today. The first time was more like being a little kid who'd snuck from their bedroom to watch the grown-ups. Sit on the floor looking down unnoticed. Um… people in small groups talking and waiters. White shirts and… oh, black waistcoats for the men and aprons for the women! Ben found a black apron in a locker today. What else? A string quartet. And I had a really specific thought.'

'What was it?'

'That I'd be so quiet nobody would notice me.'

'Which is the kind of thing a child would think or say,' Candace said. 'I remember sitting halfway down a staircase thinking nobody knew I was there, with my teddy and blankie.'

'Did you get caught?'

'Often.'

Candace gazed at Liz over the top of her coffee cup.

Instead of doing what she wanted, which was to kick off her shoes and curl up on the bed, Liz gazed back.

'And you are certain your father was one of the guests? Did you see him in both memories?'

'Just the one today.'

'What was he doing?'

He wore a black suit and his hair touched his shoulders. In his arms was an elegant woman who also wore black. A floor-length gown. Her silvery hair spilled over her shoulders, which were bare. They danced, swirling around the dance floor like they were the centre of the world.

'Dancing. With a woman. I don't know her.' Liz felt numb. 'I don't think I know anything anymore.'

'You're doing great, Liz.' Candace spoke softly. 'Memories are exhausting. Unexpected ones even more so. I'm here for you and so is the team.'

And right now, only Reuben knows the whole story and that's not fair for him to carry.

'At the risk of sounding like I've lost my mind... he looked at me. In the flashback or memory or whatever you want to call it... Kyle looked directly at me and it was like he was there. My father now. Not then.'

TWENTY-THREE

Liz felt so much better. In her entire life she'd never experienced such care and support as Operation Nobody willingly provided. She'd worked hard for everything in life, never taking for granted the success she enjoyed in the police force. It was always challenging. There were hurdles she'd never expected including the ever-present 'old boys' club' which sadly still existed. But here, at last, she'd found her home. Or at least, her work home.

Growing up she'd learned to keep her feelings to herself. Never let others see who she was apart from how she wanted to be seen. That carried over to higher education and the police force. Possibly Vince Carter was the only cop she'd ever really trusted until she met Pete. And it had taken years for her to see past Pete's own defences, to who he really is.

And now she had others. Not yet so close but getting there.

The events of the day were exhausting but after talking first to Candace, then Ben with Candace, her conviction had returned. They *would* catch Kyle. She'd been assured that none of this was a mark against her. Not the flashbacks or second-guessing or fears. It was all normal given the circumstances and Candace would work closely with Liz to support her. A shower and change of clothes had helped reset her focus. Now, the whole team was seated at the round table and there was a ton of much-needed food.

Jeff Scott was not what Liz had expected. The way Meg had spoken about the forensic scientist made him sound like a man in his late thirties. Quiet, driven, single. She'd gone as far as to imagine him living in one of the trendy suburbs taking coffee each morning and observing other humans as trams clanged their way past his window seat.

You shouldn't be pre-judging people.

Meg and Jeff had come in last and sat together. He was in his early fifties, wiry, around 160 centimetres, and was completely bald. He also wore a wedding ring and had a scar across one cheek.

So much for my detective skills.

'Everyone? I'm so happy to introduce you to Jeff Scott, who has been stolen away from his regular job to spend a few months with us.' Meg wore a huge smile.

There was a collective murmur of welcome and Jeff looked from one to the next, nodding to each person.

Ben gestured to the food. 'Please, everyone, eat. There's plenty of choice to thank everyone for such a huge effort today. And let's go around the table to introduce ourselves. Jeff and I have met previously, and I believe you said hello to Candace this morning?'

'I did.'

'In that case, let's go around and say who we all are. Annette?'

'Oh, me? Well, nice to meet you, Jeff. I'm Annette Benksi. My background ranges from being a street cop to managing records and also doing a stint overseeing interviews and interrogations in the city. I eat anything. Drink anything. And smoke... but am trying to kick the habit.'

'Me too.' Jeff grinned. 'We can kick it together.'

'I hope we can! I'm sure everyone is tired of me ducking out for a smoke.' Annette rolled her eyes. 'Sorry, team.'

Hamish was next. 'Welcome. My name is Hamish Mathers-Smythe and I have operatives training. I hope you enjoy your time here.'

Was that it? Are you learning, dude?

'Nice to meet you, Jeff. Reuben Barnes. Ex an-organisation-I can't-discuss but incredibly happy to belong to Operation Nobody. The people here are good. Really good.'

'I'm quickly getting that feeling,' Jeff said.

Phoebe was looking at her hands. 'I'm Phoebe Renshaw. A podcaster.'

'A podcaster? My dear lady, you are one of my heroes!'

The enthusiasm in his voice made Phoebe look up in surprise.

'My husband and I are subscribers and we listen all the time and try to do our own investigation… just on paper of course. A whiteboard, really. One with wheels and two sides which we keep in the living room. Joel is a master at understanding human nature and with my forensics knowledge we have quite a success record.'

Phoebe turned bright red but was smiling at Jeff. 'Thank you. Both you and your husband.'

'No, thank *you*! And your team. Very clever podcasting, if I might say. Sometimes we listen to the French version.'

'Excusez mon mauvais français. Bienvenue dans notre chambre.'

Everyone looked at Pete.

Liz had never heard him speak French and agreed with his first sentence that he should 'apologise for his poor French'. 'Not chambre but équipe. You meant team?'

'Yeah, welcome to the team. Gave it a go though,' Pete said. 'Anyhow, I'm just a normal cop. Undercover, mostly.'

'Yes, I've heard all about you.'

Jeff kept his face straight but Meg burst into laughter.

'Nice. I'll remember this, Meg. Next time you need rescuing.'

'The only rescuing I need is from your ego.'

While the two of them continued their banter, Liz reached over the table to shake Jeff's hand. 'Ignore them. I'm Liz and you are very welcome here at the hub.'

'Meg has much respect for you, Liz. When you have a little time, may we talk? I have some questions about your father which might assist me.'

'Of course. Whenever it suits you.'

She liked Jeff. His experience was going to be invaluable and take a load away from Meg. Liz finally piled some food onto her plate.

Ben closed his eyes as Ellie whispered that she loved and missed him. Their phone call was about to end because she had a restaurant to open and he had… so much work. How he longed to be home, even just for a night.

'I love you too, sweetheart.' He opened his eyes. 'Give my love to Michael.'

And that was it. His few minutes of normality was over for now. If he was lucky, Ellie would message when she was home near midnight and he'd be awake and they could talk without the pressures here. He plugged the phone in to charge and returned to the monitor where he had a spreadsheet open with status information.

There were too many columns. So many moving parts. And too many dead ends.

'Busy?' Candace was at the open door. She looked tired. And she'd been a rock today.

'Yes. But only with updating one of the spreadsheets.'

'Is there anything I can do to help?'

Ben gestured for her to sit. 'You have. So much.'

Her smile was small. 'Hard day for Liz.'

The spreadsheet could wait and Ben got to his feet and joined Candace on the other side of the table.

'I can't imagine what this has been like for her,' he said. 'A few months ago she believed her father simply abandoned his family and disappeared. A dead-beat dad but one the family were better off without. Then she's told he died years ago.'

'Even goes to his grave site.'

'Yes. And while she's coming to terms with that, up he pops. Alive and with an agenda which still isn't clear, but includes Liz.'

'His perfect child.' Candace sighed. 'She might have escaped the physical abuse he subjected her mum and sister to, but the emotional toll is fast catching up. And now with these memories emerging, she's got a lot of work to do.'

They both looked into the main room, where Liz, Meg, and Jeff were in conversation around the table, a few images on the vertical screen.

'I couldn't be so strong.'

That surprised Ben. He'd known Candace for at least a decade and considered her to be not only strong, but insightful and compassionate. She was still watching Liz with an expression he didn't quite understand. Sadness, maybe?

'She might have reconnected with her sister and – thanks in part to Pete – found her niece after so long, but Liz hasn't been allowed time to process the manipulation of her father or grieve what might have been for all those lost years. All she knows is her father wants something from her. He is unlikely to harm her but very likely to hurt anyone who gets in his way.'

'Candace, I'm struggling with having to expose Liz to Kyle. He made it clear by showing up where she runs and his stunt at Bonner Gallery that he wants her attention. She's been placed in extreme danger once. He hurt her.'

'Yes, but it was designed to disable her so she couldn't chase him. A baton blow to her stomach was awful but better than a bullet.' Candace's attention was back on Ben. 'We know he's not above physically attacking Liz but I truly doubt he'd kill her. Not purposely.' She tapped her fingers on her leg. 'She has to meet him.'

None of this sat well with Ben. He'd asked Liz to join Operation Nobody because she had a way of looking at cases which he could only wish for. Not to put her life and mental health at risk.

Candace must have picked up his concerns. 'We can manage this. He wants to have dinner at some expensive restaurant. He's also said, via his phone call to Meg that he'll tell Liz what he wants when she meets up with him. So why don't we manage the rhetoric? Liz might suggest somewhere. Might insist. If nothing else, it puts Kyle on the back foot.'

'Because he wants this desperately.'

'Yes.'

Ben's eyes moved back to the table. Pete had joined the others and his focus was on Liz. Everyone cared about her, none more than Pete. Making this happen might be harder than he thought.

'Not a chance. Over my very dead corpse.' Pete's arms were crossed as he stood with his legs apart in a pose which would warn most people to back off. 'Liz goes nowhere near that monster.'

'I'll do it,' Liz said.

She'd known this was coming ever since Kyle phoned Meg.

'Lizzie...'

'Pete, it has to happen sooner or later, and on our terms is better than Kyle's. Besides, no doubt you'll be within a short distance.'

He wasn't happy but he dropped the stance and perched on the edge of Ben's desk – until Ben looked at him. Then he found a chair and flopped onto it, re-crossing his arms.

There were just the three of them in Ben's office.

Everyone else was well occupied and with Jeff spending some time with Reuben and Hamish, Meg was busy at her own desk. She looked more like her business-like self than in the last couple of days when there'd been too much to do with competing priorities.

'The key is going to be keeping my father believing he's calling the shots,' Liz said. 'I'll go for a run tomorrow morning and see what happens.'

'And what if he grabs you?'

'How would he do that in public?'

'Just how many people do you see so early?' Pete asked. His voice was flat. 'And who are they? Other runners, probably all with headphones. People on bicycles who will have whizzed past before registering what they saw. Dog walkers. Perhaps someone coming home from a night shift and half-asleep.'

'All true. But people nonetheless, most who have phones on them. It will be in daylight.'

'For all we know he owns or has access to one of the boats at that marina.'

Ben straightened. 'Did we not check that?'

Liz shrugged. 'Who though? Quite honestly we've all been so busy I can't see how we could check that as well as the apartments in that area.'

'I'm sorry. That's something I could have had done,' Ben said. 'Let me check back to who was following up the enquiries and we'll have an answer tonight. If there's a chance Kyle can get onto a boat then forget the run. We all know what he's like on the water.'

'Speeds away, blows them up, or simply impersonates an old fisherman.' Liz knew.

'Um, you forgot about him pushing innocent lookalikes over the side of ocean liners,' Pete said.

'I try to wipe some stuff from my brain.'

If only I could. Instead, it is coming back to me.

'Actually, this gives me an idea,' Pete said. 'You didn't recognise Kyle on the fishing boat so if a couple of us are disguised then we can be close to you.'

For a moment Lis had a vision of Pete with a fake nose and

moustache. She'd have laughed except his expression was dead serious.

'Reuben is skilled in that arena and I've done okay in the past. But Kyle might still recognise me, so Reuben and what about you, Ben? You're fast. If it came down to a chase on foot, you'd have the best shot at catching the bastard. Sorry, Liz.'

'He actually is a bastard. He was raised by an unmarried mother. No dad ever in his life. At least that's what Anna was told.'

Ben frowned. 'Does Candace know this?'

'Good question. I'll talk to her.'

Was this a missing piece of the puzzle the team's profiler needed?

'Once Jeff is finished looking at weapons, can I spend some time with him?' She asked. 'He wants to talk to me about my father and if we're going to go after Kyle, then I need all the help I can get.'

TWENTY-FOUR

With Jeff settling in so quickly, Meg left it to the rest of the team to look after him for now. Each had their share of time with him to ensure he had a cross-section of information and got to know everyone. The forensic science side of things was finally going in the right direction and she was catching up on the digital world.

She had the files ready to send to Ben. There'd been a couple of dozen calls in and out of the hub across the different phones but nothing out of the ordinary. Annette, for example, called a list of numbers which Meg cross-referenced to belonging to files in the old police records – witnesses mostly plus a couple of police stations. It matched what Annette had been doing for part of the day which was locating anyone who'd worked for or been associated with the Baxters. The only phone to have received a call which Meg couldn't identify was Candace's. It wasn't a red flag. Candace had contacts all over the world so if Ben wanted to chase it up, he was the best person to do so.

The footage was uneventful. There'd been the usual movement of people to and from the kitchen, the bathrooms, and each other's desks to talk. Annette had gone up to the roof three times to smoke, staying in sight of the cameras in the stairwell and on the roof and only taking as long as one cigarette.

Too many times, though. Your poor lungs.

Only one other person left the main building during the times Ben had asked for and that was Candace, who'd also gone to the roof. It was a few minutes after receiving the call in the hub and about half an hour after the team had left to go to Heberden House. She was alone and spent less than a minute near the edge of the roof, her back to the camera. It was a bit odd. The timing was troubling. But *Candace?*

Meg glanced around to see where Ben was. Liz and Pete were with him in his office so she sent the files for when he was free. Pete had a defensive look about him which she recognised. They must be talking about Kyle and potentially how to engineer the meeting he wanted with Liz. If Pete had his way, he'd spend every waking hour tearing the city apart to find Kyle and drag him back to one of the cells within the building.

And I totally understand. The man is a monster.

Candace emerged from her office and hurried over, just as an email popped up. 'Just sent you… ah. Finally received a response from the firm handling the Baxter estate regarding the contents and whatnot.'

'Excellent. I'll take a look and then add the info for whoever needs it. Does Ben have it as well?'

'Yes. Are you able to run a trace on my phone?' Candace pushed it in Meg's direction. 'I got a call earlier and although I rarely reply to anonymous callers I suddenly wondered if it was Kyle Moorland. Like the call you got.'

'Was it?'

'No. The line was… well, strange. There was an echo even when she didn't speak.'

'She?'

'Definitely a feminine voice. She asked if I was ready,' Candace said. 'I thought she had the wrong number and asked who she wished to speak to. It isn't as though anyone has this number who isn't known to me.'

Meg took the phone. 'What did she say then?'

A look of worry crossed Candace's face. 'The thing is, she just laughed and terminated the call.'

'Well, that's weird. I'll take a look but it might well be a person randomly dialling numbers or even she was embarrassed. People laugh sometimes if they make a mistake.'

'I tried calling her back using the call-back code. From the roof because the line had been so bad before. It went nowhere that I could tell. But you have other ways to trace callers?'

'I do. And if all else fails I'll get Ben to authorise a request to our service provider. And stop looking so concerned, Candace. If it was Kyle then yes, but to my knowledge only one woman has been mentioned as a potential associate and it wasn't of him, but Marcus Bonner some thirty years back.'

Ben tapped on his window and waved at Candace.

'Thanks, Meg. I'll collect the phone later.'

Once Meg had the phone plugged in she went in search of Jeff. He'd just finished with Hamish and gave her a big smile as she grabbed his arm.

'I need to steal you. We have to talk about an earring.'

It was close to six when Ben called a team meeting. He wanted people to head home afterwards, and for once have dinner with their loved ones, or at least away from this place.

'Jeff sends his apologies,' Meg announced. 'He is fast tracking some evidence and I'll fill him in later.'

'In Jeff's absence I want to thank each of you for extending such a warm welcome. He is an asset and I appreciate your help getting him accustomed to our processes.'

Hamish nodded. 'He has a sharp mind and knows more about weapons than I expected. Although I suppose they are a big part of his work.'

'Not a big part, but he spent a couple of years working in a testing facility attached to the Army. One of his greatest strengths is his wide knowledge, thanks to working in the private sector for a long time.' Meg looked ready to keep extolling his virtues but abruptly returned to her desk to check a screen.

Ben continued. 'Everyone is being great at sending through updated information. I wanted to run through a few things and then it's time to knock off for the day, unless you have a specific task to finish. As you know, today's visit to Heberden House was productive in a number of areas. Pete?'

Meg came back, distracted.

'Apart from forcing me to spend half the day in the rain… okay, don't look at me like that, Reuben. The short version is that an unknown person was at the property not long before us. They'd let themselves in then broken through a second door. We took an evidence cast presumed to belong to this person. After demolishing a wall, we located and have retrieved several boxes with a range of items including weapons, collectables, and VHS tapes.'

'Video tapes?' Phoebe asked.

'You look too young to know about—'

'Hamish… remember our chat?' Reuben quietly cut in.

Phoebe covered her mouth but it was clear she wanted to laugh.

Hamish shut up and Pete answered her question.

'Yes, there's a whole crate of them, dated, titled, the works. A quick look at them gives the impression they were recorded at different functions. Things like birthday parties.'

'May I… I mean, I'd like to volunteer to help go through them. If I can.'

'That would be brilliant, Phoebe.' Ben had had no idea how to begin what looked like a mammoth task.

'I can.' Annette was staring at Phoebe. 'We don't get much chance to work together.'

'Boss? I actually have an idea about this. I'd need to make a phone call though.'

There was something about the way Liz spoke... almost a plea to not pass this onto anyone else.

'Sure. Let me know. Annette? What's the status with connections to the Baxters?'

Annette's eyes moved to Liz then back to him. 'Um... okay, I've made a lot of phone calls today as well as emails. Most of it isn't positive either through people disappearing – not in a missing person way but moving overseas or into aged care – or actually dying because it was a long time ago. However, I've managed to track down half a dozen people who were employed by the Baxters.'

There was a small murmur around the table. This was real progress.

'Three staff from Heberden House are living in Victoria. And the housekeeper from the Melbourne house and one of Ilona's senior staff from her business are both in Melbourne.' Annette smiled broadly. 'I think this is paying off, chasing up these kind of leads.'

'Excellent work. Tomorrow would you and Pete begin interviews? Phoebe, I listened to the podcast last night and cannot begin to tell you how much I loved it.'

'Thank you. Shall I do an update?'

Ben nodded.

'I've prepared a brief which I sent Meg just before the meeting and that includes a breakdown of the listeners – demographics such as age, country etc. The usual pattern after a podcast is a flurry of calls to our hotline and emails. This typically goes on for around two hours then peters off. But as of five pm, we are still receiving around one hundred communications every hour. My overtime bill is skyrocketing.'

Phoebe laughed and everyone looked surprised. She was a different person when talking about her work and her own small team.

'Submit an invoice to me, Phoebe,' Ben said.

'No need. People are sharing the free part of the session and we've gained hundreds more subscribers today.'

'And this is unusual activity?' Candace asked. 'What kind of responses are you getting?'

'We're filtering as fast as we can. Generally we get a lot of useless responses, based upon the listener having some old memory of a case, but almost always what they saw on television or read in a newspaper. Meg provided a clever program which looks for particular words or repetitive terms and that's helping but we also make sure a human sees every email and listens to every voicemail and it's a big job.'

Yet you are clearly loving every minute of it.

'Do you need one of us to help?'

She shook her head. 'My team thrives on this so no, thanks. In my brief I've included the transcripts of about twenty interesting calls and there's one I want to highlight… may I read it?'

Meg touched the screen on the table and a series of paragraphs appeared. 'At your service.'

Phoebe pinched one of the paragraphs to enlarge it and read aloud. 'I attended Heberden House as a cleaner after the dreadful killings. Utter chaos. Never understood why the other police never spoke to me about what I saw.'

'Wait… what other police?' Liz asked. 'Other as in a different team or an individual? The inspector?'

'Do you have the contact details for the caller?' This felt like the sort of lead he'd been waiting for.

'Yes, Ben. Gentleman's name is Bob Sampson and he's a resident at a care home in Queensland. I've included everything we know.' As if she'd expended her peopling tolerance, Phoebe's shoulders dropped and she looked down at her hands.

'Today has produced a lot to go on with. Anyone else have any comments or questions?' Ben gazed around. 'In that case, please head home. Liz, Pete, a quick word. Meg, see me before you leave? And thanks, team.'

. . .

'I think we should ask Vince and Lyndall to help,' Liz said. She'd closed the door to Ben's office and spoken immediately. 'With the video tapes. Lyndall might recognise people.'

'Have you seen how many there are, Liz?' Pete checked his watch. 'I can get on a flight to Brisbane tonight if I leave soon.'

Ben sank on to his chair and waved at them to sit. 'Pete, no. There's such a thing as a video call, so we can arrange that tomorrow with Mr Sampson. I need you managing the local interviews with Annette and you can't be in two places at once.'

'I can try.'

Liz would usually remind him how trying he was but her sense of humour was long gone today. The earlier meeting about trying to lure Kyle out ended without resolution. While Liz was ready to do whatever it took to catch him, Ben had decided – for now – to focus on the new evidence unearthed today. There'd been no contact from Kyle since his call to Meg and despite Liz's willingness to draw him out, Candace had suggested that leaving him to make the next move was best for now.

'Going back to the VHS tapes… if Phoebe is happy to help then she and I could narrow down the dates to those closest to the murders and possibly work backwards. And we know the date roughly Lyndall attended that dinner party. If she'd be willing to take a look, assuming there's footage from it, then she might be able to help identify other guests.'

Ben ran a hand through his hair. His eyes were hooded with tiredness and Liz wanted to tell him to go home and rest.

'Yeah, okay. Have a chat to Phoebe. But work it around your other priorities.'

'And Lyndall?'

'Yes. But only once you have enough footage to show her in one go. She's been through enough.'

The door was flung open. 'Sorry! But you all need to come with me.' Meg gestured madly for them to follow. 'Jeff and I have something.'

TWENTY-FIVE

Situated on a different floor than the hub, a large room had been purpose-built to Meg's specifications. It was sound-proof and had reinforced walls. There were stainless steel tables, a range of fridges, a freezer, equipment Liz couldn't begin to describe, and a glassed room kept for contagions and the like. It was state of the art and only there thanks to the generous funding provided by the estate of Inspecter Ronald Baxter.

Liz had been in here a few times to help or observe Meg. Jeff's presence added a whole new element. He was intense in a birdlike way, moving quickly from one thing to another and bringing a new energy.

'Why are we here? And so urgently?' Ben asked.

'I'm sure you didn't notice but at the team meeting I was a bit distracted.'

'We noticed.' Ben, Pete and Liz all spoke as one.

'Well if you are all so good at this, why don't you tell me why a woman willingly removes one earring?' Meg held up the earring found in the cellar. 'One.'

Ben and Pete shrugged.

'Making or answering a phone call.' Liz rarely wore the

things but had seen plenty of women do exactly that. 'Even Candace does when she's wearing hoops or those long ones.'

'Liz wins today's trivia quiz.'

'Don't mind Meg. She likes a bit of drama.' Jeff smirked at Meg. 'Although, don't we all, if we're being honest?'

I like you so much.

'So I wasn't there but I heard it was located in dirt near a wine barrel. I'd assumed it was old and probably from some tipsy ancient socialite enjoying a few too many glasses of something.'

Liz pretended to smack the back of Pete's head. 'You've spent too much time with Hamish.'

'Yeah, sorry.'

Jeff took the earring from Meg and draped it over his open palm. 'Take a look. Pick it up if you wish because we've got everything we need already. This is an extraordinary piece of jewellery. I've identified the designer and Meg has sent a query to them so we may get a reply overnight. See how there are three distinct elements being platinum, rubies, and silver. And if you look closely, what is the design?'

Everyone peered at the earring. It was one long and slightly tapering shaft with rubies set in silver in a row across the top. Almost at the top.

'Is that a sword?'

'It is, Pete. This is quite heavy and the handle of gemstones might get in the way of a phone so potentially its owner removed it and then dropped it. And I image the person was interrupted so didn't stay to search. This is valuable. Probably designed specifically for the wearer. And not new by any means. Although it is in impeccable condition there are still minute signs of ageing.'

'How old, Jeff? And where is the designer based?' Ben asked.

'Without running further tests I'd say between twenty and forty years old. And the designer is in Germany and although small, has a reputation for quality work.'

'Marcus Bonner was German,' Liz said.

'Can't see him wearing earrings.' Pete had a silly expression but it suddenly sobered. 'Or did he give them to someone? He wasn't married. We've not found a single female connection other than Lyndall.'

'May I?' Liz gently took the earring. 'Thanks to my father I've done considerable research into the dozen or so cults he followed over time… at least those which we've uncovered or Anna recalled. Swords came up a bit in some obscure esoteric societies which were often inspired by Freemasonry. The worst of them deviated considerably and followed white racial superiority beliefs. Nasty people. And he has that tattoo with a sword and snakes and stuff. Do we have access to anyone who might have a better understanding?'

'We'll find someone.' Ben made a note on his phone. 'Have you taken detailed photos?'

Jeff looked mildly affronted. 'Certainly. They are about to be printed as well as sent to the team.'

'Hold off on that, please. Send to those of us in here as well as Candace. I want everyone else to have a night off. Let's see what comes of the query.' He glanced at Jeff. 'We really threw you in the deep end.'

'My favourite place to be. Shall we get those images printed?' Jeff took the earring back. 'So the report comes just to you, Ben?'

'I'll do all of that with you,' Meg said. 'Run you through the process and…' she took the earring back, 'we'll lock this little one up for the night. And then you go home.'

'I have a hundred jobs to do.'

Liz couldn't help smiling. He was so like Meg, never wanting to walk away from his work. 'But not tonight. Most of the team have left and we'll start over early tomorrow. I'm so happy you're here, Jeff.'

His face broke out in a wide grin and he hurried around the counter and gave Liz a hug before she could react.

. . .

The hub was in shadows. Both offices were dark, as was the kitchen and most of the work spaces. Meg was at her desk with a lamp on over her keyboard. Liz and Phoebe were both in the other room, starting the long process of watching the pile of VHS tapes.

It was nice. She liked the cover of darkness. The particular quiet which accompanied the absence of people and daylight.

Perhaps I'm a vampire of sorts. Evolved beyond needing blood to survive.

Except, she did need coffee.

That was a constant and something she'd one day need to address. Caffeine addiction was real. Probably better than nicotine… at least one could get away with running to make a coffee multiple times a day rather than having to scoot outside for a puff, like Annette. People would even bring you a coffee if you sighed heavily enough.

Leaving her desk, Meg spent a few minutes in the kitchen. Ben was a generous boss, always thinking ahead and providing take-out as needed and otherwise financing a well-stocked kitchen. Meg didn't cook unless she had to. Her freezer at home was stocked with pre-made meals. But here she was spoilt. Not only did Candace enjoy baking enough to bring yummy food, but Reuben was a star cook. Even Pete was able to throw stuff together.

Makes up for the crazy hours and constant risk of being murdered.

She left her cup on her desk then carried two others to find the others. They were chatting as they sorted tapes and looked up with smiles.

'Oh, perfect, thanks,' Liz said. 'We're about to start.'

'But you won't go through each one?'

Phoebe shook her head. 'Not to begin with. I've done stuff like this before and found that by beginning as close to an important date or event as possible and then the next closest and so on, that it provides the most information.'

'How often have you done something like this?'

'Four or five? Half were audio.'

Liz gestured to three piles. 'The last one is about a week prior to the murder so we'll start there and work backwards. There are four from Heberden House that year and one from the Melbourne residence. We located two from 1991 in Melbourne plus some even earlier.'

'Oh... 1991 was the year Lyndall attended a dinner party with them?'

'It will give us insight into Marcus Bonner and his relationship with the Baxters. The other piles are a range of dates and places in between. Assuming the titles are accurate. And those will be for another time because we have no idea how long each one is.'

There were two screens set up on the table linked to VHS units. Both women had headsets available, controllers, and their tablets to record anything of note.

'Have fun, ladies. And take a break if it gets too... well, anything.' That was directed at Liz and meant if any of it was disturbing but saying it in front of another team member felt wrong. Liz knew what she meant from the rueful smile as she picked up a tape.

Back at her desk, Meg sipped her coffee, planning her next job.

With Jeff providing welcome relief from half of her workload she could hone in on outstanding tasks. One was the information about the contents from Heberden House. Another was to finish building a proper report of the events of the day of and after the murders. And although Liz was looking after the report Annette and Hamish provided on the old police reports, her focus was elsewhere. That was something Meg could help with.

You're doing it again. Stop piling the work up.

She opened the email from the estate of Ronald Baxter. This was a firm who managed the vast inheritance left by the Inspector. Part of it was meant to look after Heberden House, which they didn't do very well, in Meg's opinion. While it might cost a lot to maintain the grounds it would also keep the value high when they eventually sold it.

'So how often does anyone even visit?' she murmured.

Did they know there were potentially tunnels leading to the house and that persons unknown were breaking in and actually had keys?

The email was brief and signed by the personal assistant of one of the principals. It was little more than mentioning the attached documents which should answer Ben's query.

Meg opened the first attachment.

This was several pages long and written in legalese. No doubt they wanted to cover themselves should anyone question how they administered the estate. She left that for Ben to worry about and moved to the next document which was a spreadsheet.

It was set up with a description of every room in the mansion – at least from a quick glance – each column filled with an itemised list of contents. This made interesting reading. A lot of time had gone into recording everything once belonging to the Baxters in that home. Which raised the question about their other property... the one in Melbourne. Had this also been subject to an itemised list of contents? There was a file from records about a search of that house.

The lists were interesting. The room where Meg found blood splatter once contained a grand piano. The kitchen lacked detail and whoever had created the list must have been rushed because having been in there, she knew there were still many items in cupboards and drawers. There was mention of a washing machine being left behind.

Forget to look inside first?

She remembered the smell of decay all too readily.

What interested her the most was the main bedroom. This column included a long list of stored items. Clothes and shoes which were individually described. Jewellery. Personal products. Furniture. But no bed.

Meg sat back in her chair. How could they miss something as dominant as the bed in the main bedroom? She reread the list. Not even mention of pillows, bedding, or the mattress.

She opened a new tab and located the report regarding the original police reports. Sending a silent thanks to Annette for being so orderly and precise, Meg quickly found what she was after. Reports were written by several police who'd attended the scene and the important information was extracted and cross-referenced.

Ilona Baxter was found deceased from the gun-shot wound on the bed, under the covers. She'd appeared to have been asleep.

Joseph Baxter was face-down on the carpet at the end of the bed. He had his dressing gown partly on. It was suggested he'd got up upon hearing intruders, was putting the dressing gown on as he walked to the doors, and was shot when someone stepped in.

Great, now we have to pull up the carpet to be certain. Except that's not what happened.

The hall runner – an expensive imported piece which was mentioned in the original brief for the team – wasn't in the spreadsheet.

This was going to be a long night. Meg had no intention of going home until she located proof of the existence of the hall runner and bed and where they were now.

TWENTY-SIX

Phoebe and Liz began watching the first tape together. It would give Phoebe the chance to ask questions as she'd not been to Heberden House nor seen photographs of some of the people who might appear. And it helped Liz manage a sudden rise of panic because she didn't want more memories to emerge unbidden and sabotage her task.

'You have to wonder why these tapes exist,' Phoebe said. 'We've seen four different camera angles so far and I doubt any guests signed a release form.'

'I don't have an answer. Not yet. And considering the tapes cover some ten years and two properties… it isn't normal. Oh, that is Joseph and Ilona.'

The couple were elegantly dressed for a dinner party and he used a walking cane.

'Pause, please.'

Liz noted the time of the tape and that Joseph use the cane. 'I don't recall anything about the cane and will see if Meg can clean that up to get a better image.'

The first hour of tape was mostly of guests arriving, being welcomed, and finger food being offered. Seeing the waiting staff in black and white uniforms gave Liz a chill. Her memory was spot on.

They were running the tape through at a higher than normal speed, pausing to check anything which looked interesting such as announcements or people disappearing upstairs or outside. It all looked like a normal, if extravagant, party. There was no dining, just continuous offerings of hors d'oeuvres and wine.

Liz suddenly reached for the controller, paused and then rewound a bit.

'What did you see?'

'I might be wrong… nope. That is Marcus Bonner. I'm sure.' Liz tapped on her tablet to find his file which included images of him over the years. 'What do you think?'

They both peered at a newspaper clipping from 1994 of an event at Bonner Gallery which showed the man clearly.

'Yes, definitely him. Same jaw line and stature. You've met him, right?'

With a nod, Liz stood to stretch. 'Had a conversation with him at his gallery. He was creepy and evasive as well as charming and commanding in presence. Annette was with me and quite intimidated by him.'

Phoebe raised both eyebrows. '*Annette* was intimidated? Was he aggressive?'

'Nope. It was just at first, when we arrived there. As we were leaving she was very daring and took a photo of a painting right behind him. It helped us connect some dots about Lyndall. But until then she was very cautious around him.'

Her reaction had been odd. Annette was among the calmest of cops Liz had met over the years and could be put into a range of situations without any hesitation. She was trustworthy, solid, and kind.

Except then we started suspecting her of being an informant. Instead of seeing her for the good cop she is.

'Why do you look cross, Liz?'

'Hm? No, not at all cross. I just want to catch the killer. And my father.'

'Do you think they might be the same person?'

That hit a bit close to home and Liz returned to her seat. 'Everything about Kyle is an unknown.'

'I could do a podcast about him.'

'Sorry… what? How?'

Phoebe turned her chair to look at Liz, clearly thinking as she spoke. 'He faked his own death. Twice? Not just that, he killed to steal a new identity. He has abducted two children we know about. Depending on what I am legally permitted to discuss, it would be interesting to create a podcast about him.'

No wonder I like you. So smart and so thoughtful.

'Legally it is tricky. Kyle's never been arrested let alone charged. Although I was present when he attempted to abscond with Eliza on his boat, and when he shot Terry, putting it out in the public domain may damage the legal process. I don't know. What if I speak to Ben and get his perspective?'

'I have some experience with casting about open cases and if you need, I have access to a legal team. It matters to me that my show is above board and cannot ever be put under scrutiny… not in a legal way. Talk to Ben and then me. If you want to.' Phoebe looked at her hands.

'Thank you. I mean it. I'm struggling through all of this and your support matters.'

Phoebe glanced up.

Liz reached for the controller. 'Let's catch the killer.'

Little came of the first tape, other than the walking cane and picking up that Marcus was present. Between them, they'd flagged two dozen spots for Meg to check and they had a few queries to follow up but nothing was standing out as needing immediate attention. Liz had taken a number of screenshots showing furniture and so on.

Phoebe wanted to continue with her plan of working backwards so they moved to separate monitors.

Rather than following her own plan of keeping to that year, Liz started the first of the tapes recorded in 1991 at the Melbourne house. All she could think about was Lyndall being exposed to Marcus back then. Of course, she'd been involved in a romantic relationship with him many years earlier, before her marriage, but her trust had turned to fear at some point. By then she might well have been questioning who he really was.

This house was just as grand as the mansion in its own way but set on smaller grounds. A dining table for twelve was beautifully appointed with gold cutlery and crystal glasses. As the guests arrived, Ilona and Joseph greeted each with a kiss on each cheek. There was no sign of the walking cane. It took little time for all to be seated and Liz kept hitting pause and taking shots of faces. She opened her notebook and drew a rough plan of the table, adding names of those she recognised.

Ilona and Joseph took an end each. To Ilona's right was Marcus. Beside him was Alain – Lyndall's husband at the time and father of their two boys. Liz had only ever seen photos of him. He was animated and smiled a great deal of the time, often turning to Lyndall, who was on his other side, and making her laugh.

It hurt Liz's heart. Back then Lyndall wouldn't have known about Alain's terrible secrets. He was simply her husband. One she was to lose in just a few years, thanks to the evil machinations of Marcus Bonner.

The other couple on the same side of the table she didn't recognise, nor four people on the other side.

Her heart was pounding. She paused, then forwarded, then rewound the best image of the man sitting at the right hand of Joseph.

It was her father.

. . .

Pete wasn't a good sleeper. Not for most of his life. Becoming a cop and moving into undercover did nothing to help. And now, in a team which was the smartest and safest he'd ever been part of, he still didn't sleep well.

He'd sat at home, frustrated beyond belief at Liz's willingness to expose herself to the danger of her father.

Yet just as powerful was his pride in her.

Liz was the strongest human he'd ever met. Other people didn't always see it. Some never did. She had a way of minimising her personality to suit the situation but Liz was fierce. And the more he uncovered about Kyle Moorland, the more he admired her.

I'm going to find him and kill him. Bury him so deep the maggots won't find his rotting corpse.

It was almost midnight and Pete stood on the bank of the Yarra River. Directly opposite was the marina where Liz had seen Kyle. There had to be a reason he'd been there, but so far all of Pete's enquiries hadn't found a connection. The man didn't own or rent any of the apartments nearby. He had no interest in any of the moorings or boats. He didn't have anything to do with the handful of retail outlets in the immediate area.

So how had he known where to watch for Liz?

From personal experience Pete was all too aware of the physical abilities of the man who was almost thirty years his senior. Kyle was fit. Not only had he outrun two detectives who were at the top of their game, but then escaped underwater along a difficult river wearing a scuba tank.

What if you've been acting like yet another runner? Following her from her building?

The banks of the river were a haven for city-dwellers trying to stay fit. Every morning and evening there'd be joggers and power walkers and cyclists avoiding pedestrians, and often treating the footpaths as their own property. Pete wasn't one to run or jog. It didn't feel like any kind of fun. He boxed and surfed. Particularly the latter. And took his jet ski out as often as life allowed.

But Liz was a runner. And she was a creature of habit, so all it would take was one sighting by Kyle for him to patiently wait and plot and follow.

Pete sent a message to Liz, not caring what the hour was.

> Don't go running again for now. Please. And think about who you've seen running in the past. Or walking.

> Regulars out there on your usual routes.

> Night.

He liked his theory. Kyle might well have shadowed Liz for weeks with her never knowing. And why would she pay close attention to other people doing exactly what she was? It was probably the one thing which was familiar and safe in an otherwise messed up world for her.

His phone beeped a message.

> We already decided I wouldn't run there for a bit.

That was true. But Liz was getting into a mindset where she might well do her own thing. He could see it in her silences and it was both dangerous and productive, and she'd not yet harnessed this new way of responding to her instincts. Except now it sounded like he was mansplaining.

. . .

Are you drunk, Pete? Shall I come and collect
you?

He chuckled and dialled her number.

'I'm working, mate. But if you need a lift—'

'Lizzie, Lizzie, dizzy Lizzie—'

'Where are you.'

Pete stopped playing. 'Close to the spot that you saw Kyle watching you from the marina.'

'Why?'

He didn't know how to answer. His eyes were on the opposite side, hoping for something to make sense.

'Pete? You don't need to protect me.'

Do you have Reuben now?

He kicked at a nearby bin. It hurt.

'Hardly. I just want this case done with so I can go surfing.'

What was wrong with him? Liz had never relied on another person of any kind to protect her. She was made of steel. Mostly.

'Go surfing, dude. Catch some waves and get the wind and sea salt in your hair. Do you want to know why I'm still working at…let me check, after midnight?'

There was no reason to start crossing the river, yet Pete found himself on the peculiarly shaped footbridge. Every person who approached, as it wound its way over the river, was a suspect he evaluated and discarded with every step.

'Are you still at the hub?'

'Yes and once I can't focus any longer I'll go sleep in one of the rooms. There's so much information, Pete. So much falling down from the skies.' She kind of laughed. 'Or at least from videos.'

'Tell me.'

'Okay, so the very last one shows that Marcus was present and that Joseph Baxter used a walking stick.'

'Huh? There's been no mention of that anywhere. Not in the records I've read nor the reports.'

'Exactly. Phoebe is working backwards and she'll let me know if she finds a point where he began using one. It isn't a big deal but it is a new piece of information. In the meantime, I went the other way and looked at the tapes from 1991.'

When Lyndall was back in Melbourne.

He'd crossed the river and found a bench and sat. 'Go on.'

Liz took a moment to respond and Pete stared around himself. So late at night the locals were probably all in bed. Those visiting Crown Casino or nightclubs and wine bars were still around but not in the same numbers.

'My father was at the same dinner party as Lyndall.'

'He what?'

'I know. This tells me that she had no idea of his identity. Perhaps it was the only time they met and his name slipped her mind at the time.'

'What else.'

'Marcus was there, like she said. So was Alain. And a handful of people I can't identify but hope Meg will be able to. One interests me.'

Pete couldn't sit still and headed in the direction of the marina.

'There's a woman who doesn't appear to be attached to any other guest. She comes in alone. Leaves alone. But there is one point where she and Marcus have a brief and seemingly intense conversation away from everyone else.'

'What woman?'

'Elegant. Around Marcus' age. Stern. There's something about her, Pete. Something familiar.'

He stopped beneath the underpass. 'Lizzie? Is this from your memories from the mansion?'

'Maybe. I think so. Yes. She was dancing with my father, if I have it right. And I think… dammit I am sure I am… she is the same woman Annette met at Bonner Gallery at the age of sixteen. And there's something else. I just can't confirm it because VHS is grainy and difficult for me but again, Meg might do wonders. She's wearing earrings which sort of look like the one Ben and I found beneath Heberden House.'

'I might come take a look.'

'You'll see it soon enough and I've moved onto other things. Ben said for you to take the night off. I'd say get some sleep but I know you too well.'

'And are you going to try and sleep?'

'Sure. Later.'

With that she rang off and he pocketed the phone. Later probably didn't mean tonight.

TWENTY-SEVEN

Three hours sleep wasn't nearly good enough but better than none. Meg had woken at the first sound in the hub since she and Liz had finally quit for the night and dropped onto their respective beds. Phoebe had left around ten to have a zoom call with her various team members about the podcast the previous night.

Someone was showering and it better be Liz because nobody else should be here before six in the morning.

Meg turned on the light to jump-start her brain into activity, blinking because her eyes disagreed with her life choices. But she was already working through what she needed to do before presenting a report to Ben. She'd been down a number of rabbit holes once she began digging around about the contents of Heberden House. And Liz had wanted to talk to her but three in the morning wasn't the time.

She showered and dressed, thankful of being able to keep a couple of changes of clothes here. If it wasn't that she loved her apartment and the St Kilda Beach lifestyle so much, she could almost move here permanently.

The wonderful aroma of coffee as she emerged from her room was another consideration in favour of moving in. And letting someone else get up first.

'Here. Only just finished making it.' Liz handed Meg a cup. 'Why do you look so fresh?'

'Part cyborg. I regenerate after three hours downtime. Anyway, you look fine. Just don't sit under a bright light. Any light, really.'

'Very nice. Forgot to mention I added some arsenic to that cup of yours.'

'Old school. I'd be updating your options by having a quiet chat with Jeffrey. He knows all the latest trends in poisons, particularly ones which are insanely hard to find post mortem.' Meg winked.

'I will. You know I will.'

'Do you still have an urgent, almost childlike need to tell Mommy something right now?' Meg pulled a chair over and sat at Liz's desk. 'Not that I'm a mommy let alone American, so it would be mummy.'

'Is that how you interpreted my polite request during the night to discuss a few key points from the marathon session of watching people from the past act like they were better than us mere mortals?' Liz asked. 'Oh, scrap that. Forgot you are part robot.'

'Cyborg. Quite different. And I'm unplugged now.' A couple of mouthfuls of coffee kicked Meg into work-mode. 'What did you find?'

'I've sent a report to you and Ben, so I expect he'll want to discuss at the morning briefing. I found my father in several videos with different groups of guests. There's a woman who may be connected to Marcus and is definitely connected to Kyle. The videos are grainy and I've earmarked a number of places hoping you might be able to clean them up.'

'Oh, Liz. I'm sorry.'

'Whatever for?'

'Wanting to sleep instead of being there for you.'

Having to see your father like that.

'I'm really alright. Did you have any success with what you were chasing? I heard you on the phone a few times.'

'Yes, I'm not good at remembering some people sleep before midnight. However, twenty-four-hour businesses do sometimes answer their phones beyond normal hours, and I managed to speak to a couple of places of interest. I am now in possession of a more precise list of locations of the contents of Heberden House.'

Liz looked impressed. 'So not just what the estate solicitor sent?'

'They need auditing. If not proper investigation because the more I dug, the more emerged. These people are making a lot of money managing the Inspector's estate yet claim they don't know the whereabouts of several key items including the bed, mattress, and hall runner. No sign of a sale, disposal or storage for those.'

Meg checked her phone for the first time since waking. There were far too many messages so she ignored them all and opened one of her apps. Liz had already turned her computer on and Meg cast the information she wanted onto its screen.

'Now, one would think that itemising the contents of a deceased estate was pretty straightforward. And on the surface there's a long list all nicely laid out in the spreadsheet the solicitor sent. However…' Meg opened a different document. 'This is my list of what is missing. And I've included what Phoebe sent.'

'Phoebe? What did she send?'

'Get with the program, Liz.' Meg grinned. 'While you were checking out the earliest tapes, she was observing everything going on at those parties the year the Baxters died. And the year before. As you know there were four cameras which showed different parts of each event.'

'And she made a note of the furniture? What else.'

'Lots. Phoebe is observant and systematic and that makes for a good cop. Except she isn't a cop. Just has the nose of one.'

Liz looked away.

'I'm saying this once because everyone knows I don't do emotion and special feelings, but Liz... you are loved and respected. Kyle Moorland is not. And there is no place on this world where this is not true.'

Liz sighed deeply then looked at Meg.

'Not even in the known universe,' she added. 'And don't get me started on the unknown universe.'

'Thank you.'

They smiled at each other.

'Enough of this soppy stuff. Let me show you what I have.'

Liz might not have even bothered trying to sleep. But resting her body was necessary although her mind refused to cooperate. Pete's phone call had played on her mind too much because now she was dragging him down with her. He didn't need to be wandering around Melbourne after midnight in the hope of seeing Kyle.

She was in the kitchen. It was a safe place in the scheme of things. Here she could chill without anyone asking if she was okay. Or if they did she'd merely point to the coffee machine heating up or the oven and say everyone would be okay once the appliances cooperated.

Even better was the view. Thanks to the design, there was a half wall between this room and the main part of the hub. A row of bricks at the top allowed for a kind of pass – like in a restaurant where the chef would place the food for a server to collect. It was often used for coffee or tea and sometimes for food or glasses of wine.

Is it too early for alcohol?

The team was all here and in a few minutes would gather for a briefing. Much had happened overnight. And at this moment in time, it was more than Liz wanted to think about.

'Going okay?'

Reuben had wandered in unseen, coffee cup in hand.

'Sure. The machine is heating up.'

'I'll make one for you.'

He busied himself and Liz gazed into the main room, impressed her strategy was working.

People chatted or worked at their desks. Everything was normal.

Nothing is normal.

A cup of coffee was placed in front of Liz, and Reuben was close enough for her to inhale the musky scent of him.

'Want to talk?'

'All good, thanks.' She summoned a smile.

He took his coffee and left, but she'd seen the worry cross his brow.

She picked up her coffee and sipped without really tasting it.

'Hey, Liz. Good coffee?'

'Sure is, Candace. Machine is just heating up.'

'Not wanting a coffee right now.'

'Oh. The oven is on.'

'No it isn't. Do you want it on?'

I want everyone to stop asking personal questions.

Unlikely that would happen in a team filled with investigators.

'If I tell you something in confidence here, is it like patient confidentiality?' Liz turned and gazed at Candace.

There it was. That searching look in the other woman's eyes. She'd noticed it when Liz first met Candace and was sent by her boss to brief her in the role as profiler. Even then, without knowing each other, Candace could see her. Really see her.

It was both incredibly uncomfortable and ridiculously comforting.

'You can tell me anything. Whether I am compelled to break confidence depends on many things. For example, should someone give me a detailed plan of a terrorist attack then yes, I will be on the phone to a higher authority immediately.'

'I'm not a terrorist.'

'It was an example. Another would be someone under extreme pressure convincing themselves they need to kill their father.'

Ouch. I really need to learn how to bury myself better.

'I need to kill my father.'

'I know.'

That wasn't what Liz expected and for some reason she smiled.

Candace moved closer and put her hands on Liz's shoulders. 'Kill him. But do it for the right reasons.'

'What are right reasons?'

'Because you have no choice. Because he is otherwise unstoppable and will continue to kidnap and murder.'

Liz's heart thudded.

'What are the wrong reasons?'

For just a moment it seemed Candace wanted to pull Liz into her arms. Something flared in the other woman's eyes and Liz felt even more confused. Then Candace walked away and at the doorway turned.

'Don't kill him to avenge your mother or sister or niece or yourself. But Liz? That is my official opinion only. And I'm unlikely to break any confidentiality, but you need to keep talking to me.'

'I won't kill him. Not unless I have to.'

Candace nodded and left.

Liz knew it was a lie, and probably, so did Candace.

The briefing was long. With so much new information coming to light overnight, Ben wanted to be certain the entire team was across it. With the two cases clearly connected, every bit of evidence needed extra scrutiny. The likelihood of cross-over between people's workloads was getting higher all the time.

Liz looked exhausted but she spoke with clarity about the videos she'd reviewed. They watched a couple of minutes, which Meg had sewn together and made clearer by her voodoo.

'My focus is on why Kyle was part of this group invited to the Baxter house. Actually, both houses at different times. What was his connection to the couple whose son was a police officer? And also, who is the woman is in this particular snippet. Annette, would you mind taking a close look at her?'

The video paused on a woman talking to Marcus Bonner.

Annette leaned toward the screen, her face lined with concentration. 'I think it is… possibly?'

'Think what? We don't all have context,' Hamish said.

'I sent the context to your tablet earlier.' Meg raised one eyebrow.

'Right. I haven't read it all, so a bit of help? Please?'

Pete looked ready to say something to Hamish then Liz gave him a look and he kept quiet. The pair had one of those rare work relationships which most cops wanted. They knew each other well, likely too well, but it made for mutual respect and an ability to speak without words.

'Meg, does there happen to be a different image? Another angle?'

Annette either hadn't heard Hamish or was ignoring him.

'Sure.'

'While Meg is doing her magic, for anyone who is not up to speed about why we are showing Annette specific images…' Ben was determined not to smile. 'There was a woman at Bonner Gallery when Annette was there on a school visit, and we believe she might be able to assist our enquiries.'

'Ah yes. The one with splendid hair and an attitude who took the children into the curved room at the Gallery.'

Liz shot a glance at Hamish then to Ben. Something wasn't right and he'd speak to her later. Reuben glanced between the two of them but nobody else seemed to notice as Meg brought up more images.

'Here's two more to view. What I am doing right now,

although you can't see me doing it, is creating a 3D model of this woman. Also of every person who appears at any of the events.'

'I think it is her.' Annette straightened. 'When was this taken? What year?'

'1991.'

'So a few years before I would have met her. This woman has her hair back. She's smiling. I never saw the other woman smile. And this one is dressed almost provocatively.'

'Once Meg has more images sorted we can show you what she looks like later... but for now do you think it is her?' Liz asked.

Annette nodded. 'Pretty sure.'

'Then we need to find out who she is as a priority,' Ben said. 'Anything else you'd like to raise, Liz?'

'Only that I would like to talk to Lyndall. Face to face and with a copy of the clearest possible version of the video taken from the dinner party where she attended and so did Kyle.'

'I'll come with you,' Candace said. 'Or sit in wherever this happens.'

'Good, thanks for that. Once we finish would you both come and see me?' That was the best he could do for now. Without knowing the extent of Kyle Moorland's current network it was risky to let Liz go to Lyndall.

'Right, who is next?'

TWENTY-EIGHT

In two hours Liz and Candace were going to be in a small town between Bacchus Marsh and Geelong. It was where a stockfeed store that Lyndall regularly visited to collect supplies was located and happened to have a small and discreet café close by. The hope was that by Lyndall doing her usual thing, a meeting would go unnoticed.

It did Liz's head in to think about Kyle and how far his reach might be.

Back when she was simply a Homicide detective with a heavy caseload and a decent arrest and conviction record, she'd have treated the concept of a criminal with an invasive network as unlikely. Not in Australia. Not unless they were tied to organised crime.

But her father was different. Yes, he did seem to have ties to a number of organisations but they were religious sects rather than intricate illegal groups. If anyone had come to her with the current scenario, she'd have been doubtful. One man who'd built a clever network of seemingly normal people to work with him when it suited him. His agenda and one they followed. Yet it was real and because so few of his connections had been arrested – and of those there were even less prepared to talk – it left a lot of room for speculation.

Perhaps he was on his own now.

Or perhaps he had hundreds of people in place, watching Liz and Lyndall and Vince and Melanie.

'Lizzie? We're closing in on him.'

Pete leaned his arms on the top row of bricks at the edge of building. She'd not heard the door close behind her or his footsteps on the concrete floor of the roof.

He was staring at her. She could feel his eyes.

Hers were on the buildings over the road. The road itself. Moving endlessly in case… what? Kyle appeared?

'What if we can't catch him?' She was sick of continually seeking assurances but couldn't seem to help herself.

'Except, we will. Do you not know yet how damned good Operation Nobody is? Let alone me, personally?'

Yes, but is my father better?

'What went on at the briefing? Hamish said something and you and Ben both reacted. So did Reuben, except I reckon it was just because you did.'

'And what does that mean, mate? Why would he react because I did?'

'You'd need to ask Reuben.'

She finally looked at him. He wasn't joking for once and that was worse than if he was winding her up. Pete was good at observing people over a long period and picking up the slightest changes in patterns or behaviour. But Liz wasn't going to be drawn into whatever he thought he knew. There was nothing and she wasn't wasting breath explaining that.

'Hamish mentioned some things which he couldn't have heard us discuss. Me and Annette, that is. He'd already gone back to work with Ben somewhere else in the building but I needed to confirm it with Ben.'

'Which you now have.'

'Ben says he and Hamish were together while Annette and I

went down memory lane. No chance of him overhearing our conversation.'

'Crap.'

'Double crap. Except for all we know Annette has talked about it to him. To others even. We're jumping at shadows.'

'Which is our job, Liz. Do you want me to trail you and Candace today? I can stay out of sight. Kill any bad guys.'

The thought had already crossed her mind. It wasn't that she couldn't handle Kyle, or anyone he sent, but she had Lyndall and Candace to consider. And Pete cared about Lyndall. Somewhere not far away a police car siren blared and both of them immediately looked for the unit. It never came into view and in a moment the sound faded.

'Aren't you too busy to play babysitter?'

'Annette can take Reuben to do the interviews with the housekeeper and other staff.'

Liz checked the time. 'I have to talk to Meg. Be ready in an hour.'

The town was a hundred or so houses with one shopping street. There was a pub at either end and a dozen shops. It was off the main drag along a windy road down a hill and pretty enough, in a quaint and old way.

'I need to get out of Melbourne more often,' Candace said. She was gazing out of the window of one of the team's cars, a basic sedan on the outside but with plenty of grunt and a boot filled with weapons and equipment. 'Until about five years ago I travelled as often as my work permitted. Mostly overseas though. Europe. India. The Arctic.'

'Arctic? Who are you… some modern day explorer?'

Candace chuckled. 'Hardly. But we live on a beautiful and interesting planet.'

'So why haven't you been continent-hopping for so long? Just workload?'

Liz drove past the stockfeed store. The café was a little further down and she wanted to park away from prying eyes.

'Not workload. A loss in my life which threw me for six.'

The words were delivered evenly but a quick glance at Candace's face brought a rush of empathy. She looked haunted. Older. Then she pointed.

'There's a little carpark near those trees. We could hide the car.'

Liz had seen it. 'Not sure we need to hide it. But good spotting.'

She parked between a tree and an old flatbed ute and turned off the motor. They could easily see both the café and the stockfeed store. Lyndall's 4WD was parked in front of the latter but there was no sign of her.

'When are we going to the café?'

'I want to watch for a few minutes first. Make sure Lyndall has finished what she normally does and probably wait for her to head into the café.'

'Pity we don't have another set of eyes.'

'We will.'

Candace was confused.

'Couple more minutes and you'll see. And… I'm so sorry for your loss.' The urge to reach her hand to Candace was overwhelming and after the slightest hesitation, Liz touched the other woman's arm. She didn't know what else to say. She wasn't a therapist nor clever with words, but her heart hurt for Candace.

For a moment they just sat, Liz's hand on Candace's arm. Then Candace covered Liz's hand with hers.

'Thank you.'

They stayed that way for another minute and the air was rich with emotion. Shared understanding. Sorrow. Compassion. It finally occurred to Liz that this was a friendship. Unspoken but true.

The roar of a motorcycle caught their attention and both

turned to watch a beast of a machine slow as it came into view. The rider was in black from head to foot including the helmet and visor. For an instant, fear shot through Liz. This could well be her father. If he'd followed them…

'Is that Pete?' Candace asked. 'That's one of our bikes.'

Just not riding in like some badass gang member. Way to be discreet, dude.

'He will keep an eye on the rest of the town while we talk with Lyndall. But seriously, he might as well have brought fireworks because he's over-the-top noticeable.'

Candace was smiling. 'Smart man. Be so visible that whatever you and I do is just background noise.'

She had a good point. People were already stopping to look at Pete as he nosed the bike into a parking spot. Motor off, he sat without even looking around but knowing him, he'd clocked them and Lyndall's 4WD.

'Why don't we go into the café?' Candace asked. 'Less obvious than us moving the minute Lyndall does.'

There was still no sign of Lyndall. It made sense to go in and be prepared. Liz opened her door. 'Come on then.'

Despite being in a small town away from any main roads, the café might well have been in the inner city. The interior was dark with the walls covered in modern art and beautiful displays of plants trailing down. The menu was upmarket and on the expensive side. Yet almost every table was either currently filled or had a reserved sign.

'Do you have a booking?' A young woman with multiple facial piercings and a friendly smile asked.

'Under the name of Lyndall?'

'Oh, well in that case, of course you have a booking. Lyndall is one of my favourite customers. Would you like to order now or wait for her to join?'

'We'll wait. I'm sure she isn't far away.' Candace spoke softly. 'What a cool place you have here.'

'We love it. My girlfriend is the cook. We could never afford city rent and love the country, so here we are. Table twelve is reserved for you and once Lyndall arrives, I'll come take your orders. There's menus over there.'

The table in question was tucked at the back, with nothing behind it but a wall. It was ideal for privacy.

'I love that this place is so… out of place here. Yet is thriving. Good on them,' Liz said. She took the chair facing the front of the building. It was her natural choice to evaluate any danger and she'd done it for most of her life. Today it felt even more important as she had two civilians to watch out for.

'Oh, I almost forgot. There's definitely an apartment in my building for sale. If you're still interested,' Candace said.

'There is?'

'Two floors down and a corner apartment, so balconies on two sides. It is about half the size of mine though.'

'Sounds perfect. Who do I speak to about an inspection?'

Candace tapped on her phone and a message came through to Liz. 'It isn't on the market for another couple of weeks but Dale will look after you. Tell him I sent you.'

A small glimmer of a better future. Once Kyle was out of the picture for good, Liz could redesign her life. It was too late for marriage and kids but she longed to foster friendships and be more involved with her remaining family. Buying a home would be a good start.

'There's Lyndall.'

Dressed in her typical jeans, boots, and checked shirt, Lyndall waved to the woman behind the counter and made a beeline for table twelve. She took the seat opposite Liz but turned the chair to put its back against a wall and let her look at the other patrons.

Her hand reached for Liz's. 'So very good to see you, darlin'. And you too, Candace. Just need better circumstances.'

'We're making real progress,' Liz said. 'And I'm sorry for the precautions and how much your life has been upended.'

Lyndall's smile was tired. She looked as worn down as Liz felt and that was enough of a push to stop feeling sorry for herself. Everyone was affected. The young woman approached to take their orders, which was just tea and coffee.

Once they were alone again, Lyndall suddenly grinned. 'Noticed young Peter on his bike. Don't worry. We ignored each other but he looks pretty dapper in all that black gear.'

'If you recognised him—'

'Nobody else will.'

They made small talk until their drinks arrived and then Liz unlocked her tablet. 'We have some old video we'd like your opinion on. But I want to warn you first that this is from 1991.'

Lyndall's expression didn't change. 'From the dinner party?'

'Yes.'

'No surprise. The Baxters struck me as being security conscious, but how is there footage after all these years?'

'We located a box filled with VHS tapes in Heberden House. Although we've yet to view them all, the date on this one meant it had to be looked at because we knew you were there and so was Marcus. We're currently interested in identifying a woman who attended.'

Candace leaned a little closer to Lyndall. 'This has been edited to about ten minutes of footage showing the woman in question. But you need to be aware all of that evening's guests appear at some point.'

'You mean Alain.' Lyndall took the tablet. 'Is there sound?'

'No sound. Just press play when you want and pause if you need a closer look.'

Liz lifted her coffee and sipped, watching. So did Candace.

A couple of times Lyndall paused the screen and gazed at it, then hit play again. She watched it twice then stopped it on a clear image of the woman.

'This is Kirsten Bonner.'

'What? Is she Marcus' wife?'

'Oh no. His sister. She's a few years younger and worked with him in France for a while during my time in Europe. Not at all friendly. Quite secretive and before you ask, I have no idea where she might be today.'

This was good. A name. An unexpected connection

'Do you know this person?' Liz located a still showing Kyle.

Lyndall shuddered and handed the tablet back. 'One of the coldest and cruellest men I ever met and thank goodness it was only two or three times.'

Candace's eyes were boring into Liz and she drew a quick breath.

'His name?'

She's going to say Kyle Moorland because he hadn't changed into Garry Ford back then.

'You don't know him? Perhaps he left Australia the way Kirsten did. That man is Etienne Finn.'

'But… no.'

Lyndall nodded. 'Yes, darlin'. He was a senior member of some awful white supremist cult and his name was definitely Etienne Finn. Only person who got on with him was Kirsten. Why are you looking so upset, Lizzie?'

Blinking away sudden tears, Liz turned off the tablet and slid it into its bag to give herself a moment. Another pseudonym? 'Because that is my father. That's Kyle.'

TWENTY-NINE

'This is a goldmine,' Jeff said. He gazed at the deconstructed washing machine, now in dozens of parts which were mostly piled on top of each other but with the drum and piping on their own table. 'I can't believe you didn't dive into it the minute it arrived. This and the clothes.'

'Might be something to do with a hundred competing needs including those of my bosses and occasionally my own. Like, sleeping and eating.'

'Both overrated.'

'What have you found?'

'Blood. Enough to test for blood type. Never could do such a thing until the last couple of years, not with the age and condition of the samples. Still running trace through further testing and there's DNA to come but Meg, I've isolated three blood types.'

'Three?'

Jeff appeared to be quite impressed with himself. 'Indeed. One matches that of the male victim and another of the female victim. As for the third… that is the one I intend to put my effort into.'

Oh thank goodness. This is precisely why I needed you here.

'Sounds a bit… difficult.'

'Megan!'

She couldn't keep a straight face.

'Jeffrey!'

'Good God, only Mum calls me that. I'll have DNA results within a week thanks to not working for the police force.' He grimaced. 'Not meaning to sound disrespectful but how did you ever cope with waiting for results? Weeks if not months to get a match which might stop a killer or solve a crime?'

'Money, dude. You know as well as I do how little is made available to law enforcement, no matter which government happens to be in power.' This was something Meg felt strongly about. 'Lead times for simple results are ridiculous. The general public can get something back faster as long as they pay a private lab. Meanwhile, we're tracking serial killers and heart-breaking cold cases and have to get in a queue behind drug and drink offenders.'

Jeff held his arms wide open and Meg stepped in for a hug.

'Preaching to the converted, dearie. And why I branched out to private.'

'Maybe I should have.'

He squeezed tight then released her. 'You had some good offers but I get why you chose your path. At the heart of you, Meggie is an idealist.'

'I am?'

'You are. Finding solutions to other people's problems is high on your to do list but times are changing. Science is moving rapidly and Australia is fortunate to have clever people staying on shore to develop new techniques. I figure this team is your way of staying close to the police force but having the freedom and funds to fast track and embrace those changes. Yes?'

'Yes.'

Something dinged and they went to the source. One of several screens in the room. Jeff had brought two of his own and Meg already had several in place, all but one connected to different testing stations. The other one was a normal computer and part of her network. And that was what wanted their attention.

'Any way we can get a landline in here?' Jeff asked. 'I understand the need to keep everything digital out, but what if my husband needs me?'

Meg stopped opening the alert and looked at him. 'Oh… I'm so sorry. I'll get Ben to sort that out. You can receive alerts from your phone on this computer now, but you'll need to step out to make a call. Shall I set that up for you until we can get a landline?'

'Please. It isn't that I expect anything to go wrong but I'm accustomed to a bit less security. Don't get me wrong. Having this lab so protected makes perfect sense with the work being done.'

Taking his phone, Meg spent a few minutes creating an alert which he'd hear no matter where he was in the lab. 'There's one for your husband's phone number and a quieter ping for any other calls and messages. I'll test it once I'm back in the hub. Now, let's see what's come through for us.' She clicked the message which had brought them to the computer in the first place. 'Oh, yikes.'

'What's wrong?'

'Liz has uncovered yet another fake name her father has used. I'll need to go and start a search.'

Jeff gestured to another stainless steel table where a long row a sample bags were tagged. 'One more minute of your time?' He hurried to the table. 'These are test samples from the clothing left within the washing machine.'

Meg joined him.

'Each of these tells a story. We don't have the right equipment for one test I want to run, so with your permission I'll courier a selection to my other lab with the aim of dating the fabric and extracting other information. It isn't a quick thing by any means but if it comes to a prosecution, we'll be prepared.'

'Clever. Forward thinking and very clever. Go right ahead. And do you mind writing a quick update for me?'

'Next job. Then I'll process the evidence casts from the well and behind the house. And thank you. For the phone stuff.'

'Easy done.' Meg pushed the first door open. 'I'll call you in a minute so send me an email if it doesn't work.'

She glanced back. Jeff was reaching for the device he favoured for dictation. Knowing him, she'd have his report by the time she made a coffee and sat at her desk.

Pete was almost back at the hub when his phone rang. Although he didn't recognise the number he assumed it wasn't Kyle playing more games as he tended to mask his calls.

'Detective McNamara.'

'This is Mrs Betty Carrigan. You left your card under our front door the other day and asked about our cameras.' The voice was elderly and female.

'Thanks for ringing, Mrs Carrigan.'

'My husband and I have had a good look and found you wandering around. So we went backwards to see what you were looking for in our garden.'

'Sorry about intruding.'

'Don't be silly. We found someone else and she rattled the front door and even tried to open a window! The nerve of her. And of course we keep everything locked so she had no success, but it was obvious she either wanted to rob us or hide.'

'Do you know how long between her leaving and me arriving?'

'We do. Four minutes.'

He swore under his breath. So damned close.

'Is there any chance I can get hold of the footage? I can talk you through the process or else come over.'

'Not necessary, Detective. My husband has saved the file and says if you provide an email address then he can send it off right now.

'Mrs C, you are a dead set legend. And your hubby.'

He dictated one of Meg's email addresses they used for outside communications, thanked her again, and rang off.

If only I'd looked outside first I might have caught this person.

When the team found the broken lock at Heberden House the other day, their first instinct was to check internally. It wasted valuable minutes and allowed the intruder to escape over the wall and through the Carrigan's garden. At least his arrival might have been enough to stop the person breaking into their home and potentially causing them harm once they returned.

As he came off the freeway a steady rain began falling. Liz and Candace should already be back as he'd followed Lyndall until she was safely home. There was so much to catch up on from their meeting and this new footage to look at. Things were moving in a positive direction and now all they needed was for Kyle to show himself.

He had to stop at the alley which led to the carpark access, thanks to a homeless man struggling to push a trolley onto the footpath. The man was heavyset and hunched over and appeared to be muttering to himself. While he waited, Pete glanced to the roof of the building. Hamish was peering down and waved. How weird he was on the roof in the rain. Pete looked back at the man and was ready to get off the bike and help him when with a big shove the trolley made it. The man gestured at Pete as if telling him to go – which he did – because upstairs was a coffee with his name on it. He nosed the bike past rubbish and graffiti then used a keypad to open a roller door. Once inside he pressed the large, flat button to lower the door again, and a movement caught his attention on the security monitors.

The homeless man stood at the far end of the laneway and while Pete watched, he began to peel off his clothes. An oversized long coat. A heavy scarf. A second jacket. A pair of thick trousers. Each he dropped in the middle of the road.

'What the hell are you up to?'

Pete got off the bike and took off his helmet and gloves. The man was clearly not overweight and bent over but lean and tall. He picked up a large piece of white cardboard with black writing and held it in the direction of the camera over the roller door. It was too far to read.

'No, no, no.' Pete slammed his hand onto the button to open the door again.

The man's attention moved to the slowly moving roller door and with a broad smile he removed a beanie and sunglasses from his head. For a few seconds he stood motionless, his face visible, and then after placing the sign on the ground he strode away.

Pete tossed his helmet down and dialled Ben, kicking the roller door which was taking too damned long to rise.

'Kyle Moorland's outside the building. I'm trying to get out of the carpark. He's on foot crossing the front of the building.'

'We're coming.'

Hanging up, Pete pulled a handgun from one of the paniers, loaded it, and shoved it into the front of his jacket. The door was open just enough for him to ride out, his body flattened against the chassis to squeeze under it. At the end of the laneway he weaved around the clothes and sign and turned right.

Where are you, you mongrel?

He rode slowly, eyes darting from one side of the empty street to the other, then idling on the next corner. Four directions. No activity. Not a person. A handful of parked cars.

Kicking it into gear, Pete took off, going faster than ideal but desperate to catch Kyle. But he was on his own and going around blocks wasn't getting him results. He returned to the building where Ben and Liz were doing a foot search.

'Where's Hamish?'

'On the roof looking,' Liz said. 'Get your helmet on.'

'He was on the bloody roof when Kyle was where we are right now!'

Liz ran across the road and called up at Hamish. 'Can you see him?'

Hamish's head appeared. 'No but he ran up the road where Pete just was.'

Swearing aloud, Pete turned the bike and floored it.

He was three blocks along when something big loomed in his peripheral vision from a side alley.

As he wrenched the handles to avoid impact, the bike skidded on the wet tarmac and the ground rose.

A sickening thud and crunch.

Pain.

Nothing.

Liz had followed Pete but by the time she reached the first corner he was out of sight. She phoned Hamish as she returned to the building.

'I can see Pete but not Kyle. Too much in the way.'

'Then come down and help search. Grab a car or bike.'

'And a rifle.'

She wasn't about to argue. At this moment she'd shoot her father point blank. Twice.

Ben was jogging back and on his phone. Liz met him near the entrance to the laneway. There was a shopping trolley filled with rubbish pushed against the wall and an array of clothing on the bitumen. And a sign.

'Jeff's heading down to collect trace.' Ben was panting. 'Meg is sending an alert with the police including not to approach.'

I can't believe this. We had him right here.

Pete must have missed him by seconds.

Liz stared at the cardboard. In thick black writing was a message. With the rain already making the ink run, she quickly took a photo then lifted the sheet to lean it with the writing side against the wall. The message sent a chill up her spine.

One by one you'll see them fall.
Only you can make the call.
Do it fast, Elizabeth.
Or watch them take a final breath.

Liz's phone began ringing… not a ring. A siren sound. Same with Ben's.

Both screens were flashing in red print.

Pete's down. Tap for coordinates. Emergency assistance called.

Liz had never run so fast in her life. Her feet pounded the ground as rain drenched her hair and clothes and blurred her vision. Ben was nearby. She could hear his raspy breaths.

Pete had to be alive. He had to be alright. Nothing else was possible.

The road ahead was a mess.

The motorcycle was on its side, pieces scattered around from an impact.

There were people. Some standing. Others on phones. More running from buildings to see. Someone was on the ground.

'Pete! Peter!'

Liz pushed her way through and dropped beside Pete. He was in a loose foetal position with his arms cradling his head and there was blood on the ground. Lots of it. She moved to the other side, to see his face and got down low and close. His eyes were closed, but he was breathing.

Thank God.

Ben was right with her, checking Pete's neck for his pulse. 'Pete, we're here and help is coming.'

Liz pushed her phone at Ben when he straightened. 'I took a photo of the sign. Jeff isn't safe alone outside.'

A moment later Ben was talking to someone – Meg probably. Liz didn't listen. She lay on her side so she could see any changes in Pete's face, longing to touch it to comfort him but afraid she might make things worse. 'Don't you dare die on me. We have a party to arrange. Remember? Your place. Us all spilling onto the streets and the neighbours calling the cops. And Lyndall? Who else is going to do crap paintings at her house?'

'N..not crap.'

The words barely made it out but he was conscious.

Someone covered Pete's torso with a blanket and others held umbrellas over him and Liz. A siren was getting louder.

'Not crap? Well you'd better sort yourself out and prove me wrong by showing me one.'

'Liz… Lizzie…'

She was so close now to hear him.

'I'm here, Peter.'

'Love… you.'

'I know. I love you back. You're my best friend.'

His eyes flickered open then closed again and he kind of sighed.

Or watch them take a final breath.

Liz raised her head. 'Ben, get that ambulance here.'

THIRTY

There was nothing she could do for Pete. Not right now. He'd regained consciousness being put on the stretcher, sharp cries of agony breaking Liz's heart anew. The paramedics responded with pain relief and reassuring words.

The police arrived right behind the paramedics and had begun their job. Ben was on the phone more than off and Liz kept getting panicked messages from the rest of the team. She responded to each with a cut and paste reply that Pete was severely injured but responsive and on the way to hospital, which thankfully was only a few kilometres distance.

'Reuben and Annette aren't far away.' Ben put his arm around Liz's shoulders. 'They'll come down here with Meg to do our own investigation but for now you and I need to get back.'

The siren had faded to nothing so she nodded and they hurried the few blocks back to the building. The clothes and trolley and sign were gone and the rain had erased any trace of where they'd been. Ben input a code to open the heavy side access door beside the one to the carpark and held it for Liz to go through.

This was where she'd entered the building on the first day as a member of the team and it was rarely used. Inside were three flights of stairs and a door which looked like a wall and had a trick to activating it.

She'd thought Pete was behind sending her this way, making her work out the different puzzles to get inside. But Candace was responsible as part of an evaluation.

I blamed Pete for nothing.

The only person to blame was Kyle Moorland. Garry Ford. Etienne Finn. Or whatever the monster wanted to call himself. Her hands curled into fists.

Inside the hub was an eery quiet as everyone stopped talking. All eyes turned to Liz and Ben. Nobody was at their workstation but milling around. At a loss. Meg's glasses were off, her eyes red. Jeff was gripping her hand. Candace took a step forward and stopped. Hamish dropped his head.

You let this happen. You helped this happen.

Liz was across the room in a few seconds, stopping inches from Hamish, whose head shot up.

'Liz, I'm so sorry I couldn't get there in—'

'Why were you up there?'

'Wait, what?'

'Don't play games, Hamish.' Her voice rose and from the corner of her eye she saw Ben come their way. 'Pete said you were on the roof earlier. Was it when Kyle was waiting for Pete?'

'I have no idea what you mean.'

'Did you see my father?'

'Yes, I said so. He was running—'

Liz put both of her hands on his chest and pushed with a steady pressure which unbalanced him enough for her to force him a few steps back. He stopped against a wall, raising his own hands high in a show of passiveness.

'Liz, that's enough!' Ben bellowed.

'Hamish is going to explain why he was on the roof at the same time my father was waiting below. Aren't you?' Liz dropped her hands but didn't step back. 'Were you a lookout? Did you help Kyle pick his timing? From up there you can see one of us returning. Did you care if it was Pete? Or could it have been Phoebe?'

Hamish recoiled and the hazy cloud in her head cleared.

What the hell am I doing?

Ben was in her face. 'I said enough, *Detective*. Step away now.'

Someone was tugging on her arm.

Meg.

Why are you crying?

'You are covered in blood, Liz. Were you hurt as well?'

Liz looked down. Her white shirt was soaked in Pete's blood.

There was conversation around her. Hamish never stopped looking at her but there were tears in his eyes and that made her so ashamed.

'She's in shock. Lizzie… look at me please.' Candace's voice was soft. At least compared to Ben's. 'Let's get you cleaned up. Come on.'

Her legs wouldn't work. Not properly. They shook. Candace had her hand and someone else – Jeff – put a supporting arm around her waist. As they headed toward the change rooms the main door opened and Annette, followed by Reuben, came in. Annette's hands flew to her mouth and she burst into tears. Reuben had looked ready to go to Liz but instead, he grabbed a seat for Annette.

'This is hard on us all. Thanks, Jeff, we'll be fine,' Candace said. She tightened her grip on Liz. 'Lean on me if you need.'

'But I'm drenched in blood.'

'You are more important than what I'm wearing.'

In a moment they were in the change rooms and Liz began stripping off her clothes. The blood was on everything.

Candace turned her back. 'Once you're in the shower I'll bag everything up.'

Liz piled everything in one spot and turned on the shower.

'Do you need me to stay outside in case you feel unwell?'

I don't feel anything.

'Thanks. No. Please tell Ben I'll be out to help soon.'

She stepped under the steaming water. Would Ben fire her? Right now she didn't care, except without the team her chances of finding Kyle were drastically reduced. Not impossible. There were places she could make herself visible. The marina for one.

Liz put her head under the shower and glanced down. Blood was streaming down her stomach and legs and then her feet, the water diluting the colour. Pete's blood.

She sank onto the floor and wept.

'Are you willing to step into Liz's role? If it comes to that?'

Ben and Reuben were alone in the conference room, the door closed. He needed a moment to think. An hour would be better but time was not his to hold. In the last hour the team had been shattered and was at high risk of being torn apart completely.

'Of course. But she's solid.'

'Mate, you didn't see her. She pushed Hamish against a wall and accused him of being Kyle's watchdog.' Ben dropped his head into his hands. 'We are under threat of further attacks on the team.'

'I'll do whatever you need, boss. What first?'

A small weight dropped with Reuben's unquestioning support and Ben straightened.

'The minute Liz is back on the floor we have a team meeting. Meg has already downloaded our surveillance and is working with our other team to assess risk as well as use their expertise and bodies to close the net on this madman.'

'*Our* other team? Local police?'

'There's a second team like us in Victoria. They have their own cases and ideally, we don't cross paths. But today...' He couldn't talk about Pete without wanting to cry.

'Today we do what it takes to end this.'

Reuben was the right choice to step up. He was a calm and

steady operator with exceptional skills – not the least being his approach to handling people.

'For now would you check in with Candace? See what she needs. And ask Hamish to come and see me.'

The other man stopped at the door and looked back. 'We should have had Kyle by now. If we find whoever is helping him, then *we* can get him.'

Ben nodded as Reuben left.

Had he hindered the investigation by keeping suspicions about an insider to the core group? Why hadn't he put more effort into interviewing Hamish and Annette and getting Meg to do even more of a deep dive into their histories than she already had?

Because I'm dealing with a criminal who is outside my experience.

He'd quit. Once this was done. Let someone who could run the team with better time management and a sharper mind take over. Someone who didn't make such mistakes.

There was a tap on the door and Hamish stepped inside, closing it but not moving. His expression was blank. There was every likelihood the man would want action taken against Liz.

'Come and sit, mate.'

Hamish moved to the table but kept standing, hands at his sides.

'I'm not a traitor, sir.'

Ben got to his feet and went to Hamish, gently putting a hand on his shoulder. 'You handled yourself well before. Not traitor-like at all. Would you please sit? We need a minute off our feet.'

With a nod, Hamish took a seat and his face relaxed a little.

'The only reason I asked you in is to check on you. Kyle Moorland threw his gauntlet down today. I don't know if you are aware of the sign he left for Liz, but it reads like a threat to each of us. Personally.'

'I wasn't. So Pete was the first to be targeted?'

'Thing is, we don't know if it was Pete or just whoever was

next to get back to the hub. Candace and Liz were only half an hour ahead of him.'

Finally, Hamish properly met Ben's eyes. 'Except Kyle won't hurt Lizzie. Not until the time comes for him to realise she'll never bow to his demands. We have to kill him to stop him and then she'll be free.'

'We're going to have a team meeting very soon and pin this bastard down.'

The corners of Hamish's lips rose for a second. 'I'm offering my services to put this bastard down. Sir.'

'Pretty sure I said pin.' Ben grinned. 'Are you willing to continue working with Liz? I'd rather not stand her down with so much at stake but—'

'I have no intention of taking it further. But I'm loyal. Ben? I promise you, I'm loyal.'

THIRTY-ONE

There'd never been a more sombre group than those around the table right now. Everyone had a stool because Ben kept saying people should sit. Meg figured it was his way of mothering a broken team. For once she was happy to perch on a stool rather than stand at the end of the table.

Reuben was at the other end and watchful. It was the only word she could apply to his demeanour. Whatever Ben had said in their closed-door meeting, Reuben was different. His eyes would stop on someone and narrow, then move to another. When Liz emerged from the kitchen with a coffee, he watched her all the way across the room and only took his stool when she sat.

Liz looked awful. The blood was all gone but her eyes were haunted and skin pale.

I want to bundle you up in a warm blanket and put you somewhere safe.

Candace cleared her throat and all eyes turned to her.

'Before we start, I've just got off the phone with a doctor friend at Royal Melbourne Hospital. Pete is undergoing a series of tests to look for swelling or bleeding on the brain. He's conscious. Broken bones. There'll be further news later today including an indication of visiting protocols. I've spoken to his mother who is making arrangements to come to Melbourne.'

A chorus of 'thank goodness' and 'that is hopeful' and 'his poor mum' rose until Ben spoke again.

'I know we all feel we should be at the hospital but for now, catching those responsible for hurting Pete comes first.' Ben spoke evenly. 'We didn't see this attack coming. Our response was the best it could be in the circumstances. Mistakes were made and we are learning from them.'

Liz and Hamish stared at each other across the table. Meg had no idea if they'd spoken since Liz lost it, or if this was fixable. Thank goodness Phoebe hadn't been here to witness the confrontation because seeing Liz treat a friend like a foe was bad enough for Meg. It unsettled everyone. This was twice Liz had physically handled Hamish but to be fair, the first time she'd believed him to be a kidnapper and was protecting civilians.

My beautiful team is hurting.

Ben looked around at them all. 'I've asked Phoebe to stay home for now. She has a security guard assigned to what is already a secure building and has a protocol to follow. We have to manage risk first and foremost which might include pairing up if outside the building. Meg, Jeff and Candace will also have security guards as of this evening.'

'I don't need one,' Candace said. 'You know that nobody is getting into my apartment.'

'What if there's an anonymous call saying there's a fire. A bomb?' Liz's voice was tense. 'What if Kyle simply waits until you leave for the day?'

'Hamish is handling the assignment of security and will speak to each of us following the meeting,' Ben said. He gazed at Liz as though expecting a response but she just nodded, ever so slightly. He continued. 'Meg, where are we with information?'

'Actually, there's a fair bit. Thanks to our excellent surveillance here, we've pinpointed Kyle's moves from his first appearance to last. I've sent footage to everyone's tablet so please view it today in order to familiarise yourself with his ability to use disguise. Now I've watched at length from every available angle and believe he was in plain sight for many hours. Take a look.' She brought some footage up on the vertical screen. 'This was early this morning, before daylight.'

She zoomed in to an abandoned warehouse up and over the road. It was one the team checked regularly for any retaliatory cameras and the like and was always clean. But in its doorway was a dark shape.

'This is Kyle. See the trolley just near him? He wasn't asleep, just watching with binoculars and a camera. And he got there by walking past the building.'

Annette stood to look more closely. 'He was there all day? We drove past him.'

'The homeless are often invisible. So are the elderly and a few other demographics,' Candace said. 'Society needs a reboot but until then people like Kyle can take advantage of it. And Liz… it is quite likely this is how he knew where you were at different times. If we had time to look, we might discover him lurking in plain sight near enough your apartment to easily follow you. Any of us, really.'

Liz abruptly stood and walked to the side of the room which overlooked the warehouse.

Annette made to follow and Candace waved for her to stay.

'Now that I have this data I am running several searches as well as alerting some of our allies in different areas of law enforcement.' Meg needed to get through this. There was so much to cover. 'I still want to go and look at the scene of the attack on Pete but there's a team there right now. Jeff will be kept in the loop and has arranged for us to have access to trace, wherever possible, for our own testing. Enquiries are being made at buildings near the scene to obtain potential footage.'

Ben's phone rang and he excused himself.

'I guess while the boss is busy, I'll keep yapping on about the power of surveillance. We've had a lead pay off and it is completely thanks to Pete.'

The windows in the hub were all one-way vision. Properly done rather than the cheap jobs which allowed the 'wrong' side to still see in if there was a light on. Liz stared at the doorway a couple of hundred metres away.

You were there all along. You waited and watched and planned.

She'd driven past her father twice today.

If she was any kind of decent cop she'd have clocked him. At least, clocked there was someone there. Where was her compassion, if nothing else? It wasn't like her to ignore anyone in need.

Liz was listening to the conversation. She just couldn't be part of it right now. Her heart was heavy with shame and embarrassment and disgust at her professional lapse. She was better than that.

Meg began talking about Pete. About him being responsible for a lead.

I can't help Pete. But I can continue what he started.

She returned to the stool. Jeff was on one side and he discreetly took the hand she'd dropped on her leg and squeezed it.

'Our general email account received a lovely letter from one Mrs Betty Carrigan. She explained that she'd spoke to a delightful police officer named Pete McNamara who'd been lurking around her house a little while ago.'

A still image of a pretty garden appeared on the screen as Ben took his seat again.

'This is the property which backs on to Heberden House?' Reuben spoke for the first time since the meeting had begun. 'Pete left his card under their door.'

'Correct. It is also the property he identified on our first visit as being of interest.'

'Why of interest?' Annette asked.

Reuben's steady gaze was encouraging Liz to be involved. Or maybe he was trying to work out why he had such a good relationship with such an idiot. She wanted to cry and shout and run. Particularly, she needed to run.

Liz lifted her chin. 'He is an observer, Annette. You know this. Pete looked at the contours of the land in and around the mansion which is flattish, for the most part. But this property of about half a hectare backs onto a part of the wall which is lower there. He thought it offered a potential site where someone might climb without the need for a ladder or assistance from another person.'

'When we returned and found a broken lock, Pete and I had a quick look inside then went to secure externally. Almost immediately we found some tracks which included a clear footprint, so Pete continued to where he believed the intruder would go and I made a cast.' Reuben looked at Jeff. 'Do we have anything on it?'

Jeff beamed. 'We certainly do. It is from a female. Of this I am certain based not only on the size of the print but structure of the foot and depth to gauge someone of around fifty-two kilos weight. I've narrowed the type of shoe to one of three brands and have sent queries to my lab for assistance.'

'May I ask something?' Hamish glanced at Liz as if checking she wasn't about to fly over the table and strangle him. 'Is there anything on the print from the bottom of the well? And the piece of fabric found there.'

'That didn't yield much other than it was cotton and torn from a larger piece. Given there is a door it may be a piece of clothing was caught and ripped off.' Jeff was deadly serious now. 'What I can tell you is the evidence cast from the well shows a boot print wide and deep enough to indicate a male wearer. And it is relatively fresh.'

'Fresh? Like, really recent?' Annette asked. 'How many people are using that property for their own needs, I wonder.'

'I estimate this print is a few months old – no more than three

– but you make a good point. At least two people have accessed the property who have no reason to be there.'

Kyle, perhaps? And the mysterious Kirsten?

Meg drew attention back to the screen. 'Mrs Carrigan attached a series of short clips to her email. She mentioned her husband is good with technology and I have to agree. Each is cropped approximately ten seconds either side of movement and the camera quality is excellent.'

There were five different clips which were taken from three cameras, all at the front of the house. Watched together, they showed a figure appear along a fence, checking over their shoulder and then sprinting to the corner of the house. The person checked in the direction where they came from, then several attempts were made to open windows and there was a rushed searched under pot plants and the welcome mat, presumably to find a key. Finally, the person ran to the electronic gate and easily swung their body over it.

'She's fit and strong,' Candace observed. 'Did you notice her right ear?'

With a nod, Meg brought up several stills, all zoomed in on the woman at different angles.

Annette gasped. 'Oh my… she's older, of course, but that is the woman from Bonner Gallery. When I was sixteen.'

Liz felt sick to her stomach. The woman was familiar despite the stern, almost cold expression in this image. It was all eerily familiar, the music and the aroma of cocktails and finger food. And dancing. This woman – hair loose around bare shoulders – dancing with Kyle at Heberden House. She felt eyes on her. Reuben with those worry lines back.

Candace pointed to one clear photo of the woman face on. Her hair was back in a tight bun which exposed both ears. On the left was a drop earring which might well be a partner to the one found in the cellar. And the right ear was bare.

'I heard back from the maker of the sword earring,' Jeff said.

'They were able to provide details of the sale, as they keep hand written records back to the eighteen hundreds.'

Meg was almost bouncing off her seat. 'And thanks to Jeff's work and all the VHS tapes, and Lyndall for helping identify people and Pete for finding this footage plus all of us because we are awesome… meet Kirsten Bonner. Younger sister of Marcus Bonner, probably heir to the gallery, and currently in Australia from Germany on a tourist visa. According to my source, she hasn't been back here since 2012 and before that, 1995.'

'So why was she in the cellar of Heberden House?' Hamish asked. 'Actually, I'm going to suggest it was to access the room behind the triple brick wall. And steal the contents. After all we know there were a number of empty crates, so had she already been in there?'

'Meg, do we know anything else about Mrs Carrigan's house? Were they just out for the morning or longer?' Ben frowned. 'I'm wondering if Kirsten Bonner had been progressively emptying the room with multiple trips over the wall.'

'It would explain why the crates were at the bottom of the wall. If she was using the Carrigan property as an access point.' Hamish looked pleased with himself.

'I shall email her with some questions and see if her husband would look back further.' Meg picked up her tablet. 'I'll send it now.'

'But it doesn't make sense!' Annette pointed at the image on the screen. 'I know she was involved in the gallery but why be in Heberden House after all these years?'

Liz stood. 'I know why.'

THIRTY-TWO

Thank goodness you're back with us.

All through the team meeting Ben had kept an eye on Liz, willing her to get involved in the discussion. She'd spoken once, to answer Annette earlier. But now there was colour in her cheeks again and a fire in her eyes. Subdued, yes, but a fire nonetheless.

The energy of the entire team seemed to lift, even Hamish, their attention on her as she stalked to the window where she'd been for half the meeting.

'Most of us drove past Kyle at least once today. I did three times. Didn't see him. None of us did because we weren't looking. I don't know about anyone else but when I go home at night I check my apartment and I mean really check it. With my gun in my hand. I look in every place a man could hide expecting him to break into my apartment. I watch for him everywhere and yet there he was. Right in front of me and not for the first time.'

She wandered back.

'When we uncovered links to the European crime network which Marcus Bonner was so heavily involved with, there was much which pointed to Kyle being the Australian head of it. Entwined with his white supremacy leanings, snippets of information from people such as Tony Shaw and other minions, and Kyle's uncanny way of knowing some of our moves… is there anyone here who doesn't agree with that summary?'

A murmur went through the team and all heads shook. They'd all reached the same conclusions. Candace had her hands on the edge of the table, gripping it, leaning forward with her face unreadable.

'There's no doubt he was closely connected to Marcus. And Lyndall's kidnapping appeared to have been his doing. We saw footage of him apparently giving Marcus instructions and Lyndall overheard Marcus talking to someone we all believed to be my father. But was it? Why would Kyle go to the trouble of turning himself into an old fisherman, complete with decrepit trawler, and pulling Lyndall out of the bay if he'd engineered her being abducted? Why?'

Hamish raised a hand as if in school, then dropped it. 'Liz, sorry but are you suggesting Kyle is not running a crime network?'

'Yes.'

'He used them for his own nefarious purposes.'

Liz smiled at Hamish. 'So close, mate. So close.'

Hamish flushed bright red and nodded vigorously and Ben felt sorry for him. The young man had feelings for Liz. Probably a kind of hero worship. Her approval mattered more than Ben had realised which presented problems he couldn't think about just now.

Reuben tilted his head. 'So Kyle had a kind of influence in Marcus' organisation. Or he was some kind of consultant. Or… ah.'

'Oh my dear Lord.' Candace jumped to her feet, agitated. 'How on earth did I miss it.'

'Miss what?' Annette stared at Candace, her hands clasped together. 'I'm generally good with puzzles but you've all lost me. What is Kyle's position?'

Candace took a quick breath. 'Kyle is obsessed with Liz. We

all know this. But I'd wrongly seen this as completely to do with his beliefs because little Liz was his golden haired child, unlike his wife and older daughter, who he considered inferior. That has a factor, certainly, but isn't the whole picture.'

Slowly taking her seat again, Liz looked directly at Ben. She was hurting badly – he knew her well enough to see the pain in her eyes. It was Pete and then the terrible judgement of her actions with Hamish all compounded by what she'd worked out about her father. He hadn't caught up yet but something was falling into place. He smiled at Liz to encourage her.

Go on. We have you.

'Kyle Moorland is many things,' Liz began. 'And many people. We know him as Kyle – my father, Garry Ford – who he killed to become, and Etienne Finn. The last we have little on yet and it begs the question of whether there are more identities to find and which one is actually him? Annette, you asked why Kirsten Bonner has been in Heberden House so recently and it is such a good question. But I want to ask why *Kyle* was there.'

This caused a ripple of renewed interest.

'Meg is working hard to find out more about Kirsten Bonner and for that matter, what tied her brother to the Baxters? *That* is the problem we haven't solved. Who killed them and why? I'm wondering if the couple were part of the European crime network.' Liz took a sip of coffee which had sat for too long and wrinkled her face at it. 'Thanks for bearing with me. I'm working it out as I talk but more and more is coming together in my mind as I do.'

'You are doing well.' Candace sat again.

'Doesn't feel it. Nothing has felt right since Pete… anyway. Kyle is obsessed with me, yes. At a level of obsession which Candace would give a name to. Why would it just be me? I believe it isn't.' She looked down for a moment then seemed to pull it all together. 'Phoebe and I saw my father – who Lyndall recognised as Etienne Finn – at a Baxter dinner party at their Melbourne home in 1991 on one of the VHS tapes. Kirsten was there. I have memories of watching a black tie event at Heberden House when I was little. I don't know my age but under five. In my memories, which Candace has been helping me work through, I saw Kyle dancing. And he was dancing with Kirsten.'

There was a sharp gasp from Annette. Hamish muttered something about it all making sense. And Candace put her head into her hands.

Liz laughed. A short, angry laugh. 'Tell me I'm crazy but what if my father is obsessed with Kirsten Bonner? And what if his obsession tied him to a crime network he doesn't even like? I think she is here after so many years because her brother died and left a huge mess and my father is expected to help clean it up.'

Candace straightened. 'Kyle is caught between his two great obsessions. And that makes for an incredibly dangerous human. I think you are completely correct, Liz.'

Annette announced she needed a cigarette and took off.

'In pairs, people.' Ben said. 'Someone go with her. Please.'

Hamish followed. He'd at least share a puff with her and they could both settle their nerves.

Liz wanted to go for a long run. What would happen if she did? If Pete was here he'd go with her but complain at every step and just for once, she wanted that with her whole heart.

Her theory about Kyle sat well. Not just with Liz but the rest of the team. Now they needed to find proof and enough evidence to prosecute. Kirsten Bonner had made a mistake returning to Australia, as Meg would see to it that customs and the Australian Federal Police had every bit of information about her and would arrest her at an airport.

Except... what if like Kyle she had multiple identities?

'Liz. A minute please?'

She'd expected the call since seeing the tears in Hamish's eyes. Messing up had never been so personal. Liz would deal with being fired. With being removed from the team she'd come to love. One day she might even sleep without beating herself up for such a dreadful lapse of judgement. But if Pete died…

Ben closed the door behind them both and gestured for her to sit. She did. He checked his emails and phone and she waited.

'Update on Pete. Going into surgery tonight to repair breaks to bones in one arm. No sign of brain swelling or a bleed. Multiple broken ribs. Massive bruising. He's been bloody lucky.'

Liz felt the tears coming and swallowed hard. It didn't make a difference and they trailed down her cheeks.

'Cry. We all have, Lizzie. We love Pete and when he's back I'm going to make sure he understands never to get on a damned motorcycle without a helmet.'

That made her laugh. Kind of. She brushed her face.

'You've made a compelling argument about Kyle. Meg is trying to locate Kirsten Bonner right now and once we do, our position becomes stronger. What I need to know from you is whether you are able to continue working right now.'

'Because of how I reacted to Hamish. Fair enough. If you want me to go then—'

'Did I say that? I'm asking about your health. Mental and physical. Hamish has no intention of taking anything further so the subject can be shelved for now. My priority is keeping this team safe and preventing any more attacks, and for that I need strength and focus. If you would prefer to go to the hospital to watch over Pete and get some rest of your own, then that's fine. Just tell me.'

His voice was even but Ben looked as worried as she felt. And she'd added to his problems.

'I am so angry, boss. So. Damned. Angry.' She drew in a long breath. 'Of course I want to be with Pete but it won't make a difference. His family are coming and if he's in surgery he won't know I'm there. Tell me what to do and I won't fail you.'

'Find Reuben and the two of you rework everyone's task load. We need to cover Pete's and adjust with the new information. If I can have a list of outstanding enquiries in the next half hour?'

'Not a problem. Can we increase security for my family as well as Lyndall, Vince, and Melanie?'

Their safety had been constantly on her mind. Kyle's message might extend to anyone in her network.

'Already done.'

Liz checked the time on her way out. Almost five. In an hour the sun would set and make movement outside the hub a little bit more dangerous.

Reuben was in the conference room with a whiteboard and laptop. He was writing on the former and paused to give Liz a long, searching look. Was he disappointed in her or weighing up the chances she might attack him?

Putting down the marker, he embraced her, holding her firmly in his arms for what felt a long time. Then he stepped back. 'People need at least nine hugs a day, each of more than twenty seconds duration.'

'Even prickly, unhuggable people?'

'If you mean you… cut it out. Or I'll hug you again.'

Her heart lightened a little. 'Ben told me to work with you to reallocate the workload. How can I help?'

'Read from the spreadsheet.' He tapped the whiteboard. 'As you can see I've made a column for each of us including Pete. Let's get everything up here and we'll start using the coloured markers to draw arrows.'

Ten minutes later the whiteboard was complete and it was depressing just how much still needed doing.

'Red pen to cross stuff off?' Reuben picked it up. 'I can see a dozen areas we can cull for now. Such as the origin of the earring.' He ran a line through it. 'Here's another which you aren't aware of. It would have been raised at the team meeting but too much else needed attending. There was a zoom call with Bob earlier. The cleaner who contacted Phoebe?'

'He'd said something about not understanding why the other police didn't speak to him after the event.'

Reuben sat beside Liz and searched on his laptop. 'Here it is. Bob clearly remembers the murders as he was a casual cleaner and handyman at Heberden House. He was brought in a few days after the deaths to assist with removing a number of items damaged by blood.'

'What? Removed where?'

'To the tip.' He glanced up with a grim expression. 'This included the hall runner, mattress, and bed.'

'But... good grief! Even if all forensic work had been completed, given the gravity of the crime those things should have been properly packed and stored. Is he sure they went to the tip?'

'Yup. He drove them there. And then another cop fronted up to give each member of the staff an envelope filled with cash. His amount was five thousand dollars. They were told it had been authorised by Inspector Baxter and it was made clear not to speak to media or do further interviews with police without a lawyer present. Inside the envelope was the name and phone number of the lawyer to call. In case.'

Liz's mind raced. It sounded familiar.

'So I'm crossing off that we need to interview Bob and have sent the info to Annette to cross-reference to the police reports she still has. What's wrong?'

'Something... about a cop and money.' Liz jumped up. 'I need my tablet.'

Reuben followed Liz as she hurried to her desk. The room was busy with everyone working at their desks other than Phoebe and Pete. She ignored the feelings which rose and opened her tablet.

'What are you looking for?' He watched over her shoulder.

'Lyndall... Ben and I spoke to her a while' after she was kidnapped and she told us a lot about the time when she was trying to negotiate with Marcus who wanted the microchip returned. Her husband and older son were killed and then her remaining son taken. Wait, here it is.'

She'd been going through a transcript of the interview.

'She reported the abduction of her son and the murder of the friend who was minding him. A police officer arrived and handed Lyndall a bag and told her to disappear if she wanted her son to remain safe. There was enough money for her to build her house with its panic room and stay under the radar for almost three decades.'

Liz gazed up at Reuben.

'The same police officer? We always thought someone in the force had interfered with the investigation.'

'Sorry to interrupt but I think it was a coincidence.' Annette was at the end of the workstation. 'I got Reuben's notes and remembered reading allegations about those envelopes in the files. It was investigated but apparently Inspector Baxter *was* responsible.'

Reuben shook his head. 'How does that make any sense though? He'd just lost his beloved parents and would hardly be worrying about the staff. Particularly as there was an implication that acceptance of the money guaranteed media silence. He wanted the world to know. For people to come forward with information.'

'Happy to take another look. I'm certain though that the police officers in both cases were never named.'

Annette hurried to her desk.

'I need to get Ben the list of outstanding tasks pretty soon,' Liz said. 'Do you mind if we keep going on that?'

And I'll keep puzzling over this police officer who hands people money because something about it is terribly wrong.

THIRTY-THREE

'I've found the car! Not a car but you know what I mean.' Meg couldn't get the words out fast enough. Everyone was staring at her. 'The one which hit Pete!'

The response was immediate and chaotic with a chair hitting the ground and others left to spin into walls. Even Ben and Candace, who were both in their offices, got to their feet and followed the crowd.

Meg met them all at the table and had images up before the last person arrived.

'What's going on, Meg?' Ben asked.

'One of my searches paid off. It was for vehicles travelling away from the crash site, after the time Pete was hit. There are cameras which have to be passed no matter which route was taken. And there were five possible routes. I have had it running backwards from about two hours ago in case they took cover for a while.'

'But we don't have any witnesses who could identify the colour, let alone make,' Annette said. 'There's just offices and warehouses around the scene but then it gets a lot busier toward the main roads.'

'Yes, but my program was also searching for a matching vehicle entering the area. Now, we know Kyle arrived across the road on foot before daylight today so I worked off the assumption he was also the driver. I set parameters to allow for him to securely park, unload whatever crap he had to create his disguise, and reach his destination. It isn't a perfect way to search but it was based on the best information I had.'

Liz had gone very quiet again, her colour draining like it had earlier. In some ways Meg was surprised she was still working rather than being at the hospital, except she knew Liz. Hamish moved around the table and stood next to Liz, his arm going around her shoulder for a moment.

The entire team was watching this small but incredibly strong sign of allegiance (better word) as Liz leaned her head against Hamish. It wasn't for long but once he dropped his arm and she straightened, they exchanged a quick smile.

About time. Can't have my peeps in distress or at odds.

'Right. So I've had a decent result with this vehicle.'

She pointed to a black RAM. 'Common enough to be ignored. Big enough to cause damage without wrecking itself. This one was parked in that alley at one this morning. At least, it passed one of the cameras then. And it left two minutes after Pete's bike was hit.'

I've never been so happy with my life choices as this moment.

Years of education, training, and experience all came together to find the best lead yet to finding Kyle Moorland.

'So he was targeting Pete? How would he know he was on a motorcycle?' Hamish asked.

'Actually, no. I think he was prepared to adapt, like always. Had a person on foot got close he might well have run straight into them. Less likely if it was one of the BearCats. We know he's patient.' Meg had had enough of this man.

'This is brilliant work.' Candace peered at the image. 'What next?'

'Well, I've extracted a number plate which oddly is not stolen. The vehicle is registered to a company on the Mornington Peninsula. Same address as that of Bonner Gallery.'

'He is tied up with her,' Liz murmured. 'With Kirsten Bonner.'

'So it would seem.'

Annette looked excited. 'Are we going to the Gallery now? I'm more than ready to find these people.'

'I wouldn't suggest wasting resources that way. Kyle is smart. He might have overlooked the fact that I'm smarter but it feels unlikely he'd be hanging around the gallery right now.'

'I agree with you, Meg. For all we know Kyle might still be playing a game with us. Or at least covering the bases in case we identified the vehicle.' Reuben had his thinking face on. 'Is there any way to find it now?'

'Is that a serious question? I'm already running so many new searches you wouldn't believe it. It takes a bit of time to get approval to access some cameras but once I do, finding where he went will be my priority.'

The energy in the room was palpable. People were excited.

Ben's phone beeped and he checked the message. The colour drained from his face and he almost dropped the phone. 'No...'

Candace took the phone. 'It is an image of inside a restaurant. There's no message.'

His voice raspy with emotion, Ben spoke. 'Ellie's restaurant. And there *is* a message, look at the blackboard.'

Meg took over, casting the image to the big screen. The blackboard used for specials had been overlayed with text from the sender's phone. And the words were chilling.

Guess who is next on the menu?

Beneath the words was an arrow which pointed directly at Ellie.

• • •

Liz's instincts and training kicked in. 'Ben, go and phone Ellie right now. Ensure she and Michael are safe without scaring them. We'll arrange for a local unit to go visit.'

He nodded and rushed to his office.

'Annette, please get the local cops to drop by. Send them our best headshots of Kyle and of Kirsten and advise them to stay cool and just take a quiet look around.'

'On it.'

'Meg. Any chance of finding out when the photo was taken?'

'Minute I get his phone I can tell you. But we shouldn't assume Kyle took it or sent it. I'll go stand over Ben.'

Candace gave one of her enigmatic smiles. 'Impressive delegation. What do you need from me?'

Nobody is going to touch Ellie or Michael.

She gazed around. Hamish and Reuben were the only ones left apart from Candace. With Phoebe and Jeff securely at home and Pete… well it left the team short.

'Aren't we supposed to have some assistance from the other operation? Now would be a great time. Kyle has had plenty of time to get to Gippsland though. If he left the city immediately after his attack on Pete, then he'd be down there in just over two hours. For all we know he's sitting there waiting for a pizza.'

'We need to go,' Hamish said. 'Helicopter is best.'

'Not until we have better information than one doctored image. Reuben, your take?'

'I feel like Hamish does and want nothing more than to get down there and find the bastard. But that's a normal response and it splits the team which might be the whole motive for this. Ben needs to go. With his family threatened he's going to worry unless he is certain they're safe.'

Liz agreed. Whether this was yet another game of Kyle's or deadly serious, the team had no choice but to treat it as the latter.

'Okay, unless Ben says otherwise, we'll remain here and continue our work. Candace, would you send me the report you've been working on regarding our new take on Kyle?'

'It isn't complete but I'll go and send it to you.'

'Hamish and Reuben? Please prep two BearCats. If we have to move I want to do it fast.'

'Yes, ma'am!' Hamish almost whooped and tore off in the direction of the door.

Reuben rolled his eyes at the other man and followed at a normal pace.

Liz rested her palms on the table and closed her eyes. For the first time in a long time she was functioning at full capacity, her mind clear and emotions buried. Today she'd seen her best friend almost die. She'd treated another team member abysmally. And she'd hit rock bottom. Later… much later, she'd work through it all. But for now her team needed her.

Meg tapped on Ben's window and gestured for Liz.

He was barking orders on the landline and she had his mobile and stepped out of the office to speak to Liz.

'The image has been passed through several devices before being sent to Ben, however I'm tracking back now. The good news is it appears to have been moving between phones for at least a day, possibly longer.'

'So someone took the photo a while ago. There's no immediate threat to Ellie and Michael?'

'Correct. Ellie has checked the restaurant and has only locals in there right now. People who she's known for ages.'

'You said that's the good news?'

'Well this might be good as well but just as likely another red herring. The image message was sent from a location a few minutes from Heberden House.'

'Then we need to go and take a look.'

Annette joined them as Ben got off his call.

'Local police are popping around to see Ellie,' Annette said. 'I think you should contact them as well, Ben. Tell them what else you need.'

He began packing up his laptop. 'That's good, thanks. I've

arranged a helicopter to get me down there because I want to be back here tonight. Ellie and Michael will come with me and I've arranged for a safe house to be prepared. Something access-friendly for Michael.'

'But if Kyle isn't even there anymore, is it necessary?' Annette asked.

Meg frowned and glanced up for a second then her eyes returned to the screen as she did what it was she did to find information.

'Liz, a quick word?'

Annette and Meg got the hint and returned to their worksta-tions. Candace came out of her office. 'I've just sent you what I've done of the report, Liz.'

Ben kept packing as he spoke. 'I shouldn't be going and I'm worried this is nothing more than another ploy to split us up. Liz, you have final say while I'm gone but don't hesitate to run anything by me. I should be contactable most of the time. Treat Reuben as your 2IC. Candace, unless this building is on fire, you and Meg don't leave the building overnight. You know how to access the basement if all else fails.'

The basement was beneath the carpark and contained a forti-fied bunker.

'Meg says the image was sent from near Heberden House,' Liz said. 'I want to take a look.'

Briefcase done, Ben stopped and gazed at Liz. 'As would I. Risky.'

'No more than anything else, with all due respect. Kyle has no idea if we've tracked the phone which sent the message. It may not even belong to him but one of his people… if he still has any. I'd get Reuben to send up a drone from a distance. Have Hamish with me and take a discreet look around.'

'Talk to them both and Meg. If she believes that is a viable lead then follow it. I have to go.'

'Safe travels, Ben.'

'Same to you, Lizzie. And keep me informed.'

With Ben gone, everyone gathered in the conference room to eat. Reuben and Candace had put a platter together and it took little time to empty it.

The whiteboard had been pushed back a bit but all of the team had read it during the meal. Meg got up and wrote more beneath her name.

- *Find police officer who handed money to Lyndall and HH staff*
- *Track history of Kirsten Bonner's Australian trips*
- *Send flowers to Pete*

'Flowers from us all, of course. The minute he's allowed them.' She sat again.

'Meg, I've already gone back through the boxes Hamish and I collected with the original police reports,' Annette said. 'It was definitely Inspector Baxter who arranged the money. I guess he felt sorry for the staff, as most would lose their jobs.'

'Oh, I know you've been thorough. And I'm not surprised that's what is in the reports as we've suspected a mole in the police force regarding the case. Hamish sent through some excellent indicators of where we should start looking but there's not been time yet. But when we consider Lyndall being handed a boatload of money from a police officer and that she was also connected to Marcus Bonner… it kinda makes me jumpy.'

Me too. This is a serious connection we need found.

Meg's tablet lit up. 'Okay. Number plate recognition software has caught the RAM approximately five kilometres from

Heberden House. Let me check the phone co-ords… pretty good match.'

Liz was on her feet only seconds before Reuben. Hamish joined them with a broad smile.

'Are we going hunting?'

THIRTY-FOUR

The decision to take Annette was last minute but sensible. With Reuben managing a drone, three people on the ground improved the odds of finding Kyle. Or whoever else was there. The four of them spent a few minutes with a map of the property making a loose plan and pointing out the landmarks Annette needed to be aware of. While Liz drove, she covered off more.

'I know it sounds like I'm repeating myself but you're the only one whose never been to Heberden House and now you're going in the dark with a potential killer lurking around.'

'No, I appreciate it, Liz. I've studied the property a lot, like we all have, but you've got more experience there than anyone. Even as a child.'

'Which I have no proper memories of.'

'So what do you remember?'

'It's weird because the first time we went to the house I kept looking at the well from a top room. There's no reason on earth I'd have been near it but then again, why was I there during a party?'

'Can't even imagine not knowing that stuff. Your dad took you to an adult event and you were upstairs, watching the dancing. Didn't you long to join them? All the beautiful gowns and handsome men and delicious food. I would have loved that, I think. But I never got to have fun as a kid. My father raised me but he was busy making a living so I more or less raised myself. Not something I'd do to a kid.'

Liz glanced at Annette. 'I'm so sorry. We've known each for so long but I really don't know much about you outside of work.'

'You never asked. We're alike, Liz. All I ever wanted was my mother in my life and you missed out on having your father.'

The BearCat ahead slowed and they both pulled over. They were a couple of kilometres from the property. Hamish jumped out of the front vehicle and ran to climb in behind Liz.

'Brisk outside. Reuben needs twenty minutes to set up and get eyes on the property.'

'Where are we?' Annette peered through the windscreen as Reuben drove away. 'It looks deserted.'

'No houses anywhere along here.'

'I'm dying for a toilet stop.'

'Good grief, what are you, three?' Hamish burst into laughter. 'Did you make your dad stop all the time on road trips?'

'Very funny. We didn't do road trips. But I am going to find a private spot out there so don't leave without me.' Annette grabbed her bag and slipped out into the night, vanishing through some bushes behind them.

'Why did you ask about her dad? Not her mother?'

'Because she was raised by a single dad.'

Do I know nothing about anyone in the team?

'She worshipped him. Followed his career path and everything.'

'Wait, her father's a cop?'

'Was. Died ages ago.' Hamish looked at her in the rear vision mirror. 'Liz…'

'I'm sorry, Hamish. I am so damned sorry and would take it all back in the heartbeat. You are a loyal and brilliant member of this team and I was out of line.'

He shuffled across to better see her and she turned to look at him face to face.

'I accept your apology. But I feel I should tell you I was just going to ask if you'd heard any more news about Pete.'

'Oh. Let me message Candace as she is getting updates from her doctor friend.'

That gave her a moment to collect herself. Blurting out her apology was not the way she wanted to approach it but a weight had lifted. Hamish was smiling.

Candace replied as Annette returned.

'Good timing. Candace said Pete's heavily sedated and will have surgery tomorrow to repair and cast the arm which bore the brunt of the collision. He'd nestled his head between both arms as he came off the bike and while that saved his life, it smashed some bones.'

Annette just nodded while Hamish returned to his seat.

'We'll drive closer and get organised.'

Hamish was right. The air *was* cold and Liz added a heavy jacket over her protective gear and found a black beanie. The jacket had a hood but with an earpiece in, she preferred a light head covering.

They were closing in on the gates of Heberden House, moving slowly whenever the moon was covered. Each carried multiple weapons and a quick conversation before leaving the BearCat down the road had confirmed each was prepared to shoot, but to injure unless absolutely necessary.

'The chain is off. Someone's cut it.' Hamish's voice came through Liz's earpiece. 'Shall I open the gate?'

'No. Reuben, report.'

'The Ram is parked in the old stables. Drone's a long way back doing a circle around the main building. Lights are all off but hoping for some sign of activity.'

'Would you loop around near the gate please? The chain's been cut.'

Is Kyle in the cellar or one of the tunnels? Is that where Kirsten runs this organisation from when she's in Australia?

What if that was the key? The Baxters were part of it and for some reason they became expendable and were murdered? And then the cover up began and never really stopped, right down to bent police.

Liz used her earpiece to speak on a private line to Meg. 'Need something from you.' She held her hand up to stop the forward progress then made another signal for the other two to melt back into the bushland along the road. She was far enough away to speak now.

'Listening.'

'Do you know who Annette's father is? As in, his police rank and posting before he died?'

'A cop? Pretty sure he was a public servant… oh crap. Police are public servants. Give me a sec.'

There was the sound of an approaching car and Liz stepped behind a tree as headlights swept around the bend. But the car did a slow U-turn and once its taillights disappeared, Liz returned to the road. Annette and Hamish were doing a good job of being invisible on the other side.

The drone was just visible near the gate and suddenly lowered, almost to grass level.

'We're going to need help, Liz. There's a body behind the first tree.' Reuben was in her ear. 'Security guard uniform. He's dead. Yeah, has to be. Shot wound above an ear.'

'Dammit. There's no sign of a car down here. Or a partner. Please request a Critical Incident Response team for immediate assistance. Hamish, Annette, remain in position.'

For a heartbeat Liz wished Ben was here. That poor guard must have been on their normal rounds and found the chain cut. He'd never have seen the shooter. Someone had dragged his body out of sight, and who knew where his car was. The drone had moved and was hovering around the front of the house.

'Liz, urgent.' It was Reuben again. 'Movement in the master bedroom. Window is open a few inches.'

'Got it. Annette and Hamish. Did you hear Reuben?'

'We're checking the body, Lizzie.'

'Wait, no.'

But the gate was being opened and two figures slipped through.

'Annette and Hamish. Seek cover. Seek cover urgently. Potential sniper. This is an order. Seek cover.'

She took off in pursuit.

'Reuben, get a light into that window now. Draw any fire.'

The drone was moving, she could hear the acceleration as she reached the gates. Up ahead were the shadows of her team between a row of trees and the stone wall. It was okay. They were in cover.

'God, Liz. Annette's father was on the team investigating both Alain's drowning and the Baxter murders.' Meg's voice rose in panic. 'I think she's the mole.'

A shot reverberated through the trees and across the open ground. Ahead, one of the shadows of the team dropped to the ground like a stone.

Hamish was slumped against the wall and a few metres away, Annette was lining up a kill shot on him.

Liz fired.

The bullet hit Annette's shoulder and her gun flew into the dark and she went down with a shriek.

A second of absolute silence.

'Officer down.'

She took Annette's weapons… the one she'd lost and two others. Using her foot Liz shoved Annette onto her back. 'You move and I will kill you.'

Hamish's eyes flickered open and shut. Blood poured from a wound in his stomach, lower than the protective vest. Liz pulled off her jacket and dropping to her knees beside him, used it to stem the flow.

'Help's coming, mate. Meg, where's the ambulance.'

'Worked… it… out. She wants to be like him. Her father.'

'Yeah. Seems so. We're going to get a bed for you next to Pete. Okay?'

'Really like you. Lizzi-beth.'

His eyes closed and his head dropped.

'No. Hamish, no.'

"I had to kill him. I'm sorry.' Annette rolled onto her side, her tears making Liz want to vomit. 'Instructions.'

There was no pulse.

'Instructions from who?'

Liz moved Hamish onto his back to start CPR, flicking on the flashlight on the front of her vest long enough to see his lower stomach was haemorrhaging bright red blood.

'He's got no pulse. I think the bullet hit an artery. There's so much blood…'

'Check again, Liz.' This was Candace. 'I'll talk you through it all.'

As she followed each step Liz's heart shattered. He was truly gone. She covered his head and upper body with her jacket.

Another shot, this one near the house. The drone exploded into pieces.

'Tell me, Annette.' Liz forced her to sit upright despite a cry of pain. 'Who's instructions?'

'Kirsten.'

'But why? What the hell has been happening all these years?'

A vicious expression of hatred filled Annette's face. 'My father worked for yours. Always working. Risking his life and mine. Died for your father. Kirsten asked me to take his job and I couldn't say no. She's like a mother, even though usually absent. But I hate your father. I hate you.'

'Me?'

'Golden girl. Got to go to the ball.'

Several shots reverberated around them and Annette's head flung to one side. Liz threw herself flat. The shooter wasn't in the house.

'God, Liz!' Meg sounded panicked.

'She's dead as well. Finding cover.'

There's a second shooter. I have to get to the house.

THIRTY-FIVE

'I'm coming to find you.'

'Negative, Reuben. You have a second drone so get it working because I need eyes in the air.'

He swore. He never swore. But then a grunt conveyed his compliance. Hopefully.

The air was thick with the horror and smell of death.

There was no time to grieve. Not yet.

Liz found a thick tree trunk and squatted behind it to talk to the team, her voice low.

'I'm going to assume everyone heard Annette's confession. She said that Kirsten instructed her to kill Hamish and now I don't know if she's here alone, or with Kyle. Or not even here. Do we have an ETA on CIRT?'

'Ninety minutes. Please wait for them.'

She didn't answer and turned off the earpiece. Her heart thudded and her nerves were on fire.

An eerie quiet had fallen.

No nightbirds or wind in the trees or distant traffic.

Just Liz and her heartbeat.

Straightening carefully, she watched the sky. The clouds

would part every so often spilling moonlight on the grounds. Moving at the wrong moment might prove fatal.

During a dark phase she sprinted between the trees and wall until she was only twenty metres or so from the house. Nothing moved there. No light. No sounds.

Except there was a drone again. Reuben had it too close and was running the risk of drawing fire. Perhaps that was his intention but without the drone she was completely alone. She used night vision binoculars to scan. Nothing.

Where are you, Dad?

Getting inside the mansion was her only choice. Waiting for back-up was pointless because Kyle would have the advantage and use it when it suited him. She had a set of keys and could access anywhere on the property short of the doors inside the well and the shaft hidden in the stable. If anyone was using the passage then she'd not find them on her own.

The moon disappeared and Liz ran, covering the distance in seconds and flattening herself against the side of the building.

Her phone vibrated and softly buzzed and she quickly turned off the sound, reading the last of several messages. This was from Meg.

Stand down! Wait for backup – this is Ben's order. Confirm.

Soon. I'm safe for now.

She edged toward the back of the building and glanced around. There was a glint of metal inside the old stables building – presumably the vehicle used to mow down Pete.

I will avenge you.

Liz let herself in through the door to the mud room. It was

unlocked. Annette must have made copies of the new keys to give to her masters. The hallway was quiet. She checked her handgun again.

Clearing rooms as she moved, Liz went as far as the wall the men had destroyed and was working her way back when the music began. If this was a memory, then the timing couldn't be worse. She waited and nothing changed so she crept to where she could see the grand foyer. In the dark, two people danced.

She sank back and messaged Reuben, not prepared to talk using the earpiece.

I'm inside. Kyle and Kirsten are dancing in the grand foyer.

Wait for me.

If only she could.

The minute she stepped out in the open, light flooded the room. She blinked rapidly to adjust to the sudden glare as the couple continued their waltz.

A man in a black tuxedo and a woman in a ballgown, silvery hair soft around her shoulders. Kyle and Kirsten, their eyes on each other as though nothing was out of the ordinary.

What are you playing at?

As the music stopped, so did the dance, and Kyle bowed to Kirsten.

'Isn't she still the most beautiful woman you've ever seen?' He turned to smile at Liz like greeting a beloved daughter. 'You remember her?'

'Elizabeth didn't take to me as a child.' Kirsten spoke with a strong German accent.

And now I just hate you for what you've done.

'In my life I've had the great joy to have two perfect women in my life. Kirsten, of course. And you, Elizabeth. My greatest achievement.'

The change in the man was profound. No more the cold and calculating villain but a warm and adoring father.

Liz wanted to vomit.

'I'm arresting you both on suspicion of murder, attempted murder, kidnapping—'

Kyle threw back his head and laughed. He released Kirsten's hand and she took a few steps toward the side of the room.

'What do you want from me, Dad? What the hell has this whole game of yours been about? You've killed and injured and threatened my colleagues. My friends. You abused my mother and sister. You stole my niece. All for what?'

'For this. For my empire.' He held his arms out and slowly rotated in a circle.

Kirsten's eyebrows raised and her expression darkened.

Guess you don't agree.

'This belongs to the estate of Ronald Baxter.' Was there trouble in paradise? 'It has never belonged to you.'

'Ah, but everything in the cellar is my treasure.'

'Etienne! None of it is yours.' Kirsten's voice was sharp.

'What treasure? What empire, Dad?'

'Do you believe there's simply wine in the barrels below us? More like a fortune in gold bars, all carefully secreted by the Baxters over decades.'

'This was all for *gold*?'

'What better? Besides, they lost faith in the truth of the world so I killed them.' He half-turned to gesture at the wall. 'While Kirsten played piano, I shot them. Bang, bang.' When he turned back, there was a gun in his hand.

Now we all know what's at stake.

'Stop moving, Kirsten.' Liz raised her gun. 'I will shoot you.'

She smiled without humour and slowly drew a pearl-handled revolver from some pocket in her dress.

'I said stop. Stay still and put the weapon down.'

'You're quite safe, Elizabeth. Kirsten just enjoys displaying her smallest weapon but I'm sure if you ask nicely she'll show you her collection of sniper rifles.'

'Who shot Annette? She hated you, Kyle.'

'True, but she was useful. No, it was my true love who got tired of her. I did however appreciate the target practice with the drone.'

What monsters you both are.

'I want you both face down on the floor. Fingers locked behind your heads.'

Kyle stepped toward her and Liz turned the gun on him.

'Everything I've done since the day you were born has been for you, Elizabeth. And now is your chance, your only chance, to join me and Kirsten. To sit at our sides and enjoy the fruits of our labour. I've always loved you.'

There was a movement from Kirsten and Liz swung in her direction. The distance between the woman and Kyle was too great to keep them both in shot but he was less likely to kill her. Kirsten raised her weapon at Liz and her face was hard.

I'm going to die. It was all for nothing.

'Put it down, Kirsten. You don't get to threaten my daughter.'

'If you can't manage her, darling, then I will.' Kirsten locked the gun and pulled back on the trigger.

The bullet which whizzed by Liz came from behind and hit Kirsten between her eyes.

She dropped like a sack of potatoes.

'Nooo!' Kyle screamed and lifted his gun, spinning to find the source of the shot and honed in on Reuben, who was crouching halfway up the stairs, rifle trained on him.

Liz emptied her magazine into her father.

'Please put handcuffs on him,' Liz asked for the third time.

'He's really quite dead. I think there's a bullet in him for everyone he's ever hurt.'

Reuben had calmly taken over after Liz froze, her gun empty, the echoes of the shots slowly fading. For two dead people there was surprisingly little blood. Not like Pete.

Not even close to Hamish.

'Do you think they are vampires?'

'I think you're in shock. But if you mean the lack of blood, it was just where the bullets hit. Would you please answer your phone because there's so much talk in my earpiece I'm struggling to think.'

They sat on the stairs, Reuben's arms loosely around Liz who couldn't stop shivering. She did as he said and put the call on speaker.

The first couple of minutes was a cacophony of reprisals and questions and relieved tears from Candace and Meg. And then news.

'The place will be swarming with every unit from everywhere at any moment,' Meg said. 'It will be locked down so tight until a full new investigation is undertaken and it will be us… well, what's left of us, along with our sister team. For now though, I need one of you to get the gates fully open. I'll send through the details of the responders who are taking charge for now.'

'I'm not leaving Kyle.'

'Oh… Lizzie, I'm so sorry. I know he is your father and can't imagine what you're feeling.'

Reuben chuckled. 'Liz thinks he'll come back to life.'

'Put him in handcuffs. Ankles as well.' Candace suggested.

'I have suggested that.'

'Do it. Best to have peace of mind. Then both of you go and look after Hamish.'

The call finished, Liz leaned against Reuben and he tightened his arms. 'I let Hamish down.'

'Disagree. All of us knew the risks and we had someone

actively working against us in the team, as well as the mad genius of your father.'

I can't believe this is over. It really is over.

It was dawn before Liz was home and able to shower and dress in something not covered in blood. Ben had arrived at Heberden House in the early hours. He'd spent time with Hamish's body then begun the long job of working with other senior police to manage the situation. There was a large gathering of press outside the gates when she and Reuben finally left.

He'd been a rock. And if he'd not got to the house in time, she'd be dead and her father and Kirsten escaped again.

She stood at her balcony, holding a steaming cup of coffee and watched the sun rise.

Later she'd go to the hospital. Pete was having surgery and she'd sit in the waiting room with his mum and for a while just be someone's best friend.

The worst was behind her.

But so much death. So much heartbreak and tragedy. All because of her father, a man obsessed with greed and terrible beliefs. Before going to the hospital she was meeting up with Anna. They were free now. All of them were free.

The first rays of light peeked through city buildings.

EPILOGUE

The conference table felt far too large. Three of their own were gone, with two never returning. In the weeks following that fateful night the team had worked tirelessly. Nobody was willing to let Hamish's death be for nothing. Ben refused to take on another case until they were ready to hand everything to the relevant authorities. They were just about there.

Tonight he'd ordered pizza, and there was beer and wine on the table for the first time in ages.

He had news and wasn't sure how the team would take it.

'Shall we go around and do a quick update?' He gestured to the boxes. 'Eat, people.'

Phoebe suddenly stood and everyone looked at her.

'This doesn't feel right,' she said. 'I don't care about Annette being gone but Pete and… and Hamish.' She walked to the bar and returned with two more beer glasses.

Reuben was smiling as he opened another beer and poured a glass each for Hamish and Pete. Phoebe placed them where the men usually sat.

'What a lovely gesture, Phoebe,' Candace said.

Liz gazed at the empty chairs. It was going to take a long time before the team came to terms with the death of the brash but brilliant young ex-Intelligence officer, and none more than the detective who'd been with him as he drew his final breath. Candace reached over and squeezed Liz's shoulder.

Jeff picked up his wine glass and stood, holding it aloft until everyone joined him.

'To fallen friends.'

Everyone chorused the words.

'To Hamish. A man of too many words but a big heart.'

That was Meg and there was a round of clinks and 'cheers'.

'And to Pete,' Ben added. 'Gone too long.'

'Gone too long? Is that the best you can do? How about to Pete, the best police officer to ever wear a badge?'

Everyone swung around to look at the doorway where Pete stood with a wide grin and his arm in a sling.

'Nice of you to pour me a beer.'

In a moment he was surrounded and the chatter and laughter was more like things used to be. Only Liz hung back but her face lit up. Ben hadn't seen her smile since that awful day.

Once Pete was settled in his usual seat, he raised his glass in the direction of where Hamish used to sit.

'Give them hell, wherever you are, mate.'

For a while pizza was eaten and conversations were casual. Pete had lots of questions thrown his way, such as when was he officially returning.

'Still a bit to go with the arm. Another operation next week and physio so I'll be behind a desk for a while. Assuming Ben has a spot for me.'

'Always. Shall we fill Pete in on the current status? Meg?'

Liz was relieved Pete was here. The energy in the room had lifted. His eyes met hers a few times as though checking up on her wellbeing, which was unnecessary. She'd visited him often in hospital and a few times since he'd gone home, and poured her heart out one drunken evening about Kyle. And Hamish.

'Once we knew Annette was a long-time informant to Kyle, Kirsten, and Marcus, my job got easier,' Meg said. 'She'd dropped enough hints about Hamish to make us question him while working hard to rebuild what she must have noticed as a bit of suspicion after her first couple of mistakes. Does anyone remember her needing to leave the building to arrange childcare? Back when Lyndall was abducted?'

There were nods.

'She doesn't have any children.'

'Being involved in record management put her in a prime position to alter and even destroy evidence,' Jeff said. 'Her father helped derail the Baxter murder investigation and then Annette simply continued his work. It was his blood we've identified as the third sample in the washing machine so presumably he helped move the bodies and cut himself at some point. Whoever loaded the machine forgot to empty it.'

Phoebe looked ready to cry. 'But she treated us like friends. She was always saying how much she cared about Liz, so why would she do this?'

'We'll never know all her motives,' Candace said. 'Family pressure and being recruited by the mother-figure she never had was a powerful force.'

Golden girl. Got to go to the ball.

Liz wasn't about to repeat the last things Annette told her. It wouldn't change anything and one day, with Candace's help, she'd deal with her own guilt over all of this. Guilt which didn't belong to her, but persisted. She still couldn't read the letter from her mother. Not just yet.

'More than fifty million dollars in gold bars have so far been retrieved from those wine barrels. Vats, really.' Reuben helped himself to more of his pizza. 'We've traced it back to Joseph and Ilona who smuggled some from Germany initially and then used the connections they had in Europe to continue a slow but steady stream of transactions. Their businesses were excellent covers. Marcus and Kirsten were already involved with the European operation and at one point, all four, plus Kyle Moorland, were members of a secretive cult. It imploded, from what I can find out, but Kyle was obsessed with Kirsten so remained a part of the trail of laundering and assassinations.'

Pete looked around the table. 'Why the tunnels? What was their purpose?'

'Both the tunnel from the stables and the one from the well led to the cellar, and a stash had been removed in the past few months. Since Marcus died, actually. The tunnels are only as old as the renovations, so the Baxters presumably wanted a discreet way to move the gold.'

'Seems like a lot of effort but then again, that's a lot of gold! Do we each get a bonus?' Pete looked hopeful and everyone laughed.

After another round of drinks Ben asked if he could speak. Liz knew something was on his mind and expected he'd announce he was stepping down. The scare with Ellie and Michael had shaken him.

'Our team can't function long-term with two people gone, and Pete not operational for some time. Next week we'll have some new recruits. And once they've settled in and we put a couple more cases behind us, I'm retiring.' Ben shook his head, his eyes glistening. 'I'd rather be bored at work but with my family than keep worrying about them so far from me. Couldn't have asked for a better team and thanks to each one of you, and Hamish, we achieved the first purpose of Operation Nobody – solving the murders of Inspector Baxters parents.'

'But doesn't that mean the team will be dismantled?' Phoebe's voice wavered.

'Not at all. What it does mean is this special, elite group of experts can hone in on some of the trickiest crimes in the state. More cold cases for a start. We've proved to those who fund us that it is worth continuing.'

The room fell silent. They'd had a terrible loss. Mistakes

which almost cost more lives. New people coming. Ben eventually going. A new team leader at some point.

Liz and Reuben glanced at each other.

Whatever was ahead, it was a world without Kyle.

She lifted her glass to the team.

That was worth celebrating.

ABOUT THE AUTHOR

Phillipa lives just outside a beautiful town in country Victoria, Australia. She also lives in the many worlds of her imagination and stockpiles stories beside her laptop.

She writes from the heart about love, dreams, secrets, discovery, the sea, the world as she knows it… or wishes it could be. She loves happy endings, heart-pounding suspense, and characters who stay with you long after the final page.

With a passion for music, the ocean, animals, nature, reading, and writing, she is often found in the vegetable garden pondering a new story.

Phillipa's website is www.phillipaclark.com

ALSO BY PHILLIPA NEFRI CLARK

Detective Liz Moorland

Lest We Forgive

Lest Bridges Burn

Lest Tides Turn

Lest Nobody Lives

Lest Angels Weep

Connected to this series through several characters is

Last Known Contact

Rivers End Romantic Women's Fiction

The Stationmaster's Cottage

Jasmine Sea

The Secrets of Palmerston House

The Christmas Key

Taming the Wind

Temple River Romantic Women's Fiction

The Cottage at Whisper Lake

The Bookstore at Rivers End

The House at Angel's Beach

The Secrets of Willow Bay

Charlotte Dean Mysteries

Christmas Crime in Kingfisher Falls

Book Club Murder in Kingfisher Falls

Cold Case Murder in Kingfisher Falls

Plans for Murder in Kingfisher Falls

Festive Felony in Kingfisher Falls

Bindarra Creek Rural Fiction

A Perfect Danger

Tangled by Tinsel

Doctor Grok's Peculiar Shop Short Story Collection

Simple Words for Troubled Times

(Short non-fiction happiness and comfort book)